G.A. McKevett

Every Body ON DECK

A SAVANNAH REID MYSTERY

KENSINGTON BOOKS
www.kensingtonbooks.com

Books by G.A. McKevett

Just Desserts
Bitter Sweets
Killer Calories
Cooked Goose
Sugar and Spite
Sour Grapes
Peaches and Screams
Death By Chocolate
Cereal Killer
Murder à la Mode
Corpse Suzette
Fat Free and Fatal
Poisoned Tarts
A Body to Die For
Wicked Craving
A Decadent Way to Die
Buried in Buttercream
Killer Honeymoon
Killer Physique
Killer Gourmet
Killer Reunion
Every Body on Deck
Hide and Sneak

Published by Kensington Publishing Corporation

*This book is lovingly dedicated to
the Grandangels,
the stars in my heaven.*

Thank you, Leslie Connell, for your many years of friendship and service. For both, I will be forever grateful.

I also wish to thank all the fans who write to me, sharing their thoughts and offering endless encouragement. Your stories touch my heart, and I enjoy your letters more than you know. I can be reached at:

sonja@sonjamassie.com
and
faccbook.com/gwendolynnarden.mckevett

Chapter 1

"Savannah, that's the third disturbance call this week! You gotta get your grandmother under control, girl." Detective Sergeant Dirk Coulter switched off his cell phone and jammed it into the inside pocket of his leather bomber jacket. "I don't want the chief calling me on the carpet about her no more. I can get in plenty of trouble all on my own, thank you. I don't need any help from your relatives."

Savannah Reid didn't bother to ask for the gory details. She just sighed, turned the ruby red 1965 Mustang around, and headed out of town, toward the trailer park where her grandma had recently relocated.

"Darlin', have you ever noticed," she said, her Southern drawl even more pronounced than usual because she was annoyed, "that when she's baking you banana bread, she's 'Granny'? But the minute she does something a wee bit out of line, all of a sudden she's 'your grandmother'?"

"A wee bit outta line?" He gave a loud snort that made her jump.

Wow, he's really irked, she warned herself. Usually, when he was aggravated, he just gave the occasional cringe-worthy liquid sniff.

"She assaulted her neighbor," he said. "Clobbered him with a book."

Savannah snickered. "Just a couple of little harmless whacks about the head and shoulders with a New Testament."

"New and Old Testaments. She beat the crap outta him with the whole Bible. Large print, I believe. The thing weighed a ton. She coulda killed him. Or at least given him a concussion."

"Gran's in her eighties. Of course it was large print." She snickered. "Sorta brings new meaning to the term 'Bible thumper,' huh?"

He didn't laugh. She turned and searched his face. Not even a trace of a Dirk smirk. So she tried another tack. "Besides, it was Ol' Man Biddle. Shoot, you lived by him and his old lady for years. You know yourself what an ornery peckerwood he is. Not to mention a pervert. If my Granny Reid hit him, he deserved it."

"But isn't she a Baptist or a Methodist or something like that? Isn't hitting him with the Good Book kinda sacrilegious or something?"

Savannah shrugged. "It's what she had in her hand when she saw him peeping through her window."

Dirk opened the glove compartment and took out a plastic bag filled with cinnamon sticks. "The chief thought it was kinda cute the first time. But he took a dim view of her smacking Biddle around a second time, and with a cast iron skillet."

"Again, it's what she had in her hand. A weapon of opportunity. Biddle should've known better than to go skulking around her trailer two nights in a row. Apparently, he's a slow learner."

Poking one of the cinnamon sticks into the corner of his mouth, Dirk said, "You're going to have to explain to her that this isn't Georgia. Bible whackin' and skillet smackin' ain't as widely accepted here on the West Coast as they are in the rural South. Since she's moved to California, she's turned into a juvenile delinquent."

Savannah drove the red pony off the main highway and onto the pothole-pocked road that led to Shady Vale, one of the area's two trailer parks.

The picturesque, seaside resort town of San Carmelita had approved zoning for one mobile home park—an elegant, beachfront community, tastefully landscaped with copious palm trees, rockeries adorned with succulents, and the occasional water feature. Highly selective, the home-owners association of Pacifica Harbor Park thoroughly vetted every potential inhabitant, insuring that only the most respectable and law-abiding members of society were invited to live among them.

Granny Reid had submitted her application and was anxiously awaiting their approval. Until then, she was stuck with the rest of the miscreants in Shady Vale. The "other" park.

Dirk was all too familiar with the community himself, having lived there for most of his adult life, until marrying Savannah and moving into her small, midtown home. Better digs was just one of the many upticks that marriage had brought him, along with a steady stream of home-cooked meals, cable TV, and an honest-to-goodness love life.

He was, for the most part, a deliriously happy married man.

Except when his in-laws broke the rules of society, and he was assigned the task of corralling them.

Just outside the city limits, at the end of the bumpy and broken road, past some neglected orange groves and beyond a windbreak of ancient eucalyptus trees, sat an assortment of house trailers. A baker's dozen. Rusty and decrepit, they were unlikely to ever be called "mobile homes" again. At least, not without a hearty amount of scrubbing, some skillful bodywork, and a spray painting.

In general, the residents of Shady Vale weren't known for being overly ambitious when it came to even basic home maintenance, let alone beautification.

As Savannah drove past the row of fragrant, gray green eucalyptus trees, she steeled herself for what might lie ahead. Granny Reid was a peaceful, God-fearing, law-abiding woman who was mostly known for her piety, good humor, and the triple-chocolate cakes she baked and delivered to members of the community who were in need.

In her hometown of McGill, Georgia, many of her neighbors had found those cakes—as well as pots of homemade soup, loaves of freshly baked bread, and tins of pecan fudge—on their doorsteps when sickness, financial hardships, family problems, or death itself had visited their homes.

When Gran had first moved to San Carmelita and taken over Dirk's old trailer, Savannah had seen her extending the same warm, neighborly kindness toward her fellow Shady Valeians.

But then Ol' Man Biddle had commenced with his

tomfoolery. Some new ruffian residents had moved into the tiny community, individuals who were a bit more unruly and untidy than the less-than-stellar status quo.

The situation had been rumbling downhill ever since.

Savannah heard her husband groan, and she didn't need to ask why, as the park came into full view ahead. It looked like ninety percent of the town's law enforcement personnel was there. Several radio cars blocked the entrance, their red and blue lights flashing. Inside the property were more police vehicles, uniformed cops galore, two fire engines, copious ambulances, and a large black truck with red and gold lettering on the side that identified it as belonging to the Hazardous Materials Response Team.

"Hazmat?" they both said in unison.

"Lordy mercy," Savannah whispered.

Dirk shook his head. "What the hell's she done now?"

"I just hope she's all right." Savannah's heart was racing as she strained to see if anyone was being loaded into the ambulances. But the EMTs were nowhere in sight. The only individuals milling about were dressed in white protection garb, with hoods and self-contained breathing apparatuses over their faces.

Dirk took a long drag on his cinnamon stick and said, "I'll bet she fed that bloodhound of hers chicken livers again. She should know better. It gives him the worst gas I've ever smelled in my life."

In the interest of maintaining matrimonial harmony— at least what little there was at the moment—Savannah decided not to mention that Colonel Beauregard's chicken liver gas expulsions were not the worst thing she had ever smelled. Without a doubt, Dirk had won the blue ribbon in that contest after an all-you-can-eat buffet extravaganza at Casa Jose's. Savannah and the cats had fled the toxic cloud in the middle of the night, evacuating to the living room sofa, because the air in the master bedroom had become dangerous to any creature possessing a nose and set of lungs.

But Savannah decided to keep her mouth shut and spare Dirk that trip down memory lane.

There was, after all, a time to correct those around you and a time to just sit silently and smugly, reveling in the self-satisfaction that they were just purely wrong.

This was one of those times.

Biting her tongue, she pulled the Mustang as close as she could to the area that had been cordoned off by yellow police barricade tape. As soon as she had parked, they both jumped out and rushed to the nearest squad car. The uniformed patrolman inside recognized them and rolled down his window.

Nodding to Dirk, he said, "Mornin', Detective. Not surprised to see you show up, this being your old stomping grounds and all." He flashed Savannah a grin. "Nice to see you, Mrs. Coulter. How's the sergeant here treating you?"

Savannah returned the smile. "It's still 'Reid,'" she replied, "but I'm enjoying being a Mrs., for sure."

Never thrilled with what he called "pointless chitchat," Dirk cleared his throat and gave the officer his grimmest, no-nonsense scowl. "Whatcha got here?"

The patrolman shrugged. "Don't know. The chief said we should all stay in our units with the windows rolled up until hazmat figures out if it's safe or not."

Savannah shot Dirk a quick look. She was deeply

disturbed that her grandmother was in the middle of some sort of hazmat situation, but that concern was closely followed by her dismay at the thought of coming face to face with the police brass.

Years ago, she and they had parted company under less than cordial circumstances. While she didn't have any ex-husbands, she was pretty sure that running into the SCPD bosses felt a lot like rounding an aisle in the grocery store and finding yourself nose to nose with a previous spouse you were happy to be rid of.

If your ex had a gun and a badge and hated you almost as much as you loathed him.

The patrolman gave Savannah a sweet, reassuring smile. "Don't worry. It's the *fire* chief who's giving the orders here," he explained. "He's the only boss around. At least for now."

Savannah resisted the urge to reach inside the squad car and give the kid a hug. Like every other uniformed peace officer in the SCPD, he obviously knew about her being ousted and his sympathies lay with her. She didn't care so much what a few guys in suits thought of her, as long as the men and women in uniforms were on her side. Like this young man, who had been hired long after her departure, but he had heard her story and aligned himself with her.

Ah. Loyalty among the rank and file.

He deserved a hearty embrace.

But Dirk wouldn't approve. No doubt about it. He cast a dim eye on anything that might compromise his "bad-ass" reputation. Although he definitely had a soft side to his otherwise tough-as-nails persona, few living beings had the chance to see the sweet, mushy version of Dirk Coulter, let alone reap the benefits thereof.

That privilege was mostly reserved for his wife and the children, cats, and dogs who happened to cross his path.

In the course of his career Detective Sergeant Dirk Coulter had garnered numerous awards: a Certificate of Commendation, a Lifesaving Medal, a Medal of Merit, and even the coveted Medal of Valor.

Those honors aside, Dirk would never receive a Safe-Driving Medal or a Mr. Congeniality tiara and bouquet.

He had no problem with that.

Popularity and the good opinions and well wishes of his fellow human beings were commodities Dirk Coulter could do without.

On the other hand, having been raised as a Southern female, Savannah lived in constant fear that someone, somewhere, might not think she was the finest person walking the face of the earth. She worried about it every day, all day, and it kept her awake at night. Everyone, absolutely *everyone*, had to adore her.

Even people she couldn't stand the sight of.

She wanted to be Dirk when she grew up someday and not give a flying flapjack what anybody thought of her. But she sincerely doubted that was ever going to happen. Southern belle training went deep.

DNA deep.

She was doomed to a life of people pleasing.

"Thanks," she told the patrolman. "All I want is to find out if my grandma's okay. Did you happen to see a feisty ol' gal running around in a flowered caftan, causing trouble?"

"Silver hair, big earrings, and a bloodhound?"

"That's her!"

He nodded toward the trailer that had formerly been

Dirk's, but was now inhabited by Granny Reid and Colonel Beauregard. "When the chief cleared the area, he told her to go in there and not come out. She gave him some lip, but finally did as she was told."

"That sounds like your grandma," Dirk grumbled under his breath.

Savannah feigned surprise and indignation. "A Reid woman . . . giving someone lip? Unheard of."

Dirk snorted. "It's the 'did as she was told' part that's unbelievable."

Savannah left the car and hurried toward the trailer.

"Hey!" the patrolman called out to her. "You can't go over there. Not without a mask."

Savannah reached down, pulled the hem of her linen jacket up across her face.

Long ago, she'd been told that in a potentially toxic situation, she should tear off her bra and hold one of the cups over her nose. But she couldn't envision herself arriving at Gran's door wearing her bra on her face instead of her boobs. That would, undoubtedly, lead to more speeches about Southern belle propriety, and she wasn't in the mood. Especially if those speeches were given by a woman who had crossed paths with the law three times in one week.

From the corner of her eye, she could see a couple of the hazmat workers in their white, hooded uniforms scurrying toward her. So she quickened her step and managed to reach the trailer's front door before they could intercept her.

She gave the door a couple of brisk raps. As she waited impatiently for Gran to answer, she turned and realized that Dirk was right behind her. The look of concern on his face went straight to her heart. He might complain about her grandmother from time to time, but he loved Granny dearly and was as concerned about her well-being as Savannah was.

Glancing over her shoulder, Savannah realized that the hazmat workers were nearly upon them. This was no time to stand on formality.

Savannah pushed the door open and hurried inside. Dirk quickly followed, then closed it firmly behind them and threw the bolt.

"Gran? Granny, where are you? It's me, Savannah. Dirk's with me, so don't come out unless you're decent."

An instant later, the small trailer was filled with the plaintive sound of a baying bloodhound, as the Colonel in all of his canine glory came loping out of the bedroom. His long, silky, copper ears and pendulous dewlaps swung from side to side as he galloped toward them, eyes bright, tail wagging.

It was the most excited Savannah had seen him in years.

"I'm in here," called a voice from the bedroom, "changin' clothes. Sit yerselves down and rest a spell. I'll be right out."

Reluctantly, Savannah and Dirk sat on the old school bus seat that had served as Dirk's sofa for many years. Gran's furniture was on its way from Georgia, but until it arrived she was compelled to use what he had left behind. TV trays functioned as end tables. Stacked plastic milk crates doubled as bookshelves, chests of drawers, and dressers.

Gran had borne it all with good humor, saying that everybody ought to have a school bus seat for a couch

at least once in their lifetime. But she appeared to be in
a far less cheerful mood when she emerged from the
back of the trailer, a bundle of clothing under one arm
and a highly disgruntled look on her face. Her cloud of
silver hair, usually perfectly coiffed without one hair
out of place, was a mess. She had a smudge of dirt on
one cheek and a small scratch and slight bruise on the
other.

Colonel Beauregard scrambled to get out of her way
and slid under the bus seat. Once he was semihidden
behind Savannah and Dirk's legs, he poked his long
nose out and gave Granny a sad, apprehensive look,
his big brown eyes reflecting the guilt of a tormented
soul that had committed some grievous sin.

"Yeah, you better hide, you flea-bitten varmint,"
Gran barked at him. "You're the one that started all
this hooey, but I'm the one who'll get blamed for it.
You wait and see."

As Gran passed them on her way to the door, Savannah smelled a pungent, acrid odor—one that was all
too familiar to anyone associated with law enforcement.

"Wow, Granny!" Dirk said. "You smell like a—"

"Yeah, yeah, I know. I stink like one of those blamed
meth labs. Even after a rose bubble bath and lavender
bath spray, I can still smell that nastiness in my nose
and taste it in my mouth. Here I thought I'd left that
mess behind me in Georgia. Who'd a' thought they'd
be doin' drugs in a place as nice as California with
beaches and palm trees and all?"

Savannah stifled a grin. Drugs in California? Who'd
a' thought, indeed?

Gran opened the door and hurled the clothing out-side—a tropical print housedress and some under-garments.

Savannah couldn't help remembering one of the foremost and unbreakable Southern Belle Rules: If by necessity a lady's lingerie must be outdoors—say, hang-ing on a clothesline to dry after laundering—it should be hung discreetly, with the row of sheets on one side and large, thick towels on the other, so as not to be visible to passersby. Especially male passersby who might find such a sight overly stimulating and get themselves in a sexually charged dither.

Savannah decided that, since Granny appeared to be perfectly fine with the entire San Carmelita fire depart-ment and hazmat team having an up-close view of her flying knickers, she must be pretty upset, indeed.

"Let me guess," Dirk said with a smirk. "The Colonel sniffed out a meth lab here in the park, and all hell broke loose."

"Reckon they didn't give you that gold badge for nothin'." Gran sniffed. "You got it all figured out. 'Cept the part where that hound, cowering there under your legs, decided to bite a plug outta that drug-bakin' weasel."

Savannah looked down between her legs at the woe-begone face of her favorite canine—as sweet a dog as she had ever known. "But the Colonel has a history, a traumatic history, with meth labs," she said, pleading his case. "Sheriff Stafford used him to sniff out that one there on Cooter Hill, and the perp threw ammonia in his face."

Gran's expression softened. "Yeah. I remember."

"So does he, I'm sure. He probably thought he was

biting the same guy. They all smell pretty much the same, you know."

Wearily, Granny plopped herself onto the nearest accent chair—a folding, metal one. She sighed. "But you've only heard the first chapter of the story. After the Colonel nipped him—"

"You said, 'bit a plug outta him,'" Savannah corrected her.

Gran shrugged. "Whatever. That numbskull kicked him hard right in the rear end. So, I had to—"

"Smack him upside the head," Dirk supplied.

Granny turned to Savannah with a half grin. "Detective-wise, he ain't half bad, you know."

"It's why they pay him the big bucks." Savannah nudged Dirk in the side with her elbow.

He looked confused. "They pay me big bucks? I didn't know that."

"Well, they should." Savannah turned back to Granny. "What did you hit him with? Hopefully not your Bible this time."

"No. But it was what you people call a 'weapon of opportunity.'"

A sparkle of the devilment lit Gran's blue eyes, and Savannah was afraid to ask. But she had to. "So? What was it? Confess. Get it off your chest and you'll feel a lot better."

Granny cleared her throat. "As it turns out, I was being a good citizen, taking my dog for a walk, letting him do his business, and picking up the . . . um . . . *business* after the fact. No sooner had the Colonel concluded his business than he got a big whiff of that meth lab, coming from that old, rusty, blue trailer on the end."

"Let me guess," Savannah said. "You were picking up the *business* with something, like maybe your little garden shovel?"

Granny laughed. "My respect for the two of you is growin' by leaps and bounds."

Dirk stood, sighed, and pulled a pair of handcuffs from his jacket pocket. "There's just one more question I have to ask you, Mrs. Reid, before I arrest you for this heinous crime."

Granny looked up at him, grinned, and batted her eyelashes like a coquette who was one-quarter her age. "What is that, Mr. Po-lease-man?"

"When you smacked that numbskull upside the head with the shovel, was it full of . . . *business*? Do I have to charge you with first-degree battery and assault with a biological substance?"

Granny looked confused and shrugged. "Why, of course. If you're gonna whack somebody, especially somebody who just kicked your hound dog, you might as well make it worth your while."

Chapter 2

"As jails go, this is what I'd call fine accommodations," Granny said as Savannah walked with her to the door of her quaint Spanish cottage. Dirk followed behind, carrying Gran's suitcase in one hand and Colonel Beauregard's leash in the other.

Having scented the two cats that lived inside, the hound was in full bay, pulling with all his considerable might against the restraint.

Dirk could hardly keep his footing as he tried in vain to restrain him.

Gran glanced back over her shoulder. "You doin' all right back there, Son?"

"Peachy," Dirk huffed. "He's sure eager to get inside."

Savannah turned and took the suitcase from him, so he would have two free hands to corral the beast. Then she dropped to one knee in front of the Colonel. Grabbing him by the collar, she fixed him with her most baleful glare—the one she used to intimidate the worst of society's evildoers.

"Stop!" she bellowed. "Knock it off, or you'll be sleeping in the garage tonight instead of at the foot of Gran's nice guest bed. You'll be on a strict diet of dog food with not one bite of human leftovers to season them with."

Instantly, the baying ceased, and the dog gazed up at her, brown, soulful eyes filled with fear and remorse.

"That's better. I don't want a repeat of that shameful cat-chasing behavior that occurred when we visited in Georgia. Understand?"

The dog's head sank lower, until his chin was nearly on the ground. He whined pitifully, his tail tucked under his belly.

"Because if you harass those felines, I swear, I won't intervene this time. I'll let them have at you with tooth and claw until you look like you tangled with a herd of wild bobcats. You hear me?"

Another whine. The tail untucked and began to wag just a little. He took a step closer to her and licked the back of her hand.

"That's my good boy," she told him, stroking the soft auburn head. "If you can deny every natural and inbred instinct in every cell of your body and ignore those silly ol' cats, I'll give you a big, juicy ham bone I've been saving in the freezer since Easter. Okay?"

She rose, dusted her knee, and noticed Dirk grinning at her.

He gave her a wink. "That's tellin' 'im."

"You just watch. He'll be the perfect gentleman."

Granny chuckled. "Sure he will. At least until we get inside the house."

As they continued up the walk, Dirk cleared his throat. "A herd of bobcats?"

"Shush."

"O-o-o-kay."

They ducked beneath the always-needing-a-trim bougainvillea vines that arched over the doorway and entered the house.

Savannah ushered Gran inside first, then followed and set the suitcase on the foyer floor. Dirk followed with the Colonel, who was attempting to ignore the two cats in black satin coats, who eyed him from a nearby windowsill. He gave them one quick, predatory glance, then cut a sideways look at Savannah and focused on the floor in front of him.

She wasn't convinced. But she had to give him points for trying.

No sooner had she placed her purse and keys on the pie crust table by the door, than her assistant, Tammy Hart, came bounding out of the living room.

She didn't bound with quite as much ease and agility as she had eight and a half months ago, due to her now-enormous baby bump. But her spirit was no less perky as she hurried to Savannah and whispered excitedly in her ear. "Did you get my text? Did you? Huh, huh? You didn't answer so I figured your—"

"—phone was down. Yes. I forgot to charge it this morning," Savannah told her. "Why? What's up?"

"Then you don't know who's here!"

"No. I don't. Who's here?" Savannah asked, trying to see around her into the living room.

It took a bit more effort to look around Miss Tammy these days.

"Just come inside and see! You're going to be so jazzed! Beyond jazzed!"

After the morning she'd had, Savannah wasn't sure that anything would catapult her into the category of "jazzed," but she was trying to stay open-minded.

"You take care of the Colonel here, and I'll get Gran settled up in my man cave," Dirk said as he handed Savannah the leash. "Er, I mean, the guest room."

"I'm sorry I'm such a bother," Granny said, placing her hand on Dirk's broad shoulder. "I'd have been fine stayin' there in the trailer if that bossy fire chief hadn't gotten on his high horse about me makin' myself scarce."

"You're never a bother, Gran," Dirk told her, patting her affectionately on the head, smoothing down her ruffled hair. "We love you, and we're glad to have you, no matter what the circumstances."

As they continued up the stairs, Savannah heard him add under his breath, "This way I can keep an eye on you."

Savannah watched them retreat up the stairs and thought how dearly she loved them both. Having her favorite people under her roof—how could that be anything but a joy?

But Tammy's agenda didn't include allowing Savannah time to count her blessings. She was about to jump out of her maternity yoga pants. "Come on!" she said, giving Savannah a nudge toward the living room. "Just see who's here! Somebody who wants to hire you."

Savannah brightened. *Hire?* Now that was something to get excited about! Clients had been few and far between for over a month, but the bills persisted in arriving. So this could be a fortunate turn of events.

"It's someone you love!" Tammy was saying as she and her tummy wriggled about like a cocker spaniel with a new toy treat.

"Someone I *love*?"

Savannah had little time to consider which of her close friends or relatives might be in need of her services before she walked into the living room, keeping the meth-baker-bitin' hound from hell on a tight leash.

Sitting on the far end of her sofa, nearest the kitchen, was a woman who did look vaguely familiar to Savannah. She had a full, round face that matched her figure and wore eyeglasses that were the exact pistachio green color as her tweed Chanel suit.

But it was her hair that Savannah recognized. Unusually long for a woman past fifty, it flowed in wild, tight ringlets down her shoulders, to her elbows. A particularly vibrant shade of glistening silver, her hair was the woman's trademark, and Savannah instantly identified her visitor as her favorite mystery writer, Natasha Van Cleef.

Savannah had seen that face, and that hair, on the cover of some of her best-loved and most frequently reread books.

"Ms. Van Cleef!" she said. "What a wonderful surprise! I've read every book you've written, several times. I can't tell you how delighted I am to meet you and to have you in my home."

She reached to shake the author's hand. But that was the moment when Diamante and Cleopatra decided to leave their window perch in search of a midmorning snack in the kitchen. Unfortunately, that required them to stroll within two feet of Colonel Beauregard's nose.

Because Savannah was in prehandshake position, she didn't have a firm grip on the leash.

So, all canine/feline hell broke loose.

Mercifully, for the humans who witnessed it, the next forty-five seconds were little more than a confusing flurry of black and auburn fur, a cacophony of baying, growling, snarling, and hissing . . . followed by a long, heartrending howl.

While conducting her duties as a police officer and then a private detective, Savannah had interviewed more than her share of celebrities. Two of her best friends, Ryan Stone and John Gibson, had solicited her help when providing security for Hollywood royalty. Not to mention the fact that she lived within easy driving distance of Hollywood, Beverly Hills, Malibu, and Santa Barbara—all towns that were home to more than their share of celebrities per capita.

So, even the richest and most famous held little mystery for the country girl from Georgia.

Long ago, she had come to realize that those whom society held in the highest esteem weren't all that different than the common rabble who ate their dinners at local fast food joints and pulled on their well-worn jeans every morning one leg at a time.

Like everyone else, when the Wheel of Fortune took a turn for the worst, celebrities found themselves at the mercy of unpleasant, even tragic, circumstances beyond their control. Occasionally, fate could be unkind, and human beings, no matter their lifestyles, could be downright cruel.

As far as Savannah was concerned, it took a particularly cruel person to send Natasha Van Cleef the threatening letter that Savannah now held in her hand.

Although the two women were comfortably seated on soft, cushy patio chairs and were sipping Savannah's best icy lemonade in the shade of her wisteria arbor, the serenity of her backyard flower garden did little to dispel the tension in the lilac- and star-jasmine-scented air.

Even the gentle sound of the Colonel's snoring as he slept, peacefully curled at Savannah's feet, beyond claw-reach of marauding felines, seemed at odds with the subject being discussed.

Once again, Savannah studied the words, written by what appeared to be a standard ink-jet printer on plain office copy paper. It read:

> *Be warned. Your time is short. Soon you will die a terrible death.*

Savannah could see the fear in the author's eyes as they searched hers. Natasha was waiting for an answer to her question, and Savannah wasn't sure what to say.

"It's never easy, Ms. Van Cleef," Savannah began, "to determine how serious a threat like this is. There are a lot of nitwits out there who like to throw words around and scare the daylights out of innocent people. Some do it for kicks. Some because they're just brimming with hate and feel the need to spread it around so that others can be as miserable as they are. Some because they're bored and have nothing better to do. Then there are the others. . . ."

The author drew a deep, shuddering breath. "The ones who mean it."

"Yes. Those are the ones we have to look out for."

For several tense moments, Natasha sat quietly, twirling the bracelet on her wrist. She was nervously fingering each of many book-shaped charms that dangled from it. Savannah recognized the charms as representing the books she had published. Savannah had read all of them. More than once.

Finally, Natasha asked, "How do you tell which is which? The meanies from the crazies from the psychos?"

Many times, Savannah had been asked this question. It was an honest one that haunted far too many people in the world.

Someone had threatened someone else's life. Should they be afraid? Should they live every waking moment looking over their shoulders and sleep every night with a weapon under their pillow?

Or was it just some brutal bully trying to rob them of their peace?

It could be a question of life and death.

But Savannah had no answer.

Handling the letter as little as possible, so she could check it for fingerprints later, Savannah laid the paper on her lap and looked intently into her guest's eyes. This was no time to glance away, to speak a semicomforting half-truth. It was the time for complete honesty, unsettling as it might be.

"I've had a lot of clients," she began, "who came to me because someone had threatened their lives. I tell them all the same thing. Odds are in their favor. Most people who threaten others never actually follow through with it. It's one thing to want to kill another person, even say you're going to, but doing it . . . That's a line very, very few people actually step over. Thankfully. But you can't rely on that. You have to treat every single threat as though it's the real thing and protect yourself accordingly."

A hard glint of determination lit Natasha's eyes as she said, "I'm not going to change my life for this nut job, whether he or she means it or not. I won't give in to fear and intimidation. I'm going forward with exactly what I have scheduled."

"What do you have planned?"

"In three days, I'm embarking on an Alaskan cruise. It's a mystery-themed voyage, and I'm the star attraction. I won't disappoint the ship line or my fans. They expect me to be there, and I will be."

Savannah nodded. "I understand, and I respect your decision. Though I do think you should take certain precautions while you're 'going forward,' as you say."

"I fully intend to. That's why I've come to see you today."

A tiny light flickered in Savannah's soul. A flame of hope that one of the items on her bucket list might be checked off. A cruise to Alaska, land of natural splendor, snowcapped mountains, endless ancient forests, glistening glaciers, teeming wildlife, statuesque totem poles—

"I want you and your entire Moonlight Magnolia Detective Agency to accompany me," Natasha Van Cleef announced. "I'll need you to provide protection for myself and my entourage. Of course, I'll cover your expenses and pay you well for your services. . . ."

Chapter 3

"**H**oly cow! Did you just scream for joy or what?" Tammy exclaimed, her eyes bright with excitement. Her long, golden hair glistened in the warm light cast by the Tiffany-style dragonfly lamp suspended over Savannah's dining table as she reached across and grabbed Savannah's hands in hers.

It wasn't an easy task, because Tammy's belly was filled with a child who was just about ready to exit, greet the world, and become the newest and youngest member of the Moonlight Magnolia Detective Agency.

Savannah quirked an eyebrow. "Of course I didn't scream." She nabbed another chocolate chip and macadamia nut cookie off a nearby platter, then handed the plate to Dirk, motioning for him to send it on yet another pass around the table. "Screaming isn't professional. I quietly, calmly accepted her offer."

"She screamed," Dirk said, taking two cookies for himself and passing the platter to Waycross. "I heard her all the way inside the house. You'd have thought she'd won the lottery or at least found a box of chocolates that she'd stashed away and forgotten about."

"Okay, okay." Savannah grinned. "I might have screamed. A little. Then I quietly, calmly accepted on our behalf." She turned to John and Ryan. "Please tell me that you'll go. You can find somebody to run the restaurant for you, can't you? Natasha distinctly said she wants the whole agency to go along."

Ryan smiled his broad, handsome grin, which melted her heart every time. "Of course. We wouldn't miss it for the world. The restaurant can do without us for a few days. Francia's turned out to be a fantastic chef, practically runs the place herself." He turned to his partner, John Gibson, who was sitting next to him. "With Carlos and Maria, I'm sure they won't even miss us."

Dirk shoved a whole cookie into his mouth and talked around it. "What? No bodyguard jobs lined up? No starlet needing protection as she struts her stuff down a red carpet somewhere?"

John stroked his luxurious silver mustache a few seconds before responding to the barb. "No. Nothing of import on the agenda at the moment," he replied in his thick, aristocratic British accent. "How about you, Detective Coulter?" he asked with a sly grin. "Will the fine city of San Carmelita collapse beneath a tidal wave of crime in your absence? I can't imagine your chief parting with such a fine piece of law-enforcing manpower as yourself on such short notice."

Dirk scowled. "I got vacation time comin'. Don't you worry 'bout me."

Savannah turned to her brother, Waycross, who was

sitting next to Tammy, rubbing her perpetually aching back. Savannah was so proud of him. The baby wasn't even here yet, and he was already an amazing daddy. "Do you think you can get some days off from the body shop?" she asked him. "Our client wants everybody on deck and that includes you."

"I just finished a custom paint job on a Studebaker—a 1954 Regal Starliner. Turned out real pretty, she did." His freckled face flushed with pride as he ran his fingers through his thick, copper waves, trying to tame the haystack. "The customer was extra happy with it. He gave me a real nice tip. I can afford to take off a week or two. Even if I couldn't, I would. It's a trip to Alaska, for Pete's sake. I've never been on a cruise ship before!"

"You're going to love it!" Ryan said. "John and I have cruised a dozen times or more, and those trips have been some of our best travel adventures ever."

John nodded. "Excellent cuisine, breathtaking scenery. Cruising is by far the most relaxing of vacations."

For a moment, Savannah flashed back on the conversation she and Natasha Van Cleef had shared in her backyard. The fear in the woman's eyes. Those ugly words printed on the paper that was now securely filed inside a clear plastic sheet protector.

The threatening letter, Savannah's notes concerning the interview, information about the cruise, and personal data about the author were all neatly arranged in the loose leaf notebook that lay on the table in front of Savannah.

Before they were finished, Savannah would see to it that the notebook was bulging.

"I certainly hope this will turn out to be a relaxing

vacation for all of us," she said. "Including our client and her entourage. With the ship sailing in three days, we have our work cut out for us. I hear that Internet access can be spotty on a cruise. Phone service, too, sometimes. So, Tammy, you're going to have to get your online sleuthing done, or at least well underway, before we leave."

Tammy donned her most official, Look-Out-'Cause-Nancy-Drew's-on-the-Case face and pulled her electronic tablet from the tote at her feet. "Got it! I'll start with background checks on everyone who's traveling with Ms. Van Cleef," she said.

"Not to mention Ms. Van Cleef herself," Dirk added.

Savannah tapped her finger on the binder in front of her. "In here we have the things our client would like us to know about her."

Tammy grinned. "It's up to me to dig up the stuff she probably wouldn't want us to know."

"Exactly. Sometimes in order to keep a body safe, you have to invade their privacy."

Waycross tweaked a lock of Tammy's golden hair and gave her an adoring look. "My girl's the best in the world at that. She won't stop until we know what brand of underwear that lady's got in her underwear drawer."

Giggling, Tammy switched on her tablet. "What brand, size, color, and with or without tummy control."

"It's downright indecent when you think about it—makin' a living by diggin' up dirt on folks," said a soft voice behind Savannah.

She turned and saw her grandmother standing in the doorway.

Gran looked considerably less chipper than usual. Her shoulders were stooped, as though she was overly tired, and her usual bright smile was drooping at the corners.

Apparently, uncovering meth labs and owning a nosy bloodhound was hard work.

Savannah jumped up and offered her grandmother her chair. Once she had Gran settled, Savannah passed the plate of cookies under her nose. "How was your nap?" she asked her.

Gran shrugged. "Okay, I guess."

Yes, Savannah thought. *Something is definitely amiss with Granny.*

Many words could be used to describe her grandmother. But "lackluster" was not one of them. Unlike most people Savannah knew, if Gran was in a bad mood, there was a good reason.

"I just figured I'd stay up there in bed, instead of being down here underfoot. I know when it's time to get lost." She rolled her eyes, and for a moment Savannah saw a strong resemblance between her and the long-faced Colonel. "Far be it from me," Gran continued, "to make a nuisance of myself when there's important detective business going on."

Ah. So, that's it. Savannah smiled to herself. She glanced around the table and saw that the rest of the Moonlight Magnolia gang was having a hard time hiding their own grins.

Thirty minutes before, as Gran napped upstairs, or at least pretended to, the cruise had been well discussed by everyone in attendance at the dining table. One unfortunate detail in particular.

When ticking off the members of the agency who would be receiving complimentary passage, Natasha Van Cleef had not mentioned Granny Reid.

As far as the Moonlight Magnolia gang was concerned, that presented a problem of the most grievous nature.

As their very first item of business, the issue had been properly addressed, thoroughly discussed, and a solution had been found.

Savannah's cookie jar had been passed and was now stuffed with donations, ensuring that Granny would be onboard when they left Seattle.

Of course, Savannah would have to find a way to hide the fact that Gran's ticket had been paid for "family style." That would smack of charity and Gran's pride wouldn't tolerate such a thing.

Being officially hired to do a job was one thing. Being treated to a freebie by hardworking people with little surplus income was something else.

Savannah knew she would also have to find a way to avoid telling Gran an outright lie. Colonel Beauregard's bloodhound, meth-sniffing, super-nose couldn't hold a candle to Gran's ability to sniff out a falsehood.

Savannah cleared her throat, pulled an extra chair up to the table, and sat next to her grandmother. Amused, she watched Granny demolish one cookie and reach for another. In typical Reid-woman fashion, Gran might be upset, but never so much that it dulled her appetite.

"I hope," Savannah said, "that while you were lolling about upstairs on my guest bed—"

Dirk cleared his throat. "Uh, hmm. Excuse me, but I do believe that your 'guest bed' is now my 'man-cave couch.'"

"That's called a 'futon,' Dirk-o," Tammy told him, her pert nose elevated a couple of notches.

"Not in my man cave, it's not," he replied.

John gave Tammy an affectionate nudge. "He's right, love. There's an article in the current *Architectural Digest* devoted to this very topic. No futons, armoires, or chaise longues are allowed in a man cave."

Ryan shook his head solemnly. "Simply not done. Major decorating faux pas."

"That's right." Dirk seemed surprised at this rare, impromptu surge of male support. "None of those 'fo paws' allowed either."

Savannah groaned and turned back to her grandmother. "I hope while you were resting up there, you were giving some serious thought about what you're going to do with the Colonel while you're away."

"Away?"

Savannah caught a trace of a smile that lit Granny's face, but only for a second before she squelched it.

"Yes, away," Savannah repeated. "The cruise itself is seven days. Plus a day to fly there and the day to come back." She drew a deep breath and plunged ahead, using her best matter-of-fact voice. "If you want, I can ask Mrs. Normandy next door to watch him. I know she won't mind. She comes over here and feeds Cleo and Di when I'm gone. She talks to them and pets them and makes sure they don't feel too neglected. She loves dogs, too. Used to have a big German shepherd. I'm sure she'd be happy to entertain the Colonel over there at her house while we're gone."

At that point, even Gran could no longer maintain the cool, calm, and collected routine. She let out a shriek of joy before grabbing Savannah's hand in the

Granny Death Grip—the one she had perfected, years past, while refereeing children's wrestling matches.

Raising nine kids was definitely a "hands-on" skill, and she had perfected it.

"Do you mean to say I get to go, too?" she asked, her blue eyes lit with childlike joy, her voice slightly tremulous.

Savannah cocked her head to one side and gave her very best "tsk, tsk," accompanied by her most convincing look of pseudosurprise. "Of course. After all the cases you helped us solve, we can't set sail without you along to keep us on the right path."

Gran gave a little sniff and lifted her chin. "I figured that fancy author didn't understand the advantage of having a highly experienced detective like myself on the job. Not everybody appreciates the wisdom that a senior citizen has to offer when circumstances take a turn for the dire and dangerous."

A turn for the dire and dangerous. . . . How quaint, Savannah thought, suppressing a chuckle. Gran might mispronounce a word here and there, but she had a flair for the dramatic. She was never at a loss when it came to expressing herself.

Suddenly, Granny turned in her chair to face Savannah. She took her granddaughter's hand between her own and once again applied the Death Grip.

"You tell me the truth, Miss Savannah, and don't be lyin' to me, 'cause you know you ain't no good at it."

Savannah gulped. "Okay."

"Did that Natasha Van Cleef herself ask for me to go along? Is she the one footin' the bill?"

Time slowed.

Savannah could hear the kitchen clock ticking.

She could feel her heart pounding, and her face turning hotter by the moment.

Her mouth felt as dry as a bale of Georgia cotton in October.

This was it; the jig was up.

"Hey, Granny! Want this last cookie?" From out of nowhere the nearly empty platter appeared under Gran's nose. Dirk was on the other end. "I've already had a dozen or so. But if you don't want this last one, I'll eat it."

Granny snatched the lone chocolate chipper off the dish. "I most certainly do!" she said. "No point in me aiding and abetting you in making a pig outta yourself."

Dirk laughed and chucked her under the chin. "You are absolutely right about that. I can make a pig outta myself without any help whatsoever."

Feeling a gush of relief and gratitude toward her fast-acting husband, Savannah jumped up from her chair and rushed over to the refrigerator. "You know what?" she said with only the slightest quiver in her voice. "I'm pretty sure I have some of that homemade coffee ice cream here in the freezer! How about a big bowl, Granny? I've even got chocolate syrup and whipped cream to slap on it."

A few minutes later, as Savannah watched her grandmother finish the last bite of the decadent dessert, she couldn't help but congratulate herself—and Dirk—on outsmarting the old lady. Gran was quick, but on a good day Savannah liked to think that she, with some help from Dirk, was quicker.

"Now that I've finished my ice cream," Gran said, pushing the bowl away, "I want to take a minute to thank you all for your loving kindness and generosity toward me."

For a moment, the rest of the gang sat in stunned silence, unsure of what to say or do. Surely she didn't mean . . .

Finally, Savannah managed to say, "It's just cookies and ice cream, Granny. Nothing to get too excited about."

Gran shook her head. "No. It's about taking an ocean cruise, something I'd hoped and prayed I'd get to do sometime during my life, and not just any cruise. An *Alaska* cruise. A land of mystery and wonder if ever there was one. An adventure of a lifetime. The adventure of *my* lifetime."

She took a long look around the table, pausing on each face, her beautiful eyes conveying all the love she felt for each individual sitting there. "I don't know how you pulled it off. Probably passed a hat and took up an ol'-fashioned offerin'."

One look at the sheepish expressions around the table told the tale. Guilty as charged.

"You know I don't cotton to the idea of charity . . . unless it's a life and death situation."

Savannah reached over and put her arm around her grandmother's shoulders. "It's not charity, Granny. Not when it's from your family."

Gran reached over and ran her finger around the inside of the ice cream bowl. "Oh, yes it is," she said, before licking the residue from her fingertip. "But I'll take it. For heaven's sake, it's a cruise to Alaska! I'd take that even if it was a prize from one of those sin-ridden casinos in Las Vegas. A blessing is a blessing! If that particular blessing wants to rain down on me, I'm just gonna sit right here and get wet lettin' it."

Chapter 4

"I didn't realize your in-laws were coming with us," Tammy whispered to Savannah as they jostled along in the seemingly endless queue inside Seattle's Pier 91, awaiting their turn to pass through the security check.

"I didn't either." Savannah shifted her heavy tote to her other arm and silently cursed herself for feeling the need to bring those extra boxes of Godiva truffles. She had chided Dirk for trying to hide a twelve-pack of his favorite beer in his suitcase. But at the last moment the thought of going Godiva free for nine days had sent her into a full-blown anxiety attack.

She'd felt a bit like an addict hiding those chocolate boxes between layers of her lingerie. She was hoping the particular security agent who examined her would have qualms about rifling through a lady's unmentionables.

Glancing ahead in line at her husband, who was being a dutiful son, carrying an enormous shopping bag for his mother, Savannah felt a momentary flash of annoyance. But she did her best to quell it. Dirk had spent precious little time with his biological parents, having only recently been reunited with them. He was overjoyed to have them aboard.

Savannah told herself she should be happy for him. She was. Sort of.

Though she hoped they would understand this was a working trip for the rest of the group, and the Moonlight Magnolia gang might not be free to socialize day and night.

"When did you find out they were coming?" Tammy asked, as the line moved forward an inch.

"Just last evening, when we spent the night with them. Apparently, Richard was able to nab cheap last minute tickets."

"Cheap. Dora's favorite kind," Tammy whispered back, snickering. "What's in that big bag of hers, the one Dirk's carrying?"

"Groceries."

Tammy's mouth dropped. "Seriously? Doesn't she know that on a cruise ship there's food everywhere, and it's all free?"

"I told her, but she didn't believe me."

"What did she bring? Tuna sandwiches?"

"Peanut butter and jelly. Tuna's too expensive."

"She actually said that?"

"She did."

"Oh, dear. I'm surprised she'd buy cruise tickets, even cheap ones."

Savannah watched as her father-in-law gently guided his dithering wife up to the security check, his arm wrapped protectively around her shoulders.

It warmed Savannah's heart to see how kindly and lovingly Richard treated his wife—his wife whose company many other people avoided whenever possible. She couldn't help loving her father-in-law. He embodied the very best of Dirk's fine qualities, all rolled into one. Minus the curmudgeon factor.

"Richard bought the tickets before he told her," Savannah told Tammy. "Her birthday is Tuesday. We'll be celebrating aboard."

"That's sweet."

"Yes. He is."

"And she saved my life."

Savannah nodded, remembering that dark, horrible night, when Dora's nursing skills and calm, professional ministrations had saved Savannah's best friend. "Yes, she sure did. I'll be forever grateful to her."

That brief walk down Unpleasant Memory Lane was enough to shake Savannah out of her pouty mood. By the time they had cleared security, which turned out to be much faster and more efficient than an airline checkpoint, she was excited and looking forward to boarding the luxury liner that was to be their home for the next week.

With Dirk and his parents leading the way, Granny and Waycross behind Savannah and Tammy, and Ryan and John bringing up the rear, the Moonlight Magnolia gang in all its glory exited the gigantic terminal and stepped into the golden Seattle sunlight. Although the morning had been cloudy with occasional drizzle, it seemed as though the weather itself was wishing them a "bon voyage."

As they walked along the balcony, they could see their ship, a glistening white beauty called the *Arctic Queen*, just across the gangway. She was eight decks high, with the sapphire blue logo of the Star of the North Cruise Line wrapped around her middle—a line of eight-point compass stars, with their tips joined east to west.

The ship was being loaded, which was a study in organized pandemonium. Not only were tons of luggage being stowed on her lower decks, but enough supplies to feed and accommodate over a thousand guests in luxury for seven days and nights.

The Moonlight entourage made their way from the balcony and onto the gangway.

"I never thought I'd get to do this," Granny said as they took a couple of turns, back and forth along the metal walkway, then approached the vessel's main port side entrance. The large double doors opened into the atrium lobby.

"I've been dreaming of it since I was a girl, and here I am!" Gran said, her voice trembling with excitement.

Everyone in the group stepped aside to allow her to be the first to enter. As Savannah watched her grandmother step onto the ship, her face glowing with the joy of long-held dreams fulfilled, Savannah silently thanked Natasha Van Cleef for making this moment possible.

"Lordy, lordy," Gran breathed, taking in the magnificence of the atrium. "Have you ever seen such a sight!"

Tammy and Waycross followed. Tammy's eyes

widened, as Waycross said in a deep, Georgia drawl, "Whoa, howdy! Get a load o' this!"

Savannah could hardly blame them for being so impressed. Far grander than any hotel Savannah had ever visited, the *Arctic Queen*'s atrium lobby certainly knew how to impress her visitors.

Soaring four decks high, the massive room was breathtaking. From its stained-glass ceiling, depicting a night sky filled with stars and swirling with the colors of the aurora borealis, to the balconies of each floor with their gilded, filigree railings, to the twin, sweeping staircases that descended to a sparkling water feature in the center of the room, the ship warmly welcomed her passengers, while giving them a taste of luxurious adventures to come.

Savannah felt Dirk's big, warm hand close around hers as they strolled toward the center of the room. "This is great, babe," he said. He pointed to his parents and Granny, who had paused by the fountain to enjoy the beauty of the blue and green lights playing on the water. "It's really nice to have my folks along for the ride. Thanks for being a good sport about it."

"No problem," she said. "I seem to recall you tossing quite a handful of cash into that cookie jar for Granny. Turnabout's fair play."

She smiled and squeezed his fingers. She was glad she had chosen to be generous. Goodness certainly had its rewards, like having your husband give you a look that said he thought you were the best woman on earth.

John and Ryan left Tammy and Waycross to enjoy the fountain with the others and walked over to Savannah and Dirk. They had wide, satisfied grins on their faces.

"This is very nice, indeed," said John, nodding enthusiastically. Turning to Ryan, he added, "We've cruised on larger ships than this, but none so lovely."

"That's for sure," Ryan replied. "I predict this is going to be a very pleasant trip for all of us."

For some reason that she couldn't explain, Savannah felt a shiver run through her, as though someone had just opened a large porthole nearby and let in a cold draft.

Yes, if we can keep our client alive, she thought.

No sooner had the sentence made its chilling transit through her brain than Savannah decided to shift gears into a more serious frame of mind. With the grandeur of the ship enveloping her senses, it would be easy for her and her team to forget why they were here, and that simply wouldn't do.

With the feel of the plush, azure blue carpet underfoot, the sparkling crystal chandeliers overhead, and the aroma of fresh-baked pastries and gourmet coffees wafting through the atrium, it was hard to imagine something as horrible and base as murder could be on any of their fellow passengers' minds.

But that threatening note was real. Someone with very bad intentions had written it. Even if their purpose had been merely to frighten Natasha Van Cleef, they had succeeded all too well, and that in itself was an act of cruelty.

Added to the unpleasantness was the icy feeling that was crawling around, deep in Savannah's gut. A sense that all was not well and was about to get even worse.

She'd had that feeling many times, and because it never failed to be accurate, she trusted it. The few times she had ignored it, things had turned out badly, indeed.

Things aren't going to turn out badly. Not this time. Not on my *watch,* she told herself.

"Let's find out if Natasha and her people are aboard yet," Savannah said, leading the men past the grand Steinway and over to the reception desk.

After conferring with a purser and receiving a sealed envelope from him, she returned to Dirk, Ryan, and John. "Ms. Van Cleef left us a letter."

Savannah scanned the note, handwritten on elegant linen paper with the scrolled monogram NVC at the top. Turning to Dirk, she said, "She wants you and me to meet her in her room soon after the ship sails. She's in the penthouse suite."

"Of course she is," Dirk replied with a sniff. "You wouldn't expect her to bunk with the pigs and chickens down below."

"How about her entourage?" Ryan asked, suddenly all business. "Where are they?"

She didn't like the suddenly serious look in his green eyes. It occurred to Savannah that perhaps he, too, was sensing something less than festive in the air.

"Natasha's husband and personal assistant are in the suite with her. Her editor is aboard, too. She has a regular stateroom, like ours, one deck below Natasha's and close to ours."

"Those three people," Dirk said, "they're the only ones aboard with any connection to Natasha?"

"Presumably," Savannah told him. "We certainly hope so. But just to make certain, we have to get our hands on the ship's passenger manifest. Mrs. Van Cleef needs to look it over and see if she recognizes any other names."

John looked doubtful. "There was a time, back in

the early days of cruising, when passengers were given copies of the manifest and knew who their fellow passengers were. But the world is a far less open and trusting place these days."

"With good reason." From the inside of his jacket, Dirk took a small notebook and pen and began to scribble in it. "You wait and see. I'll get a copy of that . . . whatever you called it. I'll wave my shield under their nose, and they won't dare say no."

With a grin Savannah said, "Be sure to ask nicely and say, 'pretty please.'"

He snorted. "Oh, yeah. I'm famous for my 'pretty pleasing.'"

Savannah glanced over to the center of the room and saw that Granny was walking toward them, having left Richard and Dora to listen to the pianist, and Tammy and Waycross to gaze into the fountain.

She sidled up to her granddaughter, slipped her arm through Savannah's, and said, "Okay. Enough of this dillydallying. We're here to work, and I aim to earn my keep. What's first on the agenda? You want me to search Ms. Van Cleef's room, make sure everything's all safe and sound? I'll check under the bed and in the closets. Can't be too careful when it's a matter o' life and death."

Savannah chuckled to herself, enjoying her grandmother's enthusiasm and work ethic. "That's okay, Gran," she told her. "For the time being anyway, the rest of you guys are off duty."

"Not me," Dirk grumbled. "I've gotta wring something called a 'manifest' out of somebody before I can relax and kick back."

John pulled a gold pocket watch from his linen

trousers, flipped it open, and said, "We'll be setting sail in less than an hour. Would you like Ryan and me to take the others somewhere to get a pleasant beverage? Then we'll find us all a spot on an upper deck with a nice view of the city for our bon voyage drink."

"That would be great," Savannah told him. "I'll go with Dirk, just in case he needs a bit of Southern charm to 'sweeten the pot,' so to speak. If we get finished in time, we'll join you."

As Savannah and Dirk watched Ryan and John corral the group and head for the rear of the ship, Dirk slipped his arm around her waist.

"Since when are you the 'sweet' half of this crime-fighting duo?" he asked. "I thought when we used to play good cop–bad cop you were the mean one."

She giggled and shrugged. "What can I say? I've mellowed over the years."

Laughing, he said, "Darlin', 'mellow' is not a word I would ever use to describe you. More like a wonderful mix of piss and vinegar. . . . That's *my* girl." He kissed the top of her head. "I wouldn't have her any other way."

Chapter 5

Just before the ship sailed, Savannah and Dirk managed to locate their gang on an upper deck, port side. Ryan and John had assembled the perfect seating arrangement to accommodate the entire Moonlight Magnolia agency. Four tables, placed end to end, afforded everyone a great view of the magnificent Seattle skyline as the ship slipped away from the pier.

For a moment, Savannah allowed herself the luxury of enjoying the experience and recording it in her heart, to be savored for the rest of her life. She breathed in deeply, filling her lungs with the pungent salt air. She relished the wind's caress in her hair without worrying about the fact that she'd never get her dark curls back in any semblance of order until after the next shampoo.

Her eyes scanned the wonderful old city, unique in all the world. From the more rustic buildings that harkened back to its days of lumber mills and gold rushes, to the glistening steel and glass of the high tech skyscrapers, the iconic Space Needle and massive Ferris wheel, the Emerald City was rich in both colorful history and the promise of the future.

Savannah tucked the moment away, to be taken out like a favorite piece of jewelry at a later time and touched and enjoyed at leisure. But now, she had business to attend to.

"We've only got a few minutes," she told the group, as John placed the "sail away" beverage of choice into her hand. A mug of hot, strong coffee.

Not exactly her idea of a celebratory cocktail. But then, Tammy was pregnant, Gran a teetotaler, and the rest of them on duty. It was certainly the most sensible choice.

John saw her momentary look of disappointment and gave her a sympathetic smile. "Apologies, love," he whispered, indicating the rest of the group with a nod of his silver head. "Seattle. Coffee. 'Twas the best we could do under the circumstances."

"Gotcha." She winked at him. "No problem."

Ryan handed a matching mug to Dirk. "Did you manage to score a manifest?"

Savannah waited silently to see if Dirk would tell the truth. She wouldn't have blamed him if he hadn't. Manly man pride and all that.

"Nope," he admitted. "Savannah did." He took a swig of the coffee, licked his upper lip, and explained. "I tried to squeeze one out of a purser and nearly got us all thrown off the ship. Apparently, they don't just give those out like Snickers bars on Halloween night."

Richard turned to Savannah, quite impressed. "You got a purser to let go of a manifest?"

"No," she said. "Seems pursers have strong feelings about passenger privacy. We tried three of them."

"Then who gave you one?" Waycross asked as he removed his flannel shirt and draped it around Tammy's shoulders, leaving him to shiver in only a thin Studebaker T-shirt.

Savannah snickered. "Baggage handlers appear to be a bit less picky."

"If they're bribed," Dirk grumbled into his mug.

"Whatever did you bribe him with?" Tammy asked.

Savannah drew a deep sigh, much like the ones she had seen homicidal maniacs draw moments before confessing a capital crime. "I'd like to say I accomplished it with wit, wisdom, and feminine wiles. But do you remember that tin of macadamia chocolate chip cookies I brought for tonight's First Night Aboard celebrations?"

"No!" Dora was horrified. "You didn't!"

"Sorry. Had to."

Dora let out a soulful groan and sagged in her chair. "That's awful! What are we going to do for dessert? There's no telling how much they'll charge us for dessert on a ship as fancy as this." She turned to Richard. "We'll just have to go without. That's all there is to it. I knew I should have gone to Costco and stocked up on those little individually wrapped pastries."

Richard laughed and draped his arm over his wife's shoulders. "Babe, you're the only woman alive who's afraid she'll starve to death on a cruise ship."

"I'm more worried about gaining weight," Tammy said, stroking her enormous belly.

Savannah gulped. "I'm more afraid of you losing

weight," she said, "about seven or eight pounds. All at once."

"Me too," John said, giving Tammy a concerned, paternal smile. "I can't believe your doctor gave his blessing for you to cruise this late in your pregnancy."

Tammy smirked. "She didn't exactly give her blessing."

"She sure didn't," Waycross added. "She told her to stay put. You can't always count on these due dates being right. That's what she said. But no! You can't get this one here to listen to nobody, let alone do as she's told."

Giving Savannah a wink, Tammy said, "I've been hanging around Savannah too long."

"No, no." Savannah shook her head. "You aren't blaming me for you traipsing off to the high seas with a baby that's about to drop like an egg outta a loose goose and—"

"Stop it," Granny said, holding up a traffic cop hand. "That's quite enough of this rigmarole. There's a doctor and at least one nurse on board this ship. A whole clinic thing—"

"Sick bay," Ryan whispered.

"Whatever you call it, that's open day and night." Granny took a breath, reached across the table, and patted Dora's hand. "Plus we've got ourselves a retired registered nurse here with umpteen years on the maternity floor of the hospital, so *there*."

Savannah was moderately reassured by the confident nod and smile that Dora gave Tammy.

"Besides," Tammy added, "nature knows what she's doing. Babies have been coming into the world for thousands of years, long before there were hospitals and maternity wards. When the time comes, my body will know what to do—here on this ship or at the birthing center back in San Carmelita."

Dirk leaned over and whispered in Savannah's ear, "She talks all brave now. Let's hear what she is saying when those labor pains hit."

"Shush. They don't call them 'labor pains' anymore. Too many negative connotations. They're 'contractions' now."

"Yeah, right. I've seen women having babies plenty of times. No matter what you call those 'contractions,' they hurt."

"I heard that, Dirk-o," Tammy told him. "You keep spewing your old-coot negativity and I won't let you in the delivery room."

Dirk gave her a horrified look. "I'll take that as a solemn promise, if that's okay with you."

Savannah glanced at her watch, then out at the horizon where the city skyline was receding from sight. She nudged Dirk in the ribs with her elbow. "It's time for you and me to get back to work, big boy."

As they rose to their feet, Ryan and John stood as well.

"Are you away to Ms. Van Cleef's suite?" John asked.

Savannah nodded. "Duty calls."

"Would you like some company?" Ryan offered. He nodded toward the rest of the group, who were engaged in lively conversation. "I think this gang can keep themselves entertained on their own."

Savannah noticed that Granny and Dora were involved in what appeared to be a deep, engrossing exchange. Though with a second, more discerning look,

Savannah realized that Dora, as usual, was doing the talking and Granny the listening.

Deep in her heart, Savannah blessed her grandmother.

Gran had a mouth on her, no doubt. She was, after all, a Reid gal. But she had also lived long enough to accumulate a wealth of wisdom. Granny Reid understood the value of listening. She truly believed that she healed her fellow human beings by listening to their stories.

That made her the perfect companion for Dora Jones.

Savannah turned her attention back to Ryan. "Actually, Natasha asked that this first onboard briefing be with just Dirk and me. But we'll certainly fill you in later."

"You're right about this group here though," Dirk said. "They don't seem to need any babysitting."

Savannah added, "Why don't you gentlemen stroll around the ship, check it out, get your bearings."

Ryan gave her a wry smile. "Look for some disgruntled miscreant who might want to murder their least favorite author?"

She nodded. "Exactly."

As Savannah stepped into the elevator with Dirk, she noticed that he was scowling. Again. He had done a lot of that lately, which wasn't out of the ordinary for Dirk. He had been scowling for years.

But now that they were married, she felt it was her wifely duty to cheer him up whenever possible. Before "two had become one," she might have quietly allowed him to wallow in his wretchedness, because it was blatantly obvious that he secretly enjoyed it.

However, her Southern belle upbringing dictated that she expend every effort within reason to pull him, kicking and screaming if need be, into the sunshine of her love.

"What's the matter with you?" She punched the appropriate button for the penthouse suite with a bit more vim and vigor than the task required.

Okay, she thought. *Cheering up a grumpy guy who doesn't want to be cheered isn't the most pleasant task on the Wifely Duty List.*

But then, one couldn't always pick and choose one's responsibilities. For better and for worse, and all that matrimonial stuff.

"Tammy called me an old coot."

Savannah could swear that his lower lip was actually protruding in a classic two-year-old's pout.

"She always calls you names. But to your credit, since she's been pregnant, you've only called her 'Tammy.' You get major kudos for that."

He refused to be comforted. "She usually just calls me stuff like 'Dirk-o' and 'curmudgeon.' Not 'old coot.'"

"Curmudgeon and old coot are pretty much the same thing, you know."

"They are?"

"Yes."

"I didn't know that." He sniffed. Loudly. "For Pete's sake, I'm only in my forties. That's a long way from 'old' or 'coot,' either one."

Savannah slipped her arm through his. "It is, darlin'. It certainly is. But you have to see it from her point of view."

"Which is?"

"You're old enough to be her father."

"I am not!"

"Are too, and then some."

She watched him think it over, do the math, and reach the sad conclusion.

"Okay. I am. But only because I got an early start."

"How early?"

He actually blushed. "I think I should keep that one to myself. I'm not altogether proud of my wayward youth."

Laughing, she stood on tiptoe and kissed him on the cheek. "Somehow it doesn't surprise me that you were a bit of a naughty boy back in the olden days."

Looking a bit hurt, he said, "Why would you think that?"

"Because it would've taken you a while to get so good at your, um, technique."

She was always surprised to see how quickly his depression and grumpiness could vanish. He brightened in an instant and said, "Really?"

"Absolutely."

"Cool."

The elevator door opened, and they stepped out into an empty hallway. He wrapped his arm around her waist and pulled her tightly against him. When he looked down into her eyes, she was surprised to see that his were misty.

"You know, babe," he said, "You might think this is kinda silly, but a lot of times when we're, you know, together . . . I wish you were my first. My only. Then we could have learned it, figured it all out, discovered it, together. Just you and me. I would've liked that."

In a heartbeat she reached up, wrapped her arms around his neck, pulled his head down to hers, and gave him a long, passionate kiss.

When they finally came up for air, she said, "I would've liked that, too, darlin'. In fact, once we get all of our business done, and we're inside our stateroom, all nice and cozy and alone, I think that's exactly what we're going to do."

He looked confused.

So, she elaborated.

Tucking her chin, looking up at him with big pseudo-innocent blue eyes, she batted her lashes and said, "Why, sir, I do believe you've been attempting to seduce me for quite some time now. Even though I'm fresh as the first snowflake of winter, I reckon I might be persuaded to compromise my virtue, just a wee bit. If you play your cards right."

His deep chuckle went through Savannah like warm cognac as he pulled her tightly against him. "As it turns out," he said, "I happen to have an ace tucked up my sleeve."

After giving him one more deep, long kiss, she whispered breathlessly, "You oughta check that ace of yours, Detective Sergeant Coulter. I do believe it and half a dozen card decks have done slid down into the front of your trousers."

Chapter 6

A few moments later, Savannah and Dirk stood at the door to the ship's most luxurious stateroom, the penthouse suite, now occupied by Natasha Van Cleef and company.

Savannah patted her hair into place as best she could. Dirk adjusted his clothing. Then she rapped lightly on the door.

It was opened almost immediately by a beautiful Asian woman, wearing a black suit, a crisp white shirt, a navy blue silk vest spangled with golden stars, and white gloves. Her dark hair was pulled back into a chignon that was as perfect as her simple but stunning makeup.

Savannah's brain took several seconds to process what she was seeing. "Good gracious! You're the *butler*." It was more of a question than a statement. The moment it left her mouth, Savannah felt like an idiot.

But then, she thought, how was she supposed to

know that not all butlers were male, British, and heavy around the middle?

She cast a quick look at Dirk and saw her own surprise reflected on his face, as well.

"I never saw a butler that looked like you," he said to the woman.

The butler gave him the benefit of a coy though still professional smile and asked, "How many butlers have you met, sir?"

He chuckled. "Okay. You've got me there."

"Most of the butlers we've seen," Savannah said, "were on *Downton Abbey*."

"Then you probably haven't been served by nearly enough of our number."

She opened the door wide and gestured most elegantly with her gloved hand for them to enter. "Please come in and allow me to correct that situation. We're having champagne and hors d'oeuvres featuring ingredients from the great Pacific Northwest."

She led them inside the suite, where Savannah's eyes were dazzled by glimpses of chocolate brown marble streaked with gold and ivory veins, polished brass, glistening beveled glass, and lush tropical greenery.

To their immediate right was a bar, well stocked. Trays of canapés lined its marble sideboard, along with two silver buckets, filled with ice and dark green bottles of Dom Pérignon.

Beyond the serving area, Savannah could see an expansive living room, filled with the most inviting leather chairs and sofa. The accent tables and entertainment center were teak.

Objets d'art complimented the simple and sophisticated furniture: carved statuettes, enameled and bejeweled boxes, metal sculptures that depicted the wildlife of the Northwest, and books with fine leather bindings and gilt-edged pages.

Beyond the room and to the left, a door was open to what was, undoubtedly, the master bedroom suite. She caught glimpses of an exquisite silk bedspread, an enormous television, and the bathroom beyond with a soaking tub, fireplace, and floor-to-ceiling glass wall with an ocean view.

"Don't get used to this," she whispered to Dirk. "I'm pretty sure ours won't be anything like this."

"We'll have to kick the chickens out before we can go to bed. Is that what you're saying?" he returned.

"Pretty much."

Before they even had time to take in the sights, the nontraditional butler was offering them each a glass of champagne.

Savannah held up her hand. "No, thank you. We're on duty. We've come to discuss business with Ms. Van Cleef."

"Don't be ridiculous," said a female voice from beyond the living room where the glass walls opened onto a large veranda. "Have a glass of champagne. Two if you like, and some hors d'oeuvres."

Natasha Van Cleef strolled toward them, quite a different figure from the one who had visited their home. Gone was the formal suit and designer accessories. She floated into the room in a floor-length, brightly colored caftan that made her look like an oversized butterfly. Her magnificent silver hair lay, wild and loose, round her shoulders, and at first glance, she appeared to be a much younger woman.

It was only when she drew nearer and Savannah looked more closely that she could see the weariness on the woman's face, the dark circles under her eyes, the puffiness that hinted that she might have been crying earlier.

Her demeanor seemed far less celebratory than her words as she took two glasses of champagne from the butler and handed one to Savannah, then the other to Dirk.

"This is a cruise," she said, "and we're in one of the most beautiful areas of the world. I should know. In my lifetime, I've traveled and seen more of it than most people. As your employer I demand you have a good time."

Savannah looked into her glass and saw the tiniest of myriad, glistening bubbles that distinguished Dom Pérignon in the world of sparkling wines. *What a lovely and unexpected treat*, she thought.

"To Alaska." Natasha Van Cleef lifted her glass to them. The miniature book charms on her bracelet glinted in the sunlight. "And to the Moonlight Magnolia Detective Agency, who will be keeping me safe and sound on this wonderful trip."

"Here, here," Dirk said, joining them in the toast. "We just want to get you back to Seattle, all in one piece."

Savannah gulped. Okay, so Dirk's toast wasn't the most gracious in the world, but his heart was good. Or at least in the right place.

She stole a quick glance over at Natasha, to see if she was offended. But the author looked more amused than annoyed or nervous.

"Let's go outside on the veranda and enjoy the view

while we talk," Natasha suggested. "Sooyung, bring along
the champagne and those hors d'oeuvres, too. There's no
reason to starve just because we're discussing business."

Ah, a woman after my own heart, Savannah thought
as she and Dirk followed Natasha. *This collaboration
might work out well, after all.*

No sooner had the butler set a tray of the canapés on
a nearby table than Dirk hurried over and nabbed a
couple. He closed his eyes with rapture as the first one,
some sort of wafer with a luscious lump of crabmeat,
went down the hatch.

Savannah cringed when she saw his careless choice
for the second tidbit, a cucumber round adorned with a
dollop of some luscious cream and sprinkled liberally
with red caviar. She remembered all too well his reaction when he had sampled caviar at Ryan and John's
restaurant opening. It had not been pretty. She'd been
forced, out of a sense of common decency, to smuggle
his grossly soiled napkin home in her purse, where she
laundered it thoroughly before returning it.

Dirk despised anything that tasted, in his not-so-
humble opinion, "too fishy." He didn't even like his
fish to taste like fish.

Silently, she tried to send him a strong message
using mental telepathy and a stern look. *If you do anything other than swallow that, you're dead.*

He seemed to hear her, because he gave her a pathetic look of horror and helplessness before he began
to gag. Unfortunately, in typical Dirk mode, he had
downed his champagne in a couple of gulps and had
none left.

With a sense of great sadness, knowing it would
probably be years before she would, once again, have

the opportunity to sip Dom Pérignon, she handed him her glass. In quintessential Savannah fashion, it was still mostly full.

In their little family of two, she was the sipper and savorer of the goodies. He was the old-fashioned Hoover vacuum cleaner, slurping up everything in sight without taking time to breathe, let alone savor.

But she did feel slightly satisfied when she saw the look of enormous gratitude on his face, once he had washed down the foul tidbit.

One rather serious social faux pas averted, she told herself proudly. But then, they had set sail less than an hour ago, so there was still plenty of time and ample opportunities ahead for him to embarrass her.

She stole a glance at their hostess to see if she had noticed, but the author's back was turned to them. She was strolling to the other end of the spacious veranda, where a man was luxuriating in a hot tub. Nearby, a shapely young blonde lay facedown on a chaise longue, soaking in the sun. She was getting quite a dose of it, too, because the teeny bikini she was almost wearing blocked precious few rays.

Like many sunbathing ladies, she had untied the strings across her back to avoid the telltale white lines that would interfere with the perfect tan.

Assuming they were meant to follow, Savannah and Dirk trailed behind Natasha as she approached the other two. But neither the man in the tub nor the blonde seemed to notice their arrival.

The woman appeared to be asleep, and the man was quite obviously fixated on her. More specifically, on her curvaceous rear end.

When he did notice them, he jumped, as though

someone had just goosed his rear end, and donned the classic look of a guilty man caught in the act of ogling.

"Hi, honey," he said, far too brightly. He ran his wet fingers through his thick salt-and-pepper hair. "I thought you were inside taking a nap."

Savannah watched Natasha closely as she walked over to him, bent down, and pressed a kiss to his cheek. Apparently, she hadn't noticed or didn't mind.

"Darling," Natasha said, "I'd like for you to meet the two primary members of our security detail. This lovely lady is the famous private detective, Savannah Reid herself, founder and owner of the Moonlight Magnolia Detective Agency. This is her husband, Sergeant Dirk Coulter, a celebrated and decorated detective in the San Carmelita Police Department." She turned to Savannah and Dirk. "May I introduce my husband, Colin Van Cleef, the best husband any author could wish for. He leaves me alone when I need time to write. He brings me all sorts of delectable delights to keep my strength up when I'm facing tight deadlines, and most importantly, he never advises me on plots or characterization."

Natasha gave his right earlobe a playful tweak. "Though he does assist me from time to time with research—for the sex scenes, that is."

Savannah registered the odd and not very friendly look that Colin Van Cleef gave his wife over his shoulder. Though she wasn't certain how to interpret it.

Annoyance? Deeply held resentment? Perhaps something even deeper than that?

Something told Savannah that perhaps there hadn't been a lot of "research" going on lately.

She looked at Dirk, who was standing beside her,

and she could tell that he was watching, too. They would have to compare notes later.

Natasha walked over to the young woman, who was still sleeping as peacefully as an infant in a stroller being wheeled about a park. Tapping on the blonde's shoulder, she said, "Olive, dear, wake up. We have company."

Apparently, the sunbather had been sound asleep, because she jumped up from the chaise as though someone had lit a tiki torch beneath it. So rattled was she that she left her bikini top on the lounge and sat there, displaying her bare bosoms to all present.

"What? What did you . . . I mean, do you, do you need me to do something for you, Ms. Van Cleef?" she mumbled semicoherently.

"Indeed, I do, Olive," Natasha replied in a stiff monotone. "I need you to put your bathing suit top on. If you happen to have a cover-up nearby, please use it immediately."

Still groggy, the blonde looked around frantically, and seeing no sign of any substantial garment nearby, she snatched her bikini top off the chaise. Jumping to her feet, she scurried away toward the nearest door, clutching her bare breasts in her hands.

"That," Natasha said, "was my charming and efficient personal assistant, Olive Kelly. She's better at her job than you might think from that first impression." She sighed. "Not a lot better though, I must admit. I'll be keeping her until the end of the cruise. After that she's gone. I swear, I'm forced to change personal assistants more frequently than the hand towels in my guest bathroom."

Savannah heard a sound behind her. When she turned

she saw the butler escorting yet another woman onto the veranda. The newcomer had short dark hair and wore a black pantsuit and eyeglasses with heavy black rims.

One look at her face told everyone present that she was upset.

Instantly, Natasha hurried over to her and took her hand. "What is it, Patricia? What's wrong?"

The woman looked at Savannah, then Dirk. "I don't know if you want me to say anything. I mean, maybe we should speak alone."

"It's okay," Natasha told her. "These are the security people I told you about, Savannah Reid and Dirk Coulter. If you have something to tell me, they need to hear it, too."

Natasha turned to Savannah. "This is my dear friend and longtime editor, Patricia Chumley. You can trust her completely, as I do."

Natasha led Patricia over to a chair and gently coaxed her onto it. "Now, what is it, darling? What's wrong?"

The woman reached into the pocket of her pants and pulled out a white piece of paper.

Before she unfolded it and began to read, Savannah knew instinctively what it was.

Another letter.

Another threat.

Even Colin was concerned enough to crawl out of the hot tub, wrap a towel around his middle, and hurry over to stand beside his wife.

"What is it, Pat?" he asked. "What do you have there?"

"A letter. Someone shoved it under my door," Patricia said. "It must've been while I was unpacking, because I'm sure it wasn't there when I first entered the room."

"You've read it?" Savannah asked, though she knew from the pallor of the woman's face that she had, and it was bad.

Patricia nodded. "Yes. I thought it was for me. Some sort of bill or invitation or something from the ship's staff. But once I read it, I knew it was from the same person who sent you the other one."

Savannah pulled a clean tissue from her pocket, intending to use it as a makeshift glove to handle this new piece of evidence. But before she could make a move to take it from Patricia, Natasha had grabbed it.

As Natasha snatched the paper from her editor, Savannah could see her client's fingers trembling. Natasha held it up and read the message aloud, her voice shaking even more than her hands:

Count the hours. Hours. Minutes. Count them and enjoy them. That's all you have left.

Chapter 7

Savannah had always imagined that authors led pretty cushy lives, lounging on satin fainting couches, nibbling bonbons, sipping wine, and dictating their latest book to shirtless Chippendale-esque hunks sitting on overstuffed ottomans at their feet.

That was when they were not getting full body hot oil massages and going on trips to exotic ports of call to "research."

Hence, Savannah had always wanted to be an author when she grew up someday.

Being married, she would, of course, allow Dirk to take her dictation, as long as he did it bare chested and wearing his snuggest jeans. Since she was so benevolent and considerate, she would even furnish him with a comfortable chair.

But Savannah decided to reevaluate her opinion of the author's lifestyle as, only a few minutes after they had received that awful note, Natasha Van Cleef was sitting at her dressing table, applying her makeup and twisting her abundance of wild curls into an elegant updo.

Pretty good work ethic, she thought, *considering. Most people would be curled into a fetal position on their bed, refusing to leave their suite for any reason whatsoever.*

Savannah sat nearby, on the edge of the king-sized bed, watching quietly. But when for the third time Natasha dropped one of her makeup items, she had to say something. "Are you sure you have to go to this predinner meet and greet? I'm sure your fans would understand if you didn't show up, under the circumstances."

Natasha bent over and scooped up the mascara tube from the floor. She tossed it into the ostrich-skin makeup case in front of her. "My fans won't understand, because if I have anything to do about it, they'll never know. I'm depending on your agency to be most discreet about this horrid situation."

"We certainly will be," Savannah assured her. "But what about the other people who know? Surely you've mentioned it to the ship staff."

"The captain is aware, and yes, we had to alert the security officers."

"As well as those closest to you? Your friends and relatives?"

"No. The only people I know personally aboard this ship are Colin, Olive, and Patricia. No one else in my personal circles is aware of this. That's the way I want to keep it."

"Then I hope everyone involved respects your wishes and protects your privacy."

Even as Savannah uttered the words, she knew it was a case of "Hope springs eternal, but people have loose lips."

It was a bit naive to think that people would keep something as spooky and juicy as anonymous death threats to themselves, even personal assistants, editors, husbands, or ship security staff.

Natasha glanced at the clock. "I'm going to have to get dressed. I'm expected in the library in ten minutes."

Savannah stood. "Then I'll leave you to it. But first I just want to ask you one quick question."

Natasha reached into her makeup bag and pulled out an amber medicine bottle. She removed a small tablet and popped it, then pushed her makeup case away from her and turned to face Savannah. "I usually don't have to take a pill before an appearance. But you're making me nervous, and that is not what I hired you for."

"I'm sorry. Truly I am. But it's just a simple, standard question under these circumstances, so please don't take offense."

"Usually people say that right before they utter something highly offensive."

Savannah chuckled. "That's true. But I have only the best of intentions. I'm just trying to keep you safe."

"Ask."

"From the moment you stepped on this ship until right now, have Mr. Van Cleef and Olive been with you?"

The expression on Natasha Van Cleef's face went from guarded to serious in a heartbeat. "What kind of question is that?"

Savannah locked eyes with her client and gave her the same sapphire blue lasers that she usually reserved for hardened criminals. "Necessary. That's what kind of question it is, and I need an honest and accurate answer."

Natasha rose and walked over to stand uncomfortably close to Savannah. The two women were nearly nose to nose.

"If you start questioning the characters and intentions of the people closest to me," Natasha said, her amber eyes flashing, "you and I are not going to get along very well or be working together very long."

"So be it," Savannah replied with equal intensity. "For as long as we *are* together, you need to help me protect you. The best way you can do that is to be completely honest with me. Did your husband or your assistant leave your sight at any time since you boarded this ship?"

Natasha stood, glaring at Savannah, her fists clenched at her sides, for what seemed like forever. Finally, to Savannah's relief, she said, "Yes."

"Which of them?"

"Both."

"Together?"

"No."

"When and what reason did they give?"

"I sent Olive to buy a couple of pens. Bold markers that I like to use for book signing. She forgot to pack them."

"Was she gone long?"

"Yes. Olive's a nitwit. It takes her forever to do anything."

Savannah drew a breath and nodded. "Okay, and your husband?"

"I asked him to go buy us some Bonine. She forgot to pack that, too."

"Bonine? What's that?"

"Motion sickness medicine. I highly recommend it, if you intend to enjoy your cruise."

Savannah filed that tidbit away for future reference. "How long was he gone?"

Natasha sighed, exasperated, and glanced again at her watch. "About as long as it would take to run downstairs and purchase such a thing. I now have seven minutes, Ms. Reid. Are we quite finished here?"

"We are. For now."

"Then, hopefully, you and I won't be seeing each other until tomorrow afternoon at the earliest."

"Tomorrow afternoon?"

"That's correct. This evening I'll be dining at the captain's table. I can't imagine that anything terrible would befall us there. Then tomorrow morning I'll be having breakfast in my suite and a nice long massage afterward, again, here in my suite."

"That sounds lovely," Savannah said without enthusiasm.

"I'm sure it will be. So I won't need to be babysat until tomorrow afternoon at the earliest."

Savannah smiled, but her eyes were anything but friendly. "Oh, no, Ms. Van Cleef. You'll see me again in just a few moments when you step outside this suite.

In fact, you'll see me every time you step outside the security of this suite. That's just part of the protection that my agency is determined to afford you."

Natasha's cheeks flushed red with indignation. "Now how is that going to look? Everywhere I go on this ship, I'll have you tagging along behind me? Certainly nothing suspicious about that."

"I understand," Savannah said in the most soothing tone that she could muster. "We'll compromise. It won't be only me following you. My agency members will take turns. No one will be the wiser, I promise."

Natasha didn't look happy, and she certainly didn't look convinced.

It occurred to Savannah that perhaps this was why John and Ryan were doing less body guarding these days and spending more and more time in their restaurant. More than once they had told her stories of clients who paid for their protection, then balked at the lack of privacy that required.

"It's going to be okay, Ms. Van Cleef. Really. You won't even know we're there, unless you need us. You're going to have a wonderful time on this cruise. Your fans will be delighted to meet you, and we're going to keep all of you safe and sound."

Once again, Natasha glanced at her watch. "I now have six minutes to dress and get downstairs to greet my most loyal fans, who have spent thousands of dollars to go on this cruise and to meet and chat with me. Do you mind if I do that?"

Savannah bowed her head in a gracious nod, then headed for the door. "I'll be waiting outside to escort you down."

* * *

As Savannah took yet another sip of her Alaska king crab and brie soup, held it in her mouth, and delighted in every nuance of the multilayered flavors, she silently thanked the woman who was seated at the next table. The captain's table.

So near, and yet so far away.

For the past twenty minutes, as Savannah and the other members of her agency sat at the noncaptain's regular ol' table, she had done her best to catch Natasha Van Cleef's eye, if for no other reason than to reestablish their former rapport. But Natasha had quite successfully avoided her gaze as she chatted happily with the ship's handsome captain, who was seated next to her.

Apparently he was quite charmed by her, as he neglected his other eight dining companions seated at the large, circular table and focused his full attention on his celebrity guest.

Being invited to a captain's table on any ship was a cruiser's dream. But until their dying day, the lucky folk at his table tonight would be sharing their memory of the auspicious occasion with observations like: "It was okay, I guess, sitting at the captain's table, except for that loudmouthed author. I swear, the more wine she drank the louder she got. The rest of us didn't have a chance to get a word in edgewise."

"That Natasha gal was pretty miffed at you," Dirk said between bites of soup. "What did you say to her there in the bedroom that got her so mad? She didn't speak a single word to us all the way down to the library."

While Savannah was relieved to see that he was

using his very best table manners—she might have mentioned something about torture, death, and dismemberment if he picked his teeth at the table—she wasn't in the mood to share every nuance of that miserable bedroom conversation with the entire table.

She shrugged and tried to deliver the briefest of explanations as casually as possible. "I asked her if she knew her husband's and personal assistant's whereabouts from the time they boarded until they got that ugly note. Now she's a mite peeved."

Granny nabbed another hot roll from the basket, snickered, and said, "I reckon she was. That's pretty much like asking, 'Do you reckon your husband's got it out for you? Think he might be intendin' to bump you off?'"

Tammy picked at her salad, searching for the darkest green leaves. "Actually, it's not that outrageous of a question, considering," she said.

Savannah could practically feel her own ears perking up. "Considering what?"

"Considering what I read on the Internet."

"By all means, do tell!"

As Waycross selected his own darkest leaves and transferred them to Tammy's plate, she explained, "I found several gossip columnists claiming that the Van Cleefs are splitting up. More specifically, that she's leaving him."

Savannah nearly choked on her soup. "When were you going to tell us this juicy little tidbit?"

Tammy shrugged. "You know how it is. Those gossip mongers aren't always right. I thought I'd wait for corroborating evidence before I leveled such an accusation."

Granny gave her an incredulous look. "I applaud your good intentions and noble ethics there, girl. But a body's gotta be sensible about these things. If you've got dirt on somebody, and they're being threatened with a killin', you spread it around, pronto."

"Gran's right there, Tamitha," Savannah said. "If you've got anything else that you're holding back, for some goofy reason like common decency, spill it. Here. Now."

Tammy drew a deep breath. "Okay. He's having an affair with that silly little personal assistant of hers. He's a degenerate gambler—gambled away all of his own money. He's been embezzling Natasha's. And he got drunk and slapped her at a backyard party they were giving a couple of months ago for their family and closest friends. Everybody there saw it happen and figures she'll divorce him before the end of the year. Other than that, I gather he's a pretty nice guy."

Everyone at the table sat in stunned silence. Finally, Savannah found her voice. "Tammy, I have to tell you, I'm surprised and disappointed in you, keeping all this good stuff to yourself. I thought I raised you better."

But Tammy didn't appear to be particularly devastated at the news that Savannah was unhappy with her. Waycross had just delivered his spinach and watercress to her plate, along with a rose radish and spiral of carrot, and she was happily devouring them.

Shaking her head, Savannah finished the last spoonful of her soup and reached down into the tote that she had stashed beneath her chair. "Which reminds me," she said, addressing Tammy, "I do appreciate the fact that you were able to make copies of that manifest earlier."

"You're welcome," Tammy replied, nonchalantly munching on a bit of cucumber. "Any time."

Savannah selected two of the four copies and slipped them into a manila envelope. Since each copy was several pages long, it made a fairly hefty package.

Thick enough anyway, she decided as she rose from her chair.

"I'll be back in a minute," she said. Then to Dirk she added, "If they bring out the main course before I get back, don't you dare touch mine. Remember what I told you about dismemberment. Fingers in particular."

"Your dinner's safe with me, sugar," he told her. "Though if it's got any fresh vegetables in it, Miss Preggers over there might bury her face in it."

Savannah walked quickly and directly from their table to the captain's. Natasha Van Cleef didn't notice her approach. In fact, Natasha didn't see Savannah at all until she was leaning over her left shoulder.

Natasha glanced up, jumped, and couldn't have looked more startled if she had found herself cheek to cheek with a werewolf. "You!" was all she seemed able to say.

"Yes, ma'am, just little ol' me," Savannah said, slathering on the Southern drawl and charm. "Remember earlier when we ran into each other in the lobby? You said you'd be willing to read those first three sample chapters of my novel and give me your opinion?"

Savannah shoved the manila envelope under Natasha's nose. "Here it is. I have to tell you this is such an honor. I'm just tickled pink that you'd take the time to do this for me, considering how busy you are."

Savannah turned to the captain, who appeared to be

almost as surprised as Natasha at this impromptu inter-
ruption of their fine dinner. "Isn't she wonderful, Captain?" Savannah gushed. "To take time to help the little
people, and her so famous and all. It just restores a
body's faith in humanity. It truly does."

Tapping Colin on the shoulder, she told him, "I
would be plum thrilled to death if you'd take the time
to give it a look-see, too, Mr. Van Cleef. You never
know, there might be something there that would interest you, as well."

Sensing that Natasha was about to hit her over the
head with the nearest wine bottle, Savannah decided it
was time to make a graceful exit.

As graceful as possible under the circumstances.

As she backed away from the table, she delivered a
closing remark. "Just look it over, Ms. Van Cleef. I'll
check back with you later to see what you thought of it."

She hurried back to her seat, convinced that she
could feel eyeball darts stabbing her in the back as she
scurried along.

When she sat down in her chair, she glanced across
the table and saw that Dirk was grinning at her, a look
of amazement, respect, and disbelief on his face. "You
didn't."

"I did. That's what she gets for ignoring me and giving me the cold shoulder. We need her to look over that
manifest, and him, too. If they recognize any of those
names, we might have our wanna-be killer."

Savannah glanced down the table at her father-in-
law, a retired police officer himself. He was giving her
a smirk that was very similar to the one on his son's
face.

"Well done, Daughter-in-law," he said with a wink.

"I can see why my son enjoyed having you for a partner back in the day." Then Richard turned to Ryan.
"Did you get anywhere with the chief security guard
about a possible camera in that hallway outside the editor's room?"

"Absolutely nowhere," Ryan replied. "It was a total
waste of time."

John nodded. "Not only was he a bloody unpleasant
fellow, but they have no cameras installed in their hallways. Not a one."

Richard looked surprised. "Seriously? For some
reason I thought every inch of this ship would be under
surveillance at all times."

"You would think so, would you not?" John said.
"Lately, the odd bit of skullduggery aboard such ships
has popped up in the news far too often."

"You'd think they'd be scared of somebody suing
'em," Waycross added. "If every Tom, Dick, and Harry's
all-night convenience store can afford a camera, you'd
think a ship like this could fit it into their budget somehow."

"You would," Ryan agreed. "Some ships have full
surveillance of all public areas. But it seems the only
cameras they have aboard this ship are the ones at the
entrances, to capture the likenesses of everyone entering and leaving, and some others positioned over areas
where money is being exchanged: shop cash registers,
the bars, the casinos, et cetera."

"That's a bite in the hindquarters," Granny said.

"No kidding." Savannah was about to say more, but
the waiter had just slid an amazing plate of food in
front of her.

A perfect filet of delicate grouper was surrounded

by a mound of mashed potatoes, a generous portion of sautéed spinach, and a juicy, slow-roasted tomato. It was a mountain of food, and Savannah considered it a worthy personal challenge to eat every bite.

"That's it? That's all you're giving us for dinner? I never saw such a skimpy portion in all my life."

The grumpy voice reaching her ears from across the table annoyed her almost as much as the grumpy face across the table.

Her husband wasn't pleased with his dinner. It wasn't quite enough to feed a platoon of starving soldiers, so his knickers were in disarray.

What a rarity, she thought. *Alert the media.*

"Maybe Tammy knows a gossip columnist who would give a diddly-squat," she muttered.

The waiter hovering over the disgruntled Dirk seemed as upset as he was. "What is it, sir? You aren't happy with your dinner? Perhaps when you taste it, you will enjoy it more and—"

"I'm sure it'll taste fine," Dirk grumbled. "All three bites of it, that is. It isn't enough to feed a grown man. I have a healthy appetite, you know."

"There's nothing healthy whatsoever about his appetite," Tammy said, eyeing Savannah's spinach.

"There is no problem, sir," the waiter assured him. "You may have as many entrées as you like. Would you enjoy another grouper, or would you prefer the roasted veal chop?"

Dirk's face lit up like a Halloween bonfire with a gallon of gas sprinkled on top. "Do you mean I can have them both?"

"Wait a minute! Wait a minute!" From the other side

of the table Dora was waving her arms, like she was trying to flag down a train. "Son, I don't know what's going on here, but think this through before you regret it. There's no such thing as a free lunch, so you know very well there's no free dinner. I don't care what this man here says. Sooner or later that food is going to show up on your bill. You're going to feel pretty stupid if you find you paid one hundred dollars for a veal chop."

She reached beneath her, pulled out her purse, and held it up for Dirk to see. "If you get hungry, you just let me know. I've got half a dozen peanut butter and jelly sandwiches in here, and more in my suitcase."

"No, madam. Truly, there is no charge," implored the waiter. "You may have all the food on the ship you want without extra cost. Except for your alcohol, everything is included."

The waiter hurried away to get a second meal for Dirk, and for the next ten minutes Dora Jones chattered on excitedly about the miracle of having a week's worth of delicious, free food at her fingertips.

Normally, Savannah would have found that moderately entertaining, but something else had caught her eye. Something far more interesting.

A man was walking through the restaurant, from one side to the other, studying the occupants of each table as he passed. Those diners who caught his eye gave him wary looks. Not just because he was an enormous man, standing at least six feet, five inches and weighing well over three hundred pounds. Not just because his face bore the scars of more than one severe beating.

It was the intensity of the man, a distinct sense of

menace that radiated from him and appeared to intimidate everyone in his vicinity.

Savannah couldn't remember when she had seen
someone quite so scary. Her first thought upon spot-
ting him was, *I sure wouldn't want to tangle with the
likes of him.*

"Holy cow! Get a load of that guy," she heard her
brother say. "How many poundings do you reckon it
took for his face to look like that?"

"Something tells me," Granny added, "that over the
years he's given more than he's got."

But it wasn't the man himself or the reactions of the
diners he passed that set Savannah's heart racing. It
was the reaction of one diner in particular when the
giant passed the captain's table.

She watched, spellbound, as Colin Van Cleef looked
up from his veal chop and saw the monstrous man with
the battered face.

Savannah had seen men so frightened that they fainted,
so scared that they vomited or urinated. Occasionally,
even worse. But she had never seen a man look like he
might do it all at once.

"Did you see that?" she heard Dirk say. "Did you
see the look on Van Cleef's face?"

"I did," she replied, even as she studied her client's
expression. Natasha gave the strange man the same suspicious look as everyone else in the vicinity. But her face
had not turned gray, like her husband's, and she didn't
look like she was about to have a heart attack on the
spot.

"We have to find out who he is," Ryan said.

"No doubt about it," John replied. "I do believe we
have our first suspect."

"I know who it is."

Everyone turned in their seats to look at Dirk's father. Richard sat there, staring at the passing man, a cop-stern look on his face.

"Who is it, Dad?" Dirk asked. "What's his name?"

"He's an enforcer for a Los Angeles syndicate. He works out of LA and Vegas, collecting gambling debts for the mob. As you can tell by looking at him, he's very effective. His name is Frank Bellissimo."

"Bellissimo?" Ryan asked, then turned to John and they both snickered.

"What's so funny?" Dirk wanted to know.

John told him, "'Bellissimo' is Italian for 'the most beautiful.'"

"Talk about a misnomer." Savannah noticed that the man appeared to be leaving the room by way of the side door. "We can't let him out of our sight until we know more about him. What room he's in. What he's up to."

Ryan and John instantly jumped to their feet. "We'll follow him," Ryan said.

Waycross rose, too. "I'll tag along. The three of us, we can leapfrog him, and he won't know he's being followed."

Waycross looked down at Tammy. "You gonna be okay, sweet cheeks?"

But a waiter had just placed an eggplant soufflé in front of her, and she hardly even heard the voice of her beloved. She dismissed him with the wave of a hand and, "Okay. Sure. Whatever."

As Savannah watched Ryan, John, and her brother discreetly follow the mountainous man out the side door, she turned to Dirk and said, "Do you think they'll be okay?"

"Sure." Dirk picked up his knife and fork and attacked his veal chop with a vengeance. "As long as he doesn't figure out they're following him. As long as they don't piss him off. If they do, God help 'em."

Chapter 8

When Savannah awoke the next morning, she was disoriented and for several moments couldn't remember where she was. The stateroom was so tiny that, at first, she thought she had fallen asleep or passed out in somebody's closet.

It had been a long time since she'd done that.

The only source of light in the small space was the dim, narrow beam that outlined the edge of a door.

A bathroom door, she recalled, when she heard the toilet flush.

Seconds later, she was blinded by eyeball-searing light as Dirk threw the door open, walked the two and a half steps to the bed, and hurled himself onto it.

"Good morning, gorgeous," he said, far too chipper for a dude who hadn't had his morning coffee yet.

Gorgeous? Without makeup? Without benefit of a hairbrush? Without caffeine?

Not likely, she thought. *Not in a pig's eye.*

Then she remembered.

The hot, steamy, adventurous, darned-near-kinky whoopee they'd made the night before when finally hitting the sheets of their diminutive, no-frills stateroom.

"No wonder you're in a good mood," she mumbled, trying to turn away from him and hide her face with the blanket.

"Oh, no you don't." He grabbed a pillow and smacked her on the rear with it. "We're docked! We've arrived! Alaska is waiting! Forests and glaciers are waiting! More importantly, the b*reakfast buffet* is waiting. Shake a leg, babycakes."

"If you hit me again with that pillow, I'll shake your leg. Then I'll whack you on the head with it."

He leaned down and nibbled her neck. "You were a lot sweeter last night," he said, "you know, when you were still a virgin."

"Yeah, well, since you 'deflowered' me, you have to face the consequences. Us wanton women can be ornery, especially in the morning before we've had our coffee."

She rolled onto her back and gave him a quick kiss. "Why don't you go on down to breakfast and get started without me? Your parents will be there by now, and Tammy and Waycross, too."

He perked up instantly. "You don't mind?"

Do I mind? she thought. *Do I mind the chance to wake up gently, to shower in peace, to put on my makeup without watching somebody bounce impatiently around the room, asking, "Can we go yet? Can we go yet? Can we? Huh? Huh?"*

"I'll miss you somethin' awful," she said with just

the right amount of bogus sincerity, "but I know how hungry you are this time of the morning. You go on ahead, and I'll be down as quick as I can."

"You're the best, darlin'," he said, pressing a kiss to her forehead.

"Yes, I am. Don't you forget it."

Less than three seconds later, he was sprinting out the door, in search of the perfect Alaskan lumberjack's breakfast.

She giggled, turned back onto her side, nuzzled her pillow, and pulled the blanket snugly around her shoulders.

Ah, peace, quiet, and treasured solitude, she thought. *This cruising gig is a wondrous thing.*

When Savannah entered the buffet restaurant on the lido deck, the first thing she noticed wasn't the endless cornucopia of breakfast delectables that stretched in both directions, seemingly into infinity.

Her eyes and imagination were instantly captured by the view from the massive floor-to-ceiling windows. Her first impression of Alaska would always be dearest to her heart. The tiny village of Saaxwoo was little more than a large pier and simple row of quaint, rustic buildings lining the shore, painted in brilliant shades of goldenrod, brick red, robin's egg blue, and hunter green.

Rough hewn, hand-carved signs identified the various establishments as souvenir stores, fur galleries, and jewelry shops, along with the occasional bar or restaurant.

The waterway in front of the town, its only connection

to the outside world, hummed with activity as fishing boats jostled for space with private yachts and tenders transporting cruise passengers to and from their ships, while floatplanes took off, taxied, and landed.

Behind the town and its water, providing the quintessential Alaskan backdrop, was a range of thickly forested, mist-clouded hills.

Behind those, lording over it all, rose the ragged tops of snow-covered mountain peaks, glistening coral and gray blue in the morning sun.

Alaska. Alaska. Her soul breathed the word over and over again. *You're here, Savannah girl. A poor kid from the Georgia cotton fields. You're actually here!*

"Hey, Savannah!" Someone grabbed her by the elbow. "You're not going to believe all the food, and it's free!"

Dora. Just had to be. Savannah turned to greet her mother-in-law. No one else she'd ever known got that excited over a complimentary waffle.

"Good morning, Mom," she said, putting on her best smile. It wasn't much of a smile, but the best she could manage precoffee. "I'm glad you're enjoying yourself."

"Wait until you see the waffles!"

Yes, somehow she'd known it was about the waffles.

"They're big and fluffy and golden brown and covered with this fresh berry medley, raspberries, strawberries, and blue-berries. Even Tammy had one because of all the fruit . . . you know how she is about only eating healthy things, which is a good idea anytime, but especially when you're pregnant, and they'll put either butter or whipped cream or sour cream, whatever you like, on it, and I'll bet if you asked nice, they'd probably put all three, because they really want to please their—"

That was when Dirk rescued Savannah.

He grabbed her other arm, shoved a mug of dark coffee into her hand, and said to Dora, "Sorry, Mom, but I've gotta talk to her about some important stuff over here and . . ."

There was only the briefest of tugs-of-war before he won.

So what if a bit of coffee slopped onto the front of her shirt? 'Twas a small price to pay for freedom.

"Thank you," she said as he guided her toward a large table by the window where the rest of the Moonlight gang was eating and enjoying the view.

"No problem. It was the least I could do for the young woman who so graciously surrendered her maidenhood to me last night."

Savannah paused and looked up at him with a coy smile. "You quite enjoyed that, didn't you?"

He snickered and nodded. "It was a hoot. A hot hoot."

"Then we'll be sure to do it again sometime, but only if you promise to stop talking about it."

"Soon? Can we do it again soon?"

"All right. Sure. Whatever."

"When would be soon? Tonight? Next week?"

"If. Only if."

"Okay."

Savannah slid into the empty seat next to Gran, assuming it had been saved for her. Granny Reid had been saving the chair to her right for Savannah as long as she could recall. "One of the few perks of being the oldest of nine young'uns," Gran had always said. "Them that does the most work gets the seat of honor."

"Good mornin', sugar," Gran said. "Is that all you're havin' for breakfast? You'll faint away dead in the street if that's all you eat."

"Breakfast is the most important meal of the day," Ryan said.

John added, "The Irish say, 'Food is gold in the morning, silver at noon, and lead at night.'"

Granny laughed and spread an indecent amount of butter on her waffle. "I reckon we Reids don't hail from Ireland then, 'cause we consider food to be pure gold morning, noon, and night."

"Especially if your granddaughter's cooking it," Dirk said, far too enthusiastically.

Of course he loved the meals that Savannah shoved under his nose on a regular basis. But she also knew when she was being buttered up for nefarious, lascivious reasons.

She also knew the moment that his fleshly lusts turned from sex to gluttony. His mother walked up behind him and shoved a grossly overburdened plate onto the table in front of him.

"There you go, Son," Dora said. "I just picked up a few things I thought you'd like."

The "few things" consisted of an oversized omelet, some cinnamon rolls, French toast, and several slabs of thick, smoked ham.

She sat down beside him with a plate of her own that was similarly laden, and in seconds mother and son were shoveling in the grub with gusto.

As Savannah watched them, virtual mirror images

of each other, it occurred to her that if the researchers were sitting in her chair at that moment, the age-old question of "nature versus nurture" would have been settled on the spot.

Attempting to ignore them both, she turned to Richard, John, and Ryan, who were quietly sipping their coffees. "How did your leapfrog surveillance endeavor turn out last night?" she asked them.

"A waste of time." Richard sighed and ran his fingers through his hair, which, like his son's, appeared to have a hard time waking up in the morning. "We could've been out on the deck, staring up at the sky, watching the northern lights for all the good it did."

"You can say that again." Ryan shook his head wearily. "That guy roamed this ship for over two hours. He was obviously looking for somebody, but he didn't find them."

John added a sugar cube to his coffee. "If you think he was in a bad mood when he passed through the dining room, you should've seen him when he finally slipped into his suite and put an end to it."

"Frankly, we were hoping we wouldn't have to tangle with him," Ryan said. "A guy that big, that cranky . . ."

"Without a weapon or even a pair of cuffs," Richard added. "It wouldn't have been pretty."

Savannah chuckled. "You would've needed Granny and her Taser along. Let's just say she's come in handy on previous occasions."

"I'll bet she has," Richard replied solemnly. "But let's just say that since we didn't have her along for protection, we were glad when he went into his suite and stayed there the rest of the night."

"Don't tell me you guys watched that door the whole night," Savannah said.

"Until half-six this morning." John yawned. "Of course, we traded watches. But it still made for a less than restful night."

"You should've gone to the magician show with Granny and me," Dora said around a mouthful of pancakes. "That guy was amazing, sawing girls in half, pulling roses out of his jacket and giving them to the ladies sitting closest to the stage, and of course we were right up front, because we got there early and grabbed the best seats, and the most amazing thing of all is that they didn't charge a penny for the show, a show that was fit for Broadway, for free I tell you!"

Eventually, she had to pause for a breath. The instant she did, Savannah turned to Tammy and Waycross, who were seated at the far end of the table. "How did the two of you fare, getting Natasha back to her suite?"

Neither of them replied. In fact, Savannah was pretty sure that Tammy was deliberately ducking her head, so as not to look her straight in the eye.

"Did everything go okay?" Savannah prompted when she got no response. "You didn't have any problems with her, did you?"

"No," Waycross replied. "She was downright ladylike about it. Didn't give us no problem at all. 'Course we didn't ask her any embarrassing questions, like you did. We just walked behind her, bringin' up the rear, so to speak."

Yes, something was definitely wrong. In spite of the fact that Tammy was staring down at her plate, and her golden hair was covering much of her face, Savannah could tell that she had been crying.

Tammy almost never cried. Even throughout her pregnancy she had been sunshine and daisies, puppies and kittens.

In the years that Savannah had known her, she had never seen her down in the dumps or out of sorts, unless something quite serious had occurred.

Savannah opened her mouth to ask the obvious question, but something in her brother's eyes warned her not to. Apparently, this wasn't the time. But Savannah was determined to find an appropriate time. Soon.

With his sharp green eyes that missed nothing, Ryan had seen the exchange. As though intending to change the subject, he said, "What did you and Dirk do last night after we split up?"

Savannah didn't dare look at her husband. She was fairly certain that if she did he would burst into giggles, possibly guffaws.

That was the last thing she needed first thing in the morning.

"We walked around the ship," she offered, too quickly. "Got acquainted with the layout. Checked out any potentially dangerous areas, suspicious people, et cetera, et cetera."

Even she could hear the overly flippant, blatantly false tone in her voice. Ryan looked at John. They both looked at Dirk. She looked at Dirk and realized that he was going to start tittering at any moment.

A sexy smirk played across Ryan's handsome face. "Yes, I believe that, considering the lack of security cameras onboard this ship, a couple could 'et cetera, et cetera' pretty much anywhere they wanted."

"Except for the shops," John said, "and the bars, and the casino. But those areas are probably a bit too crowded anyway."

Granny put down her fork and gave them all disapproving looks. "I wasn't exactly following what y'all were saying, because I was payin' close attention to my bacon and eggs. But I think you were talking dirty, and I don't allow such stuff at the breakfast table. There's a time and a place for such rigmarole, but this ain't it."

The caffeine was beginning to hit Savannah's bloodstream, making her feel just a bit feisty. She grinned at her grandmother and nudged her with her elbow. "So, Granny, exactly where is the time and place for rigmarole?"

Gran demurely dabbed her lips with her napkin and replied, "Apparently, anytime and anywhere there ain't no cameras."

Chapter 9

As Savannah and Dirk walked down the hallway that led to Natasha Van Cleef's luxury suite, he said, "I thought she told you she didn't want to see our mugs until afternoon at the earliest."

Savannah glanced at her watch. "It's five minutes until twelve. That means that in six minutes it'll be afternoon. Close enough. Yesterday, she was pretty tight lipped about her itinerary. I want to know, once and for all, what her schedule is. How else are we going to protect her if we don't even know where the heck she is?"

As they neared the suite, Savannah glanced to their left where, looking over the balcony, she could see the multistoried atrium lobby. More specifically she could see passengers leaving the ship and heading ashore for an afternoon of shopping and sightseeing.

Most of the passengers had already left earlier in the morning. These were the stragglers, disembarking with the day already half gone.

She was beginning to wonder if she or any of her own entourage would be able to go ashore, or would they have to be content enjoying Alaska's magnificent natural beauty with their noses pressed to the ship's windows.

When she and Dirk rounded the final curve and were twenty feet or so from the penthouse suite's door, they found they weren't the only ones who had come to conduct business with the Van Cleefs.

The butler, Sooyung, was standing with her back to Savannah and Dirk, and she was knocking quite vigorously on the door.

"Hello, again," Savannah greeted her. "How are you this fine day?"

Sooyung jumped and whirled around, a look of deep concern on her pretty face. "Good morning, Ms. Reid, Detective Coulter," she said. "I'm relieved to see you. I'm worried about our guests."

"Who?" Dirk snapped. "Mr. and Mrs. Van Cleef?"

Sooyung nodded and pointed to the privacy sign hanging on the door. "I'm not really supposed to bother them when the sign indicates that they want to be left alone. But I'm beginning to wonder if something's wrong."

Savannah felt her heart start to race and her face flush with heat. No. No, she thought. They're okay. They are. There has to be a simple explanation.

"Tell me why you're worried, Sooyung. What's going on?" Savannah asked, trying to sound far more calm than she felt.

"A couple of things," Sooyung replied. "First of all, they asked to be served breakfast at eight-thirty sharp. They had chosen a particularly lovely meal, and our executive chef spent a lot of time personally preparing it for them. But when the waiters and I brought it up, the privacy sign was still on the door. I knocked, but they didn't answer. So we left, thinking they would call when they were ready to eat."

"That doesn't sound all that bad," Dirk said, using his seen it all, hard to impress, cop persona.

"But there's something else," Sooyung told him. "Ms. Van Cleef had ordered an in-room massage. She was quite adamant about having one. Yesterday, as soon as she boarded, the first thing she did was have me schedule it for her."

"I can understand a woman being passionate about a massage," Savannah said. "They certainly are one of life's pleasures."

"Precisely. Also, she was very particular about who was going to give it to her —someone who had experience with deep tissue massage and acupressure. She appeared to be really looking forward to it," Sooyung explained. "But when the therapist arrived, the privacy sign was still up. When he knocked no one answered for him either."

Savannah gave Dirk a quick glance and saw that he, too, was becoming concerned.

"What time was that?" Savannah asked.

"Shortly before ten. The appointment was for ten o'clock."

Dirk hurried to the door and jiggled the doorknob, though no one present expected it to open.

"Can you get us in there?" he asked.

Sooyung nodded, but looked unhappy at the prospect. "I can. I'm not really supposed to. Perhaps I should call the chief security guard."

Considering the way Savannah and Dirk had locked horns with that particular fellow before over the manifest, Savannah wasn't excited about drawing the ship's head of security into the situation.

"Let's don't bother him," she said offhandedly. "Let's check inside the suite and just see what's going on. We don't want to call him down for no reason."

Sooyung thought it over. "It is a busy time for the security guards, with passengers leaving and returning to the ship and going through the checkpoints."

Reluctantly she walked to the door, pulled a key card from her pocket, and unlocked the door. To Savannah's surprise, the butler stood aside and allowed her and Dirk to enter first.

Savannah steeled herself for whatever she might find inside the luxury rooms. But as she hurried from the living and dining areas into the bedroom and then back out onto the veranda, she saw no signs of violence.

She also saw no signs of the Van Cleefs or Olive.

"So far, so good," Dirk said, speaking her thoughts aloud. "No overturned, broken furniture. No dead bodies."

She gave him a quick, moderately perturbed look. Sometimes she preferred that her scariest thoughts remained inside her head. Having them uttered frequently made a bad situation seem even worse.

But *was* this a bad situation?

She couldn't tell for sure.

Savannah turned to Sooyung. The butler looked as relieved as Savannah felt.

"I guess I was worried for nothing," Sooyung said a

bit sheepishly. "Apparently, they're okay. They just stepped out or whatever."

Dirk was standing by the glass door, perusing the vacant veranda. "Or somebody tossed them overboard," he said.

Savannah looked around for the nearest nonbreakable or least valuable objet d'art to smack him with.

"Maybe they're just downstairs at the breakfast buffet," she offered, though the words sounded ridiculous even to her.

He gave her his most condescending look. "Yeah, right. They order a gourmet breakfast, prepared by the executive chef, and then they head for the lido deck to sample the common swill."

"Okay, okay." She searched her brain for a more plausible explanation. "All three of them left the ship first thing this morning to do some sightseeing."

Again, Dirk had a less than comforting response. "Right. They wanted to go slide down some glaciers and eat some bear burgers. They decided to go on this little excursion without a single member of the private security detail they're paying a bundle for."

"The day after Ms. Van Cleef receives another death threat," Sooyung added.

Savannah wouldn't accept any of it. Logical or not, her mind wasn't ready to go there yet.

Instead, she walked around the suite, taking in the simple, everyday details the occupants had left behind.

One empty glass sat on the bar. It appeared to have held water. Looking closely, Savannah could see a light shade of lipstick on its rim. She recalled that Natasha Van Cleef wore a nearly nude lip gloss. Her personal assistant, a strange shade of orange.

Nearby, the coffeepot was full. But when Savannah touched it with her fingertip, it was cool. "Did you fill and set this coffeepot?" she asked Sooyung.

"Yes, I did. Last night."

"What time was it scheduled to brew?"

"Eight-fifteen."

"Did someone give you that time?"

"Yes. Ms. Van Cleef told me that's when they would want it."

Dirk had joined them in the bar area. "Apparently, they don't take their coffee as seriously as we do. Three people and nobody drank a single cup."

"Or maybe they left in a hurry," Savannah suggested.

She walked from the bar to the living room. Nothing was amiss. The space was as pristine as it had been yesterday.

"I'll search the veranda," Dirk said. "You know, check for scuff marks on the railings."

Savannah gave him a quick glance to see if he was teasing. The gleam in his eye told her that he was. Though she was sure that he was as concerned as she was.

This set of circumstances didn't make sense on several levels.

When things didn't add up, there was usually a reason. In a situation where death threats had been made, the reason was seldom a good one.

As Dirk walked past her, heading for the door, his hand lightly brushed her arm in a brief but comforting gesture. "Try not to worry, Van," he told her. "It ain't bad news until—"

"Until it's bad news," she supplied.

"Exactly."

He walked out onto the veranda with Sooyung following close behind. It occurred to Savannah that perhaps she, too, was worried about that "over the railing" possibility.

Don't trouble trouble till trouble troubles you, she told herself, quoting one of Gran's favorite sayings.

Entering the bedroom, she looked around, registering every detail. The rumpled bed had been slept in. Both sides. The armoire doors were half open. Savannah opened them further and looked inside. Two thick, white, terry robes, no doubt supplied by the ship, hung on hooks mounted to the doors. Both looked as though they had been worn. A woman's and a man's garments were neatly arranged on hangers and folded on shelves.

Savannah recalled having heard that butlers unpacked for the passengers in luxury suites. It appeared that Sooyung was good at her job.

Savannah walked over to the dressing table and noted that Natasha's makeup items were still arranged in the same manner as they had been yesterday. Most were inside the open ostrich skin case, and a few items, like her brushes and an eyebrow comb, stood in a small, marble vase.

"If she's gone," Savannah whispered to herself, "she intends to come back."

Any time a female went missing, Savannah always looked for the makeup stash. A woman might leave her husband, her kids, her jewelry, and maybe even her money behind, but if she was leaving for good, she always took her makeup.

A search of the bathroom yielded nothing of any interest either. A fine travel bag hung from a hook on the back of the door. Unrolled, it featured numerous see-through, zipped pockets that contained the standard toiletries that a man and woman would use on vacation: toothpaste, deodorant, body lotion, sunscreen, and a small box of motion sickness medicine.

She couldn't help noticing the hemorrhoid ointment and the vaginal cream.

Definitely more information than she needed about her favorite author.

Turning to leave the room, she happened to glance down and saw something familiar in the waste can.

It was a sheet of paper.

White copy paper.

Grabbing a tissue from a dispenser on the counter, she reached down and used it to avoid touching the paper with her fingers as she pulled it by its corner from the can.

Of course, it was just standard paper. But it was folded a certain way. In thirds, like a regular letter going into a number ten business envelope, and then folded in half.

She had seen that pattern before. Recently, in fact.

"Whatcha got there?" Dirk asked, stepping into the room.

She held it up to his eye level, so he could see.

"What's that?" he asked. "I thought you took that back to our room yesterday. Didn't you tell me you put it in a plastic bag and stuck it in that little safe there in our closet?"

"I did," she said.

"Then how . . . ?"

He shot her a look that was as unsettling as the thoughts running through her brain.

With the use of a second tissue, she managed to unfold the paper.

"What does it say?" he wanted to know, leaning over her shoulder.

"Excuse me," said a soft female voice just outside the door. "Did you find something?"

"Hold on, Sooyung," Savannah called out. "We'll be out in a minute."

"Yeah. Just keep looking around if you don't mind," Dirk said as he gently pushed the door closed. "You might find something important."

Savannah unfolded the sheet of paper and held it up so they could both read the now familiar format of few words, printed in a common font with a terrible and uncommon message:

I have her. She's alive. For now. Meet me and I'll let her live. Don't, she dies.

"Damn," she whispered.

"What the hell's that supposed to mean?"

"Somebody's in trouble. Bad trouble."

"Natasha?"

Savannah shrugged. "Maybe Olive. But probably Natasha."

He thought for a moment, then said, "The coffee that was brewed at eight-fifteen wasn't touched."

"Plus they didn't answer the door at eight-thirty or ten."

"They probably got this bright and early this morning."

Savannah looked at her watch. "It's now after twelve."

"That's four hours."

"At least."

His eyes searched hers. "Do you think we're too late?" he asked, his face as somber as she had ever seen it.

"It ain't bad news till it's bad news," she told him.

And herself.

Neither believed her.

Chapter 10

The day before, when Savannah and Dirk had attempted to weasel a copy of the passenger manifest out of Chief Security Guard Poole, she had thought him a condescending, dismissive jerk. He also had a prominent wart on the end of his nose that had two shockingly long, black hairs growing out of it.

If he had been a pleasant fellow, she probably wouldn't have held that against him.

Nobody was perfect.

But since he had not deigned to give them two minutes of his time or even a smidgen of professional courtesy, she heartily disliked Poole. She couldn't stand his wart, and she positively loathed the hairs. Both of them, but the one on the right the most because it was longest.

When he addressed her, regarding the missing passengers, he lifted that nose at least two notches and said, "Ms. Reid, Detective Coulter, if you can't keep track of your charges, that really isn't my problem. If you'll excuse me, I have duties to attend to."

He started to walk away, leaving them alone next to the fountain in the atrium. But Savannah grabbed the sleeve of his crisp, white uniform. "Excuse me, sir," she said in a low, menacing voice, "but you need to know that if anything happens to Natasha Van Cleef, it's going to be on the evening news all over the world. When I speak to reporters, and I will, I'll be sure to tell them that we tried to help her, but received absolutely no help whatsoever from the security staff on this ship. Specifically no help at all from you, sir. I'll tell them that you were as helpful as a trapdoor in a canoe."

Poole glanced over at Dirk, who gave him a solemn nod and said, "She will. I guarantee you. That's exactly what she'll tell them. She'll even make sure that the reporters spell your name right."

Savannah jostled his sleeve. "I have a vindictive streak a mile wide," she told him with a smile that was slightly maniacal. "If something awful happens to Natasha Van Cleef, and I couldn't get to her and help her in time, it'll be on your head."

At that moment, they were joined by another man whose name tag identified him as Allan Martell, the cruise director. Tall and blond with a shaving commercial chin, he was as handsome as Poole was homely. Unlike the chief security guard, he looked more than concerned. The expression on his face was full-fledged alarm.

"Excuse me," he said to Savannah, "but I couldn't help overhearing you suggest that something bad may have happened to Ms. Van Cleef. Is that true?"

Savannah gave him her warmest Southern smile.

Allies appeared to be few and far between at the moment, so she figured it couldn't hurt to butter this one up from the outset. "I certainly hope not, sir," she told him. "But we have reason to believe she might be the victim of foul play. Possibly her husband and personal assistant, too."

Dirk had already removed his badge from his inside jacket pocket. He waved it under the cruise director's nose. "I'm Detective Sergeant Dirk Coulter, and this is my wife, Savannah Reid. We were hired by the Van Cleefs to provide additional personal protection for them on this cruise. Now they've gone missing, and we're attempting to get a little help from the good chief here."

"All we want," Savannah added, "is for him to check and see if they left the ship this morning. You scan passengers' cards when they come aboard and again when they leave. There are cameras surveilling the security checks. I'm sure you could tell us whether or not they're still on the ship."

Martell turned to Poole and gave him a less than friendly look. "Yes, we most certainly *could* give you that information," he said, his tone calm, but firm. "I'm sure Chief Poole would be happy to help you with that most reasonable request. After all, he knows how important Ms. Van Cleef is to our passengers on this particular cruise. Many of our guests are sailing with us specifically because she's aboard. They're looking forward to interacting with their favorite mystery author at the numerous functions we've scheduled that involve her. They're going to be very disappointed if she isn't with us."

Poole bristled and Savannah wondered which of the

two men had the highest rank. The security chief's epaulettes were decorated with three bars each, but the cruise director was wearing a simple navy blazer and charcoal slacks, so it was a bit hard to tell.

She had a feeling that, rank or not, the cruise director would have his way, based upon the quiet forcefulness of his personality.

Which, in this case, was just fine with her.

Seconds ticked away as Poole weighed his decision. Finally, with a most disgruntled look on his face, he turned his back to them and strode to the security checkpoint, where passengers were being screened, both coming and going.

He spoke briefly with a female guard there, then hurried away without a backward glance toward the three of them. As the woman walked their way, Dirk said to the cruise director, "Nice fella. I'll bet he's popular aboard."

Martell gave Dirk a smile tinged with something like distaste and said, "Let's just say that Poole takes his job very seriously. Considering the gravity of his duties, that's probably a good thing."

"Perhaps," Savannah replied thoughtfully. "Though I can't see how having an important job keeps you from being a decent person. An ounce of civility and a bit of cooperation go a long ways toward making everybody's job easier."

"That's true." Allan Martell reached into his jacket pocket and pulled out a business card. He placed it in Savannah's hand and said, "I certainly hope you locate Ms. Van Cleef and that she's fine. Would you please let me know when you do?"

Savannah slipped the card into her purse. "I certainly will. Thank you for your help."

He gave her a slight, gracious bow. "It was my pleasure. Nice meeting you, Ms. Reid, and you, Detective Coulter. If I can be of any assistance whatsoever, please don't hesitate to call me."

Martell walked away as the security guard approached.

"I understand you need to find out when a certain guest left the ship this morning," she said.

Her attitude seemed a bit cool, and Savannah wondered what Poole had told her. She decided to slather on the Dixie charm.

"We sure do," she told her in her thickest drawl. "If you could help us, we'd just be ever so grateful."

Savannah glanced over at Dirk and saw him roll his eyes.

Hey, she thought, *whatever works.*

It did work. The security guard, whose name tag identified her as Marcia, melted on the spot. "No problem at all," she assured them. "Just follow me."

As Savannah and Dirk followed Marcia into what felt like the bowels of the ship, heading toward what she called the "engine control room," Savannah sent a text to each member of the Moonlight Magnolia gang. She asked them to assemble in the library in fifteen minutes and wait until she and Dirk could join them.

Marcia led them down the hallways that were far different from the public corridors. There was no plush, brightly colored carpeting here. Only gray, commercial-grade, no-frills coverings. The walls were a bland white, and the doors bore signs with strange symbols that Savannah didn't recognize.

Near the end of the long hallway, Marcia entered a complex code on the keypad on a door marked Restricted in large, bold lettering. The door swung open for them.

Once inside, Savannah saw a wall of computers, monitors, and numerous men and women in white uniforms manning them. On the screens were graphs, numbers, dials, lists, and live footage of mechanical parts that she assumed were sections of the ship's massive engine.

Although she understood absolutely nothing of what she was seeing, she couldn't help being impressed. *So, this is what it takes to propel a massive ship through ocean waters*, she thought. *Who would've thought it could be so complex?*

Marcia steered them toward a door to the right. In an instant Savannah recognized the symbol on that door—a bright yellow triangle that surrounded the black silhouette of a closed circuit television camera.

This was where the feed from security cameras was viewed, collected, and stored.

With any luck, the questions concerning her client's disappearance would be answered behind that door.

Marcia led them inside and directed them to take seats near one of the larger computers. Sitting down at the keyboard, she said, "Okay, I need the name of the first person we're checking."

"Natasha Van Cleef," Savannah said.

She held her breath as Marcia entered the name. They waited only two seconds before the information appeared on the screen.

Marcia pointed to the time given. "Ms. Van Cleef is no longer aboard. She passed through the security check at 0822."

"Was her husband, Colin Van Cleef, with her?" Dirk asked.

"He passed through less than one minute later."

Savannah turned to Dirk. "Okay, so they left together. I guess that's good. At least no one dragged her, kicking and screaming, off the ship."

Marcia gave her a crooked grin. "Nobody drags anyone off this ship, kicking and screaming. We're a little better at our jobs than that."

"I'm sure you are," Savannah replied. "Can you please check Ms. Van Cleef's personal assistant, Olive Kelly?"

Marcia nodded and typed in the name. "Olive Kelly cleared the checkpoint at 0806."

"Hmm," Savannah murmured. "Before the Van Cleefs."

"Just out of curiosity," Dirk said, "how about our big, ugly friend Frank Bellissimo?"

Tapping her finger on the screen, Marcia replied, "Franco Bellissimo's card was scanned at 0736."

"Before the other three," Savannah observed. "If you don't mind, one more, please. Patricia Chumley."

Marcia pulled up the information, then sat back in her chair and folded her arms over her chest. "Your Patricia Chumley left at 0802."

Dirk had been writing the times in his pocket notebook. Glancing over the numbers, he said, "Bellissimo was the first to leave. Then the editor, Patricia. Then Olive, the dingbat assistant."

"The last ones to leave were Natasha and Colin," Savannah added.

"What does that tell you?" Marcia wanted to know.

"Not a helluva lot," Dirk replied with a sigh. "For all we know they're all out there somewhere, shopping for bear coats, muskrat hats, and gold nuggets. Meanwhile, we're sitting in here, doing this boring crap, instead of having a cold beer at the Red Moose Tail Saloon."

Savannah thought that over for a moment. "Do moose actually have tails? I can't say that I've ever seen a moose tail."

"What's the plural of moose?" Marcia mused. "Mooses? Meece?"

Savannah shook her head, thinking she should have had at least three more cups of coffee before beginning this day. "Marcia, could I ask one more big favor?"

"Ask away. I'd much rather be down here with the two of you than up there scanning cards and searching bags."

"Could you please show us the actual video footage of each of these people leaving? It might help if we could determine, say, their demeanor. If anything looks out of the ordinary."

"Sure. Give me a minute."

Marcia's hands flew over the keyboard, and a few moments later they were watching as Frank Bellissimo passed through the checkpoint.

Studying the screen, Marcia said, "He looks grumpy."

"That appears to be his natural state," Savannah told her. "Actually, he appears to be in a better mood than he was last night."

"Not saying much," Dirk added.

"Here's your Patricia Chumley." Marcia pointed to the screen where the editor was calmly moving through the line. She looked upbeat, as though anticipating a pleasant day ashore.

"Moving along to Olive Kelly," Marcia said.

Carefully, Savannah studied the footage, noting that, unlike Patricia, Olive did not appear to be looking forward to her land excursion.

"She's a nervous wreck," Savannah said. "Look at that card shake when she holds it out to be scanned."

"She's looking over her shoulder, too," Dirk observed, "like she's expecting somebody to come up behind her."

"Maybe she's sneaking away from the Van Cleefs." Savannah had seen a lot of people up to no good in her day. Her intuition told her that whatever Olive Kelly was doing, she didn't want to get caught doing it. "Okay, let's see the last ones, Natasha and Colin."

It took a few moments for Marcia to find that particular video, long enough for Savannah's anxiety level to build. More than anything she wanted to see her favorite author and client walking casually off the ship, arm in arm with her husband, ready to enjoy a day in the magnificence of Alaska, America's last frontier.

Somehow she knew that wasn't going to be the case.

Her worst fears were confirmed when she looked at the screen and saw the Van Cleefs' faces. Colin looked worried, nervous, and jumpy, like Olive. He had the appearance of a secretive man who was doing something that he wanted to keep private.

But it was Natasha's face that haunted Savannah. Her favorite author, and more importantly her client, looked deeply frightened. So frightened that Savannah studied the film closely to see if Colin was gripping her too tightly, perhaps forcing her along. His hand was on her back, but the gesture seemed natural enough for a husband and wife.

Savannah watched each frame carefully until the Van Cleefs were outside the ship and had disappeared from sight. She saw nothing to indicate the cause of Natasha Van Cleef's fear. But Savannah had no doubt whatsoever that the woman was in danger.

She appeared to be running from someone.

Somehow, someway, in this tiny, unfamiliar village, Savannah had to find her missing client. And she had to locate her before whomever Natasha was afraid of found her first.

Chapter 11

When Savannah and Dirk entered the library, they found the Moonlight gang had assembled, just as requested. They had arranged a semicircle of chairs in front of an enormous window and were enjoying the view of the village and its busy waterway.

But their festive mood turned somber the moment they saw Savannah and Dirk's faces.

John jumped up from his chair and offered it to Savannah. "What's up with you two?" he asked.

Granny reached over and put her hand on Savannah's knee. "What's the matter, Savannah girl? You look like you've lost your best friend."

"Not my best friend exactly," Savannah told her. "But I've misplaced my client, her husband, and her personal assistant. Their suite was empty this morning and no one's seen them, including their fancy dandy butler."

"We found another of those threatening letters in the bathroom garbage can," Dirk told them.

"Oh, no," Granny said. "That can't be good no matter how you slice it."

For the next ten minutes, they filled everyone in on the depressing new developments. Savannah noticed that, while each member of the group took the news seriously and with concern, it was Tammy who appeared to be the most upset.

But then, Savannah had noticed that her young friend appeared distraught even when she and Dirk had first entered the room.

She cast a quick glance at her brother and realized that he was watching her. More accurately, he was watching *her* watch *Tammy*. Savannah quirked one eyebrow and gave him a questioning, big sister look.

He shook his head slightly, then looked down at the floor, as though to warn her against saying anything.

A new fear, even sharper than the one she was feeling for Natasha Van Cleef, sliced through her.

The baby? she thought. *There can't be anything wrong with the baby. That would just be too, too terrible.*

With a tremendous effort, she pulled her attention back to the business at hand.

Dirk was handing out assignments. "Ryan, John, and you, Dad . . . how would you feel about taking Bellissimo duty again? Find him if you can, trail him, and see what he's up to."

"You've got it," Ryan agreed.

"Done." Richard might have been retired from the police force for quite a while, but Savannah observed that the expression on his face, so like his son's, was all "cop."

Only John looked the slightest bit reluctant. "With luck we won't find it necessary to actually lay hands on himself. A fierce big bloke he is, and no doubt nasty tempered as well." He glanced around at the others, then shrugged, looking a bit sheepish. "You understand, of course, I wouldn't be concerned if we were carrying any weapons. Even a small Taser would be a comfort under the circumstances."

"I understand completely," Savannah said. "Don't take any chances. If there's a problem, contact the local authorities. Let them deal with him."

"Yeah," Dirk added. "They're used to wrestling grizzly bears. They have wolf steak for dinner. What's one measly mobster from Los Angeles when your family pet is a wolverine?"

Ryan chuckled. "Exactly. In a rugged, masculine place like this, Frank Bellissimo isn't the top of the food chain anymore."

Savannah tried not to make it obvious that she was worried about Tammy when she said, "Waycross and Tammy, would you mind very much staying here on the ship? It would be very helpful if you would hang out in the atrium and watch the security checkpoints. We need to know if any of these people return to the ship."

"Sure, Sis," Waycross replied. "No problem. We'd be happy to."

Instead of her usual, over-the-top, bubbly response, Tammy simply stared down at her hands, which were folded demurely in her lap, and gave a little nod.

"Thanks," Dirk said. Savannah noticed that he was staring at Tammy, too.

In fact, everyone in the group was watching her and looking most concerned.

After a long, awkward pause, Dirk turned to his mother and Granny. "Mom, would you and Gran go ashore and see if you can get a line on Olive? Just ask around, try to find someone who noticed her, who can tell you what she was doing. She's a distinctive gal. Men in particular would probably remember her if they saw her."

Savannah said, "Everybody keep an eye out for Patricia Chumley, too, Natasha's editor. She's the one with the dark hair and black eyeglasses."

Dirk added, "On the security video she appeared to be pretty happy, just leaving the ship to have a good time. So she's probably out shopping for smoked salmon to take back to the relatives. But let us know if you see her."

"We have pictures of all these people." Savannah began sending the photos to their phones. "They're courtesy of a security guard who treated us like gold this morning, unlike that stinky Poole fella. Her name's Marcia. If you see her, give her a big hug."

Dirk grimaced. "She's kidding."

"No, she's not," Gran said. "She's Southern. We hug good folks. Tight. Kiss 'em, too. Sometimes whether they want it or not." She turned to Dora. "Let's hit the shore, girlfriend. Raise a ruckus if we can."

Dora jumped to her feet. "Let's do. This sounds like fun. If we find her right away, we could go shopping for some cheap souvenirs or take one of those free historical walking tours. Or would you like to have lunch

at one of those exotic eateries, Gran? One with reasonable prices, of course. I can't imagine myself eating a
bear burger, but I'd try a moose steak, if it was on the
menu. Would you, Granny? I would if you would, even
though I've never—"

"I'd try just about anything once," Granny said, in-
terrupting the flow of words that would have, undoubtedly, gone on for a very long time.

Savannah was most grateful. This new friendship
that was forming between her grandmother and Dirk's
mom was proving to be beneficial in more ways than
one.

Granny turned to Tammy and Waycross. "If you want,
we can come back to the ship after an hour and trade off
duties with you. That way you'll get a chance to walk
around town, too. Soak in the local atmosphere and all
that good stuff."

"No, that's okay," Tammy said, still staring down at
her hands. "We'll be fine here, surveilling the security
station. You go ahead."

Yes, there's something wrong, Savannah thought.
Very wrong.

Since when did her little Nancy Drew wanna-be
prefer the boredom of surveillance duty to hardcore
"sleuthing," as she liked to call it?

The other members of the team were gathering their
things, forming their groups, and leaving the library, so
Savannah stood and picked up her purse.

She said to Waycross, "I'm fixin' to go over there to
the coffee bar across the room and grab a few cups. I'll
see if they have some chai for our Mom-to-Be. Would
you give me a hand?"

He gave her a half smile that showed he hadn't

bought her ruse for a moment, but he joined her anyway.

No sooner did she have him out of Tammy's earshot than she began the interrogation. "What the heck's wrong with Tamitha? She's droopier than Colonel Beauregard's face. Did you two have a fight? Is there something going on with the baby?"

"No," he said sadly. "Nothing as bad as all that. But she's in a dither, for sure. She finally got her folks on the phone this morning. Couldn't get them to return her call for months now. At first she was all happy to talk to them, but then, her and them, they had a . . . Well, I reckon you'd call it a fight."

Tammy fighting with someone? Savannah couldn't imagine it. Other than the occasional testy, siblinglike banter between her and Dirk, Savannah had never heard Tammy utter a cross word to anyone for any reason.

"What about?" Savannah asked, realizing she was being too nosy, but unable to help herself.

Waycross shrugged his broad shoulders and hung his head. "I reckon I shouldn't say. She'd probably talk to you about it if you asked her."

Savannah was torn. One of the half dozen people closest to her heart was in pain, and she didn't have time to even talk to her about it.

"I can't, Waycross," she said helplessly. "I have to—"

"Of course you do," he said. "You can't be worrying about stuff like that. That author lady could be in bad trouble right this minute."

He glanced ahead at the coffee bar. "Did you really want to get coffee?" he asked. "Or was it a lame excuse?"

"A lame excuse."

"That's what I figured. Let me see if they have some green tea for her and then we'll go on down to watch that checkpoint for you."

"I'll make sure you get some shore time, too."

"Don't worry about us, Sis. You got enough on your hands as it is. You just take care o' business, hear?"

Savannah stood on tiptoe and kissed his ruddy, freckled cheek. "I love you, sweetie."

"I love you, too, Savannah," he said, his eyes shining with affection and respect. "Hightail it outta here. Go get your bad guy and let me take care of Tammy. That's what you do best, and taking care of my girl and our baby is what I do best."

"You got it, sugar."

She left him by the coffee vendor and hurried over to Dirk. Grabbing him by the arm, she said, "Let's get going, Mr. Detective, sir. Time's a'wastin'."

"This isn't the way I'd envisioned my bucket list visit to Alaska," Savannah told Dirk as they made their way down the gangway. "I was supposed to be all a'twitter with excitement, not filled to the gills with dread."

"I hear ya," he said, slipping his arm around her waist and giving her a little squeeze. "Maybe we'll have to do this again sometime, when we aren't worried about people getting murdered and stuff like that."

"Yes, that crap's a bit of a buzz-kill."

"Think how bummed out we'll be if we spend our whole day walking around this place, looking for them, and can't find them."

She drew a deep, shuddering breath. "I can think of worse things."

"Me too. But I'm trying not to."

They made their way past the Visitor Center with its long line of tourists, waiting to ask their questions and collect their maps and brochures.

They threaded a zigzag path through a multitude of tour operators, holding signs that advertised bus tours, floatplane tours, hiking tours, and the occasional lumberjack show, all calling out the virtues of their particular adventure, like barkers at a carnival.

"Do you suppose we should poke our heads into the nearest station house and give local law enforcement a heads-up?" Dirk asked.

"And say what? Some passengers who left a cruise ship are probably walking around your town! God knows what they're up to! Put out an APB! ASAP!"

"Smart-ass." He cleared his throat. "But if we told them about the threatening letters . . ."

"Celebrity gets weird letters from a fan. News story at eleven!"

He reached over and ruffled her hair. "It's good for you that you've got dimples and a cute, big butt. Otherwise, I wouldn't put up with all this abuse."

She grinned up at him, employing those high-ticket dimples. "Yeah, you got it bad, boy. You suffer."

"In silence."

"Never, never in silence. Just ain't your style, Coulter. Never was."

They paused on the sidewalk and looked up and down the street, lined with quaint stores and eateries.

"Where do you suppose they went?" Dirk asked.

Savannah shrugged. "They passed up a gourmet

breakfast, prepared by the executive chef, so they couldn't have been too hungry."

"True. Maybe they wanted to go shopping."

"They're millionaires. What would they need that they could buy here?"

"Smoked salmon?"

"They'd have it shipped in from Scotland."

"Furs?"

"If Natasha wears fur, I'd imagine it would be a full-length mink. I can't picture her in a beaver-lined Elmer Fudd hat."

"Also true. So, what does that leave?"

Savannah glanced around at all of the eager tour operators. "Sightseeing."

"If you had a lot of money, like the Van Cleefs, would you get on a bus full of tourists to ride around and look at the scenery?"

"No way. I'd hire a private car."

They both looked around at the traffic driving by, the nearby parking lots, and the taxi queue halfway down the block.

"Not a luxury limo in sight," Dirk said, stating the obvious. "Next idea?"

"In a pinch, I'd get a cab. I'd hire the driver to take me wherever I wanted to go."

"That's a lousy idea. A long shot at best."

"Have you got a better one?"

"Nope."

"Then that makes my idea positively sterling."

He rolled his eyes, reached down, and grabbed her hand. As they walked toward the taxi queue, she squeezed his fingers and said, "One of these days, darlin', your eyeballs are gonna roll right outta your head.

Then you're not going to be able to find them, 'cause you have a hard enough time finding things with your eyeballs in their sockets, let alone with them rolling around on the floor."

Placing a kiss on the top of her hair, he said, "No problem. I have a wonderful wife who's great at finding things."

"Like your toothbrush when you leave it in the toaster?"

"Absolutely."

They spent the next half hour leaning into taxis with open windows and questioning the cabbies. They showed them the pictures of Natasha and Colin and asked if they had seen either or both of them that morning.

The answers had been nothing but a string of depressing nos.

They were considering taking another tack, when at long last they were surprised and delighted to get a yes.

An older female cabbie, wearing a green and blue plaid shirt that was three sizes too large for her, said, "Saw them earlier this morning. Right about here, as a matter of fact, waiting for a ride."

"Did you give them one?" Dirk asked.

"No. But the guy behind me in number 436 did."

"Bless you!" Savannah gushed.

The cabbie gave her a wry smile. "That's mighty kind of you. Blessings are nice. Cash spends better though."

Dirk pulled a five-dollar bill from his pocket, reached through the window, and handed it to her.

"Gee," she said, shoving it into her oversized shirt

pocket. "Now I can buy that vacation home in Florida I've been dreaming of."

Giving her a curt little salute and bright smile, Dirk said, "That's wonderful. I feel like a fairy godfather."

She growled under her breath, then moved her cab forward, nearly running over their toes.

They hurried to the next taxi in the queue. Instead of leaning through the passenger's window, they rushed around to the driver's side.

"Hang back a few steps and let me take this one," Savannah said, when she saw that the cabbie was a fellow who was probably in his fifties.

She did well with guys in their fifties, sixties, and upward. She wasn't particularly sure why, and she wasn't especially proud of it. But she'd decided long ago that, when you've been given a natural talent, it's your duty to use it to full advantage.

She leaned down just enough to expose a bit of cleavage—yet another natural gift that had been bestowed upon her. She deepened her dimples with a cutesy smile and said in a sorghum sweet voice, "Why, hi there, sugar! As it turns out, you are *just* the man I been lookin' for!"

He looked at her. Her ample bosom. Her bright blue eyes. Her ample bosom. Her deep dimples. Her ample bosom.

Grinning from ear to ear, like a roadkill-possum on a hot Georgia highway, he said, "Really? Then I guess this is my lucky day!"

Chapter 12

"I'm surprised that you have a car rental agency here," Savannah said when the cabbie parked the taxi in front of an establishment, which the sign identified as LARRY'S RENT-ALL.

"It ain't Alamo or Enterprise, but it'll do," replied the driver, who had become somewhat less enamored with Savannah the moment Dirk had climbed into the cab and sat beside her. But he'd been pleasant enough and had offered them an interesting tidbit of information.

Natasha and Colin had asked him to take them someplace where they could rent a vehicle. They had expressed a desire to do their own driving tour.

Savannah wasn't sure if she was relieved or further puzzled by that, but she was determined to pursue it.

"You'd be surprised what we've got in this little town," the driver was saying as Savannah paid him for the ride. "Why, we've even got fast food joints. Three of 'em."

"That's wonderful," she said, adding a generous tip.

"I wouldn't say 'wonderful,' because they're all fish joints. Boy, what we wouldn't give one that served beef, like a McDonald's or a Burger King. Better still, maybe an Arby's!"

As she and Dirk crawled out of the cab, Savannah said, "Tell you what. My husband here likes to buy lottery tickets. If we ever hit the big one, we'll come back here and open up a restaurant that specializes in hamburgers. We'll even name a burger after you. How's that?"

"Wonderful! Now *that* would be wonderful!"

She saw the stars glittering in his eyes when he looked at her, and she realized that he was, husband or no, in love with her again.

Yes, it was a gift. God given? Probably not, but handy all the same.

While she and Dirk walked up to the door of Larry's Rent-All, she pinched his rear and said, "It's not just my boobs, you know."

"What?" He genuinely looked confused.

"This effect I have over men."

"I know that. I'm a man, remember?" He gave her a lusty once-over. "It's the *whole* package, gal. That's what has 'em fallin' at your feet. Those bright blue eyes. The soft, Southern drawl. That prissy little wiggle when you walk. You've got the *whole* shebang."

"How sweet! Thank you."

"Yes, you *can* thank me. You know how!"

"If you stopped talking about it. *If!*"

"Oh, yeah. I forgot that part."

Thankfully, they had reached Larry's entrance. Savannah jumped when she turned the knob and the door swung open. An eardrum-splitting buzzer sounded, alerting Larry that they had arrived.

He came rushing out of the back room, a toaster in one hand and screwdriver in the other. Wiping the sweat off his brow with his forearm, he said, "Hi. Whatcha need?"

Savannah glanced around at the shelves that lined the walls, holding a plethora of household appliances, tools for machinists and woodworkers, not to mention every odd apparatus used by homemakers and weekend handymen.

Apparently, Larry rented far more than automobiles.

She wouldn't have been surprised to hear he had a fishing boat on a shelf in the back room.

The place smelled of dust and oil, a combination that Savannah had always liked. It reminded her of men, good men, who fixed things that were broken.

On a top shelf a CB radio squawked, rattled, and squeaked out the mostly unintelligible messages flying back and forth on the airwaves between the local police and other emergency responders.

Savannah heard an exchange about a lost dog, last seen behind the fish-packing shed.

Apparently, Saaxwoo was a sleepy, basically crime-free town.

Savannah walked over to Larry and stuck her phone under his nose. "We understand that these people rented a car from you this morning." She showed him the Van Cleefs' photos.

"Yes, they did." He laid the toaster and screwdriver

on the counter, yawned, and ran his fingers through his rumpled hair. Savannah was pretty sure he had been taking a nap in the back room. The toaster and screwdriver had been a prop to convince his customers that he actually worked for a living.

"I don't wanna sound rude," he said, sounding like he was about to be rude, "but how's that *your* business and not just theirs and mine?"

Dirk pulled out his badge. "I'm a police officer, and I'm conducting an investigation."

"An investigation?" Larry went from lazy to alarmed in a heartbeat. "What's wrong?"

"They're missing."

"Missing?"

"Yes," Dirk said, "and since they're missing with your car, I figure that might be of interest to you."

All drowsiness gone, Larry was fully attentive. "Did they take off with my car? Did they steal it?"

"Might have," Savannah said, mentally crossing her fingers behind her back. "Did they say where they were taking it?"

"Yeah. They were talking about driving up to see the glacier."

"What glacier?" Dirk asked.

"Tongass Glacier. The only one we have within driving distance around here. It's one of the main reasons the cruise ships stop here. We're not exactly known for our fine hotels and restaurants."

Something about the way he said that last sentence made Savannah think of bedbugs and buffets serving week-old food. Suddenly, she was very thankful to be traveling aboard a luxury cruise ship.

"How long does it take to drive up to Tongass Glacier?" Savannah asked.

"About twenty minutes at the height of the season, when the traffic's bad. Fifteen if it's light, and the weather's good."

Dirk picked up an electric nail gun from the shelf, looked it over, and then replaced it. "How long do people usually stay up there at the glacier, poking around, doing whatever it is you do when you're looking at a glacier."

Larry thought it over for a moment, then said, "An hour maybe. An hour and a half tops, if you take a bunch of pictures. Cruisers take a lot of pictures of glaciers. I'm not sure why. If you ask me, it's just a great big chunk of dirty ice."

Savannah opened her mouth, ready to defend the geological importance, not to mention the scenic grandeur of glaciers, but decided it would be wasted on Larry, so she closed it.

"What time did they leave here with the car?" Dirk asked.

"About nine-ish."

Dirk was starting to lose his patience. Savannah could tell by the squint of his eyes and the tightness of his jaw. He looked like he wanted to pick Larry up and shake him until his teeth rattled.

Leaning deeply into Larry's personal space, Dirk said, "I'm not conducting a 'nine-*ish*' sorta investigation here, Larry, my man. So, if it wouldn't be too much trouble, would you please aid the cause of law and order by hauling out the book where you wrote down the *exact* time that they left with your vehicle.

I'm sure you have one back there somewhere. Maybe under the dust bunnies?"

Larry sighed wearily and leaned down to rummage beneath the counter.

"While you're doing your civic duty," Dirk added, "being an exemplary citizen and all that, could you also tell us the make, model, and color of the vehicle?"

As Larry continued to search, he said, "It's a bright red, 2006, Chevrolet HHR. Its vanity plate is LARRYS BB."

"Larry's baby?" Savannah asked.

He looked slightly embarrassed. "Okay. So she was really cute when she was new."

She nodded. "Weren't we all?"

Larry pulled a battered and, as predicted, dusty notebook from beneath the counter and spread it open. He flipped through the pages until he found the morning's entry. "Okay, here it is. They left at ten till nine." He snapped the notebook closed and gave Dirk a look filled with attitude. "Like I said, nine-ish."

Savannah glanced at her watch and saw that it was, as Larry would say, one-thirty-ish.

She did a bit of quick math. The Van Cleefs had been gone four and a half hours since picking up the car.

Fifteen minutes to the glacier, fifteen minutes back. Ninety minutes spent looking at the glacier, tops, if you took plenty of pictures.

That was two hours. Which left another two and a half hours unaccounted for.

She looked over at Dirk and realized he was doing the same mental arithmetic.

"I know. But it doesn't mean anything, Van," he said

softly. "They could've stopped along the way, got something to eat, checked out some other natural wonder and—"

"There ain't no other natural wonders around here or places to eat neither," Larry opined. "Just woods, mountains, creeks, and rivers. Those are all a dime-a-dozen in Alaska." Suddenly he looked serious. "You think my car's all right? That's the most valuable thing I own. I'd hate for something to happen to it."

"You're all heart, Larry," Savannah told him, "all concerned about your customers that way."

"Hey, I love my fellow man as much as anybody else, but that car's my bread and butter. If anything happened to it, I'd have to move back in with my in-laws, and if you knew them . . ."

Larry the Rental Man continued to prattle on about the shortcomings of his wife's parents, but Savannah wasn't listening to him anymore.

Her attention was focused on the squawkings and sputterings coming from the CB radio on the shelf.

"10-4, dispatch. This is Eagle Eye. We got a 10-55 here on Copper Creek Road just south of the glacier Visitor Center," said a male voice that sounded like every other cop Savannah had ever heard who was trying not to appear upset when he was.

"10-52, Eagle Eye?" asked the female dispatcher.

"Negative, dispatch. 10-79."

"Oh. Uh, copy, Eagle Eye."

Savannah's heart sank. It felt like it had just hit the dirty, dusty floor. She whirled to face Dirk and saw that he had the same stricken expression on his face that she was sure she was wearing on hers.

"No," she whispered.

"It's not. Not necessarily," Dirk said, stepping closer to her and putting his hands on her shoulders. "Don't go there, Van. You don't know."

But she did know. Deep in her soul.

"Do you have another vehicle to rent?" she asked Larry.

He hemmed and hawed a moment, then said, "Not as nice as the Chevy."

"What do you have?" Dirk demanded. "Speak up, man."

"An oldie. It's a 1984 Bronco. She's rusty and looks awful, but she'll get you where you wanna go."

"That old nasty thing I saw out front when we pulled up?" Dirk asked. "The green one with the purple fender and yellow driver's door?"

"That's the one."

Dirk was already pulling out his wallet. "How much for the day?"

"I don't know. I haven't ever rented it out, and—"

Slapping two twenties on the counter, Dirk said, "Gimme the keys, dude. Now!"

When Larry hesitated, Dirk added, "Unless you want me to just commandeer it in the name of the law."

Savannah held her breath. She knew that Dirk had no authority to do such a thing in Alaska. It might even be iffy in California, since he wouldn't be using the vehicle to pursue a fleeing felon.

But Dirk had never let little technicalities like that get in his way when he was riled up.

"Okay. Okay." Larry pulled a large ring of keys off his belt and thumbed through it until he found the right one. As he peeled it off the ring, he said, "I'm doing you a big favor here. If it happens to be my pretty red car that's wrecked up there, you let me know as soon as you can, okay?"

"Sure." Dirk grabbed the key from him, and he and Savannah rushed to the door.

She paused a moment before leaving and turned back to Larry, who was fondling his twenties. "Which way to Copper Creek Road and that glacier?" she asked.

"Out the driveway, turn right. Half a mile down to the road. Turn right again. The glacier's about four miles down."

"Thanks." She sailed out the door with Dirk.

It wasn't until they were in the old Bronco and hurtling down the bumpy road that she said, "Eagle Eye refused an ambulance."

"I know, honey."

"And a 10-79."

"I heard."

"Send a coroner. That's as bad as it gets."

Dirk said nothing. He just nodded.

"It's her." Tears filled Savannah's eyes and squeezed her throat until she could scarcely breathe.

Dirk reached over, grabbed her thigh, and gave it a shake. "You don't know that, babe. It ain't her till it's her."

"I do know. It's her."

Chapter 13

Long before Savannah caught sight of the crashed vehicle, she smelled the horrible, acrid odor of it and saw the black cloud of smoke staining the otherwise perfect blue sky.

Neither she nor Dirk had spoken since their initial conversation when they had left Larry's.

The silence inside the Bronco was deafening.

"Probably around this next corner," she heard Dirk mumble to himself as he guided the rented jalopy around a tight curve in the two-lane road.

Savannah tried to steal herself for what she would see. But if she had learned anything, it was that some sights were just too terrible. No amount of armor could protect the heart from such soul-scarring visions.

Once seen, they would always be remembered.

In the course of her career she had seen things that still caused her to wake in the middle of the night in a cold sweat with tears streaming down her face.

Instinctively, she knew that within moments she would be adding one more to her ever-lengthening list of nightmares.

No sooner had Dirk rounded the curve than they saw it. There, at the bottom of a long, steep hill, sat the wreckage of a red vehicle.

Or what was left of one.

She could tell that it was a Chevrolet HHR, but only barely.

Having apparently missed the sharp left turn at the bottom of the incline, the SUV had left the road and crashed into the thick forest of old-growth evergreens.

Nearby sat an old fire engine and one patrol car with an Alaska State Trooper insignia on the side. Three firemen and two troopers were milling about, peering at the wreckage.

"Not much of a turnout," Dirk remarked. "I guess that's what you get in the way of response from a town that's less than a mile long."

Savannah couldn't reply for the lump in her throat that felt like it was choking her. Her eyes burned, and it wasn't from the smoke in the air or the awful stench.

As they drew close to the wreck, she could see that the front end of the vehicle was completely destroyed, having been virtually cut in half by the trunk of the large fir tree it had struck, head on.

What she could see of the exterior of the car was badly scorched by what must have been a terribly hot fire. There was little left of the exterior paint to indicate that the vehicle had once been red.

Only the last two letters of the license plate were visible: "BB"

Deep in Savannah's brain, the part reserved for thinking nonsensical things at the most inappropriate times, she wondered why she was surprised to see those letters, those telltale letters that further confirmed her worst fears.

The moment Dirk stopped the car, she jumped out and ran toward the wreckage. But before she reached the car, one of the troopers approached her, his hand raised.

"Hey! Stop right there, ma'am. Don't come any closer."

She ignored him and tried to get around him.

He reached out and grabbed her by the arm. "I told you to stop, lady!" he said, tightening his grip. "You don't want to go over there. Believe me."

"I have to."

"No, you don't."

"You don't understand. I know them," Savannah told him.

"All the more reason why you shouldn't," the trooper replied, his tone softened, his face registering sympathy and compassion. "Believe me, there's nothing you or anybody else can do for them right now."

Dirk walked up and gently, but firmly, put his hand over the trooper's hand and pulled it off Savannah's arm. "I've got this now," Dirk told him. "Thanks."

With an understanding nod, the young man released her.

Dirk showed him his badge and read the trooper's name tag. "Corporal Riggs, I'm Detective Sergeant Dirk Coulter. This is my wife, Savannah. We have reason to believe some people we know are in that vehicle, and we'd like to confirm their identities."

Riggs cast a doubtful glance over his shoulder at the

wreck. "I'm sorry, sir, but you're not going to be able to identify those folks. The only way you'll get a positive ID on them is with dental records."

"That bad, huh?" Dirk said.

"Very, very bad, sir."

Savannah stood there, listening to their exchanges, saying nothing. She was waiting. Waiting for another part of her brain, one that was normally dormant during day-to-day life, to come to the fore. It was the purely intellectual, logical, nonemotional, and professional part that dealt with death. The mystery, the horror, the complexity of it.

Few people had seen as many dead bodies as she had, and for that, she envied them. Death was an alien entity to most folks. The occasional wake and funeral, the grief of missing a loved one, mourning the loss of their beloved presence . . . that was what the average person knew about the Grim Reaper.

But Savannah had seen his work firsthand, before the hospitals and undertakers had a chance to sanitize it. She knew all too well the brutality with which he sometimes harvested his victims.

"We have to see them," she said softly.

Corporal Riggs leaned closer to her. "I beg your pardon, ma'am?"

"I have to see her," she said more loudly. She looked directly into his eyes and added, "It doesn't matter how bad they are. My husband and I are trained crime scene investigators. We were charged with protecting the author, Natasha Van Cleef, and we have every reason to believe that she and her husband, at least their bodies, are in that car."

In a moment of unexpected familiarity and intimacy,

even for her, she laid her hand on the young trooper's cheek and gave it an almost affectionate pat. "I know you're trying to spare me, darlin', to keep me from seeing what you just saw yourself and wish you hadn't. But you can't protect me. Not this time. We're going to do at least a preliminary investigation of this scene. Let's just say that if you try to stop us, it's not going to be worth your while."

Riggs seemed to know that he had met his match, because he reached up, took her hand from his face, and patted it. Then he moved aside and allowed them both to pass.

As they neared the vehicle, the horrific stench grew stronger and stronger with every step, and for a moment, Savannah thought she would surely vomit. But she fought the urge with all her might. The last thing she needed was to be sick in front of these male cops and firemen. Though she wouldn't have been surprised to hear that they'd done the same thing when they'd first arrived.

Most vehicle fires produced a dreadful odor, and the SUV was no exception. Burning rubber, electrical wires, petroleum products, not to mention scorched carpet and upholstery, combined into a toxic mix of fumes that human lungs were loath to breathe.

Savannah also resisted her body's demand that she pull her shirt collar over her nose and mouth. This wasn't the time or the place to appear delicate.

"Good God," she heard her husband say behind her. "Anybody got an extra couple of masks they aren't using? This stinks bad enough to gag a skunk."

It was only then that she realized the firemen were wearing full face respirators. Even the second trooper, who was bent over, looking into the vehicle, had a white, industrial-grade dust mask over the lower half of his face.

But before anyone could supply them with masks, Savannah moved around to the passenger's side of the car and looked through the broken window.

In an instant, all concerns about the nauseating stench and toxic fumes left her mind.

The interior of the vehicle was like a muddy, macabre collage of grays, blacks, and dingy whites. It was hard to discern any of the ruined forms and name them for what they once had been.

But after a few moments, Savannah's addled brain was able to make sense of the horror she was seeing.

Once seen, she wished for the impossible. That it could be unseen.

Two human bodies, genders indeterminable, sat in the front seats amid the incinerated rubble. Little remained of the living creatures they had once been. Charred far beyond recognition, they were little more than ash and blackened bones.

She wanted to look away, but she couldn't. The sight held her mind and heart hostage. Only vaguely was she aware of Dirk standing at her right shoulder, his hand on her back.

"Is it them?" His voice sounded far away, as though he was standing at the opposite end of the long, dark tunnel.

"I don't know," she heard herself whisper. "Can't tell. They're mostly . . . they're almost completely . . ."

She thought of the vibrant woman who had sat in her backyard under the wisteria arbor, drinking lemonade. Frightened as she was that day, Natasha Van Cleef had courageously announced that no one would keep her from fulfilling her duties to her adoring public.

Unfortunately, she had been wrong. The person who had penned those threatening notes had done exactly what they said they would do.

Natasha Van Cleef had, indeed, died a terrible death.

Savannah thought of the author sitting at her dressing table, trying to twist her thick silver curls into some semblance of a formal updo with hands that were trembling.

Her fans expected it, and she was determined she would meet their expectations.

Now those gleaming curls were gone. The brave, vital woman, who had written so many books and given so many people hours and hours of pleasure, was gone.

Savannah knew that the author would be mourned by thousands and thousands of people who had never met her but, because of her writing, felt they knew her well.

"Hello, I'm Sergeant Bodin," the older trooper said as he walked around the back of the car to join them. He removed his mask and added, "Corporal Riggs says you knew these people."

"I knew her well," Savannah answered immediately, and she meant it.

After all, she was one of Natasha's readers and, like all writers and readers, their hearts had touched on some level. The intimacy of that contact was something understood only by authors, who spilled the very essence of themselves onto paper, and their readers, who absorbed their words deep into their own souls.

"Are you sure it's her?" Sergeant Bodin asked.

Savannah forced herself to look into the car again,

specifically at the left wrist of the body sitting in the passenger seat.

There it was. The charm bracelet.

It was badly burned, like everything around it, and the miniature books were indistinguishable one from the other. But it was a highly distinctive piece of jewelry.

"I'm certain," she said sadly. "It's Natasha Van Cleef."

"Hey, I've heard of her," the sergeant said. "My wife reads her books all the time."

"We suspect the driver is her husband," Dirk told the trooper. "His name is Colin Van Cleef. They were both aboard the *Arctic Queen*. They came ashore this morning and rented this car from a place called Larry's Rent-All."

"Yes, I know Larry well," Bodin replied. "You two, you're from the ship, also?"

Dirk nodded. "We were hired to provide extra protection for the Van Cleefs on the cruise."

"Why did they think they'd need extra protection?"

"She received several death threats," Savannah replied.

No one said anything for several long moments. Savannah didn't need to ask what the trooper was thinking. The same thing that she was, no doubt. That she had done a lousy job of protecting these people, who had just lost their lives in one of the most grisly ways imaginable.

"They left the ship without telling us," she heard herself saying in a voice that sounded weak and defensive, even to her own ears. "We were told to leave them alone in their suite until noon. How were we supposed to know they were out here doing"—she waved an arm, indicating the carnage in front of them—"doing this?"

The trooper gave her a look that was far more sympathetic than accusatory. "Before you go feeling too guilty, ma'am, let me say that I'm pretty sure this wasn't foul play. As awful as it may look because of the fire, we have accidents right here on this curve fairly frequently."

He turned and pointed up to the top of the hill. "People come roaring down this incline all the time. Especially tourists who don't know the road. When they get to the bottom here with this tight curve, they spin out and hit a tree. These are old growth trees, and they don't give one little bit. We lost a whole family here two years ago, a wreck that was a lot like this one. I think that's what happened to your friends."

Savannah wanted desperately to believe him.

She left him and Dirk and walked behind the car where the firemen were gathering up their hoses and extinguishers. Squatting, she studied the pavement, searching for any sign of tire marks. Surely, someone approaching a tight curve at a high speed would have realized their error at some point and applied their brakes.

She saw none.

As she walked back to the car, she forced herself to breathe the foul air more deeply and attempt to discern its components. Yes, there was the scorched rubber and the particularly terrible stench of burnt flesh. But there was another smell. Not as strong, but equally distinct.

She returned to Dirk and the trooper and told them, "There're no skid marks on the pavement, and I smell gasoline."

The trooper shrugged. "Not surprising. It's a car wreck. Probably a broken fuel line somewhere."

Savannah shook her head. "No. It's too strong for just a broken fuel line."

"Then maybe the gas tank ruptured."

She gave him a doubtful look. "When was the last time you saw a gas tank rupture in an accident? It happens, but very rarely. Those things are built like army tanks now."

The younger trooper, Riggs, had joined them. "What are you saying? You think somebody used an incendiary liquid? Are you suggesting this was arson?"

"No," Savannah told him. "I wish that's all it was. I'm suggesting it's far more than just simple arson. It's cold-blooded murder."

Chapter 14

Sitting in their rented Bronco, Savannah and Dirk watched as the burned-out SUV was loaded onto a flatbed truck.

"That's pretty bad," Savannah said, "when the coroner doesn't even take the bodies out before the vehicle's moved."

"They couldn't help it, Van." He patted her hand. "Those bodies are, well, you know, really fragile. I doubt they're coming out of the car intact, and that's not something you'd want to do out here in the road."

"I know, I know." She could feel the sting of tears in her eyes, or maybe it was a reaction to the fumes from the still-smoldering vehicle. She figured it was probably both.

"What do you think of that coroner?" he asked.

Savannah watched as the tall, thin man with graying hair, wearing a dark suit, climbed into an old station wagon and drove away. "At least they called him

'Doctor.' That was a relief. I was afraid in a town this small the coroner might be the village dogcatcher. Maybe he's a real, honest to goodness medical examiner. Wouldn't that be nice?"

Dirk seemed less impressed. "He seemed kinda weird."

"He seemed okay to me. How would you act if you'd just been told that you had to do autopsies on bodies in that condition? How many murders do you suppose he deals with annually in a peaceful little place like this?"

"The more likely question is, has he ever investigated a homicide?"

She groaned. "Now you're just trying to cheer me up." She held her arm up and sniffed her shirt sleeve. It reeked of the accident. "I need a shower," she said, "and a change of clothes."

"I need to eat. It's hours past my lunchtime."

She looked at him incredulously. "Are you kidding me? Seriously? You could eat after seeing, smelling . . . that?"

He returned her look with equal astonishment. "Well, yeah. Duh. I see a gruesome sight and now I'm never going to eat again? Get real."

Shaking her head at the never-ending source of wonderment that was her husband, she said, "Let's head back to the ship. We'll round up the gang and see if anybody's come up with anything new."

"And break the bad news to them."

"Yes. Bad news is always best delivered in person."

As though some form of telepathy was at work, her cell phone rang. She looked at the caller ID and said,

"It's Ryan. Maybe he has some news that's better than ours."

"Wouldn't take much."

"No kidding." She answered the phone with a cheerless, "Hello, Ryan."

"Hi," he replied in a hushed voice. "I'm calling to give you the latest report on Bellissimo."

"Let 'er rip."

"We just thought you might like to know that for the past hour, John, Richard, and I have been following him up and down Main Street. Leapfrogging. I'm watching him in a store right now. I'm about twelve feet from him. You're not going to believe what he's doing."

"At this point, I'd believe about anything. What's he up to?"

"Are you sitting down?"

"As a matter of fact I am. Lemme have it."

"He's shopping for a diamond engagement ring. That's what he's been doing all afternoon so far. We've followed him in and out of half a dozen shops. Now he's back at the first store he visited. Looks like he's got one picked out. A pretty big rock, too. She must be a really special girl."

"She must be an especially *dumb* girl if she's marrying a hoodlum like that."

There was a long pause on the other end of the phone, and Ryan said, "Are you okay, Savannah? If you don't mind me saying so, you sound a little droopy, not your usual bubbly self."

Savannah sighed. "To be honest, I've had better days. Like when I was eight years old and had the measles. Like when I broke my foot, tripping over a cat."

Dirk nudged her and whispered, "Cleo or Diamante?"

"Naw, a stray cat. I was chasing a pervert flasher down a dark alley. It was before you and I met."

"Who are you talking to?" Ryan asked.

"Nobody. Just Dirk," Savannah told him. "Why don't you, Moe, and Curly find your way back to the ship and wait for us near the Visitor Center? Leave our buddy there, Franky the Most Beautiful, to pick out his girl's ring in peace. We'll meet you in twenty minutes or so."

"Then you're going to tell us what's the matter, right? 'Cause you know John and I worry when something's up with our girl."

She smiled a little, feeling the love. "Yes, darlin'. I'll fill you in on all the gory details. See you soon."

She hung up and looked at Dirk. He was wearing his weird, crooked, little smile. It was the one he wore when absolutely nothing was funny.

"Gory details? Truer words were never spoken."

"Let's just get back to town," she said, staring out the passenger window at the dark, misty, and mysterious forest. "I think I've had about enough of the Alaskan wilderness for the time being."

It took Savannah and Dirk a bit longer than she had anticipated to reach the town's waterfront area. Plus it was at least five minutes before they found a parking place for Larry's multicolored Bronco.

By the time they made their way to the Visitor Center, Ryan, John, and Richard were there. So were Granny and Dora.

"Let's go get a bite to eat over at that little outdoor café," Savannah suggested.

Dora was horrified at the idea. "But why? If we eat on the ship, the food's better and, even more important, it's *free!*"

"Yes," Savannah admitted. "But if we sit at one of those outside tables, we'll be able to keep an eye on everyone coming and going on the ship's gangway. If we go aboard, we're not going to be able to eat in the atrium, and that's the only place where we'd be able to—"

"Okay. Okay. I got it." Dora held up her hands in surrender. "It's just that when you've got a week's worth of free meals available, it seems like you're flushing good money down the toilet when you . . ."

Richard had taken his wife by the hand and was leading her toward the café whose billboard advertised two-dollar beers and one-dollar hot dogs. "Don't worry about it, honey. I brought a few extra shekels along, just in case."

"Just because you have them, doesn't mean we need to spend them, you know. A penny saved is a penny earned."

Savannah glanced over at Dirk to see if he was embarrassed by his mother's behavior. But if he was, he certainly didn't show it.

She turned to John, who was watching the entire exchange and grinning broadly beneath his silver mustache.

"'Twasn't a windy day when that acorn fell from

the tree," he whispered to her as he nodded toward Dirk and then Dora.

"What? Oh, right," Savannah replied. "We use that down South, too. But we say when that 'nut' fell from the tree."

"Truth be told, that's how we say it, too. I was attempting to be kind, love." He laced his arm through Savannah's and escorted her toward the café, while Dirk, Granny, and Ryan brought up the rear. "I heard earlier that you're the sad one today," he said. "Any particular reason that you'd care to share?"

"I will, as soon as we're settled at a table," Savannah replied. "Have you heard anything from Tammy and Waycross?"

"Not a word. I shudder to think of the mischief they've created aboard ship in our absence. They may be under the chief security guard's lock and key as we speak."

She laughed. A little. The last time she had seen Tammy and Waycross, neither looked like they had the energy or gumption to create any sort of havoc. "One can only hope," she said.

When they were all seated at a large table, with some extra chairs and a clear view of the gangway. Savannah took her cell phone from her purse and called Waycross.

"Hi, Sis," he said, his voice as sad and listless as she had ever heard it. "What's up?"

"We just sat down here at the café beyond the gangway. We can see anybody who's coming or going. So you two are off duty now. Come on down and join us for a bite to eat."

She heard Waycross muttering something to Tammy, and although Savannah couldn't discern her actual words, her friend's lackluster tones said more than enough.

"Uh, if you don't mind, we're gonna pass this time. Tammy's kinda tuckered out. We're fixin' to go up on the top deck and set a spell. They've got comfy chairs up there with cushions and everything."

"Okay, I understand," Savannah told him, wishing that she truly did understand. She had a pretty active imagination and it was working overtime, coming up with new possibilities that ranged from inconvenient to horrific.

"By the way, we haven't seen anybody come in or go out, except for that Patricia Chumley gal, the editor. She just came back to the ship about five minutes ago. She had a whole heap of shopping bags with her and looked pretty happy with herself and what she bought."

"That's great, honey. Good work. You tell Tammy I appreciate it. Are you sure you won't join us?"

"No. Thanks. My girl's got her heart set on those deck chairs and some peace and quiet."

Although Savannah's mood was pretty low, she felt it plummet even further. Since when did that otherwise amiable and cheerful couple decline a social invitation?

More than anything, she wanted to jump up from her chair, rush aboard the ship, and find out what was wrong with her chickadees. But at the moment Mama Hen had more urgent issues to attend.

"Okay, pumpkin," she told him. "You guys just relax and kick back. We'll meet up with you later."

Then, because she had a feeling he might need it, she added, "I love you."

"We love you, too, Sis," he said.

She could swear she heard tears in his voice.

As Savannah tucked her phone back into her purse, Dirk asked, "Is everything okay with those two?"

"No," Savannah said. "I'll have to give them a good talkin' to later and find out what's up."

Granny leaned close to Savannah and said, "I noticed Tammy seemed a bit puny myself, and we can't be havin' a lady who's expecting in a state. If you need any help with that 'talkin' to' business, you just let me know."

"I sure will, Granny. Heaven knows, you are the best at it. Always have been."

"No, I haven't. It's a gift that comes with age." Granny took the glass of sweet tea that the waitress handed her and gazed into its depths like a fortune-teller studying a crystal ball. "The years bring a lot of gifts, if you're lucky enough to be alive to receive them. Arthritis, lumbago, bunions, to name a few. But some of them are worth havin' and pretty much make up for the rest."

"Like what, Gran?" Ryan asked, intensely attentive to her every word.

"Oh, like peace of mind, acceptance of your own faults and those of others, faith that all things happen for a reason. I reckon the best of all is the confidence that you can get through anything, 'cause you've already been through most of what life can throw at a body. Even if some of it knocked you down, stomped on you, and squashed you flat as a flitter, you still manage to get back up."

Savannah nodded thoughtfully. "Okay, Gran. We're going to tell you what happened earlier this afternoon. And if you can, I'd sure appreciate it if you could explain to us how it happened for a reason, and how it's gonna work out for the best in the end. Because right now I just can't see it."

Chapter 15

By the time Savannah and Dirk had related their sad story, the mood of the Moonlight gang was far less festive. The seeming nonstop flow of sweet tea—with nary a beer, in honor of Granny and their work ethic—and hot dogs galore had done nothing to raise their spirits.

"Where does this leave us?" Ryan asked.

Dirk leaned back in his chair, his arms crossed over his chest. "It's pretty straightforward," he said. "We have a double homicide with only one suspect—"

"Who, we're pretty sure," Richard inserted, "is more interested in proposing to his girlfriend than doing a hit on a degenerate gambler."

"He could do both," Granny suggested. "You young folks seem to think highly of what you call 'multitasking.' Though I think it should be called 'doing more than one thing, and not doing anything all that good.'"

"When did you fellas pick up his trail?" Savannah asked.

Ryan, John, and Richard conferred for a moment. Then John said, "About half-one, give or take ten minutes."

"That was about the time we heard about the accident," Dirk noted. "So he could have had something to do with it, after all. At this point, as far as we know, he doesn't have an alibi for the time someone would have done their dirty work."

"Whatever the 'dirty work' was that they did," Ryan offered.

"If any dirty work was done at all," John added.

"There was!"

Savannah realized, the moment the words left her mouth, that she had shouted them, and she felt terrible about it. The group had every reason to doubt that foul play had been done, just as the trooper at the scene had.

"I'm sorry," she said. "Really, I am. I've just . . ."

"Had a terribly difficult day," John offered. "We understand, love."

"No, that isn't it." She wiped her hand wearily across her forehead and paused a moment to find the right words. "I don't know how I know the Van Cleefs were murdered. I just know, as stupid as that may sound."

Gran leaned over and grabbed Savannah in a tight, grandmotherly embrace without a thought for the rest of the diners who were now watching to see what might happen next.

"You've had an awful shock to your system, Savannah girl," she said. "Your feelings are strong on this subject, as one well might expect under the circumstances. But you've got to figure out if what you're feeling is ol' unreliable emotions, born of some sort of misplaced guilt, or true intuition. It's mighty easy to mistake one for the other at a time like this."

Savannah tried to absorb what her grandmother was telling her, but her wits were too scrambled. "What does my guilt have to do with it?"

"Guilt's a powerful thing," Gran told her. "It's a good thing if we genuinely did wrong and need to make amends and learn from our errors. But when it's false guilt, it lies to us and makes us think all sorts of awful things about ourselves that ain't true. Lies like that don't do nobody no good."

"Listen to your granny, babe," Dirk said. "She's telling you the truth. Whatever happened to the Van Cleefs, it's on them, not you."

"It is," Richard agreed. "What kind of person hires a team of people to guard them, then tells them to stay away? Then they leave the safety of the ship and go driving around in rural forests without their protectors?"

"That's true." Savannah looked into her grandmother's face. "What does your intuition tell you, Gran?"

"My intuition ain't saying much. Sometimes, unlike my mouth, it's quiet. But common sense tells me there's reason to suspect the worst."

"Me too," Dora jumped in from the other end of the table. "Especially considering what we saw today, while we were out and about."

Granny grinned broadly. "That's right. Us gals have

something to report, even if all you fellas came up with is a guy shopping for an engagement ring."

Savannah experienced the first positive emotion she had felt since entering that empty suite hours ago. She was about to hear something good. Emotions or intuition, she just knew it.

"You ladies are holding out on us?" Ryan asked.

"Let's hear what you discovered," John said.

"As it happens," Gran said, swelling with importance, "us more mature ladies didn't exactly spend our afternoon sightseeing. Although, that isn't completely true. We did see us some sights, didn't we, Dora. One in particular."

"We sure did." Dora giggled. "We saw that dark-haired woman with the black glasses. She was shopping like she was afraid they were going to sell out of T-shirts with grizzly bears on them and those little Inuit dolls with the fur coats. Why, we saw her buy ashtrays with the map of Alaska and—"

"That's not the important part, Dora," Gran snapped. "Stop with the chitter-chatter and tell 'em what we saw. Tell 'em the part that mattered, or I will."

Savannah half expected Dora to fly into a huff, but she was too excited to take offense.

"We didn't know for sure what we were seeing," Dora continued, "because we had no idea what you were going to tell us about the car accident and the fact that you smelled gas and that you think—"

"Okay, that's it." Granny drew a deep breath. "That dark-haired editor gal wasn't doing nothin' but shopping, but that other one, she was up to no good."

"Which other one?" Savannah asked. "The blonde? Olive, Ms. Van Cleef's personal assistant?"

"That's the one. We spotted her driving past in the backseat of a taxi cab. She had a serious, up-to-somethin' look on her face, for sure. So we kept an eye on her."

"That's right!" Dora was practically bouncing up and down on her chair. "Then we saw that she was waving the cab driver to pull into a service station. There's one right there by the place that's got those grizzly T-shirts five for twenty dollars. I thought about buying some, but I don't know five people who'd wear a bear on their chest like that, especially a—"

"When the driver stopped," Gran interjected, "this Olive gal jumped out of the cab and ran into the service station. A couple of minutes later, she came out with one of them gas cans that you keep in your trunk. You know, for in case you run out of gasoline."

Savannah felt her heart begin to pound. Her brain started to race with this small but tantalizing amount of information.

"Then," Gran continued, "she looked like she was talkin' all sweet to the fella that works there at the station. Sidlin' up to him, she was, friendly like a female hound dog who just met a male hound dog that she's taken a likin' to. The next thing you know, he's pumpin' gasoline into that can of hers."

"Then she paid him," Dora added. "I couldn't see how much she paid him, but you've just gotta know that she was *way* overcharged. Probably paid too much for the can, too. They know they've got you at their mercy in a little place like this. They'll just gouge you any way they can."

Richard leaned close to his wife. "What. Happened.

Next?" he asked her. "What did she do once the can was filled and she paid him too much money?"

"She carried the can over to the taxi and tried to get into the backseat with it," Dora said.

"The cab driver made it clear, even to us, as far away as we were," Gran said, "that he wasn't havin' none of that. The two of them argued for a while. Then the cabbie got out, opened up the trunk, and let her stick the can there in the back."

"Then they took off, and we couldn't see them anymore, so we don't know what happened then." Dora picked up her glass and drained the last of her tea.

"Which direction did they go?" Dirk asked.

In unison Gran and Dora pointed south.

Granny unsnapped the clasp of her white patent leather pocketbook. Reaching inside, she said, "But there is one more little thing you might like, so that you don't have a complete dead end on your hands here."

She pulled out a piece of paper with some pencil scribblings on it and pressed it into Savannah's hand. "I may just be an amateur detective, not a professional one like most of y'all sittin' here. But I know a thing or two, and I aim to earn my keep on this here trip of ours."

Savannah looked down at the piece of paper and saw several numbers scrawled across it. "What is this, Gran? Don't tell me it's the plate number of the taxi."

"Of course it is. It ain't my grocery shoppin' list. That other one, 592, that's the number of the cab itself. You know how they've got the number painted on the back there where you can see it."

Dirk jumped up from his chair and gave both his

mother and Granny hearty hugs. "I can't believe you two gals were sitting on this all this time. We're here stuffing our faces with hot dogs and swilling down tea, and you've got the best break of the day."

"The *only* break of the day," Granny said, smiling.

"Okay. The *only* break." He turned to Savannah, an excited look on his face. "What you say, babe? Let's pile in the Bronco and let these ladies take us to the service station. We'll see if Blondie said anything to the station attendant while he was selling her the can and pumping her gas. Then we'll take a drive to the taxi office and find out what we can about that cab and his schedule today. Maybe they can tell us where he dropped her off."

Savannah wanted to go. She desperately wanted to go. But she thought of the sadness in her brother's voice, of him and Tammy sitting on that deck alone, troubled by a problem that seem to be getting the better of them.

Finally, she said. "But before I perform any other duties on behalf of the Van Cleefs, I've got something I need to do for my own family."

Dirk's eyes searched hers. "Tammy and Waycross?" he asked.

"Yes. I have to talk to them. Figure out what's going on. Then I'll find a way to join you."

"I understand. You take care of business, and we'll hook up later." He leaned over to give her a kiss on the cheek, and when he did, he whispered in her ear, "You tell them that I'm thinking of them, and that whatever it is that's bothering them, it's gonna be all right."

As everyone stood and gathered their belongings, getting ready to go their separate ways, Granny reached out and grabbed Dirk's hand. "Would you mind too much, Grandson, if it was just your mama who took you to see that gas station? I'm worried about those young'uns myself, and if Savannah's gonna give them a talkin' to, I'd like to be along."

Dirk tweaked her nose. "Not a bit. We'll be just fine. You've already earned your keep and then some today. Go tend to your family."

Granny reached over and took Savannah's hand in hers. "That's all we've ever done, ain't it, Savannah girl? It's a job I don't think we'll ever get to retire from."

Savannah thought of Tammy and Waycross's child. Soon the baby would be entering the world with needs of its own. There was never an end, it seemed, to the long line of people to love, people who needed you. Usually at the most inconvenient times.

"I believe you're right, Gran," Savannah said. "I reckon this is a life sentence we're serving."

Chapter 16

On an upper deck, Savannah and Granny found Waycross, but he was without Tammy and looking most forlorn.

He was standing at the railing, staring down at the busy waterway and town with a grief-stricken expression on his face. His broad shoulders were slumped and his head low. Savannah couldn't recall ever seeing her brother so sad.

Of her eight siblings, he was one of her favorites. A good man who always tried to be even better. Yet, throughout his life, Waycross always seemed to get the short end of any sticks that were being handed out.

Until Tammy.

Tammy Hart was a jewel, a treasure, a queen. Though Waycross had always felt unworthy of her, he was infinitely grateful that she hadn't felt the same.

"Hey, sweetie," Savannah said as she walked over and stood to his left at the railing.

Gran positioned herself on his right. "Where's your honey bunny?"

He nodded toward the rear of the ship. "Back there. Sittin' all by her lonesome."

"Why?" Savannah asked. "Why aren't you with her?"

"I got the idea that's what she wanted. To be by herself."

"I doubt that." Savannah patted his back and felt him draw a little sob. "Tammy likes company, and she loves you, so I don't know what'd give you that idea."

"She told me, 'Just leave me alone, Waycross. Just git away and leave me be. I mean it. Git.'"

"Oh." Savannah glanced behind him and looked at Gran.

Granny lifted one eyebrow and shrugged. Then she said to her grandson, "I reckon I can see why you might take that from what she said. But then, she's expecting. Women don't always mean what they say even on a good day, let alone on a day when they're pregnant."

"No. She means it. She's been sayin' it for a while now. I think she's pretty much done with me."

Big tears began to stream down his freckled cheeks and he began to cry in earnest.

Granny put her arms around his waist and pulled him to her. "There, there," she said. "Don't you cry, my strong, brave boy. I don't care how things look right now. They'll all work out for good in the end. You just wait and see."

"Not this time," he said, bending down and resting his head on his grandmother's. "It's over. I'm losin' the best thing that ever happened to me. The two best things. Tammy and our baby, and I won't ever get 'em back."

Savannah's heart sank. How could things have gotten this bad so quickly? Only a month ago, they had given Tammy a baby shower, and she had been overjoyed to be having a child with Waycross.

Although . . .

Savannah and everyone else had been wondering when they were going to set a date for the wedding. As the pregnancy had progressed, there had been less and less said about it.

Now that Savannah thought about it, she didn't recall any mention of a ceremony for weeks.

Maybe Waycross had reason for concern after all.

"You stay here with him," Savannah said to Granny. "I'm fixin' to go find Tammy."

Gran nodded. "You get to the bottom of this, hear?"

"I will. Don't worry about that. I've interrogated a lot tougher cookies than our Miss Tamitha."

As Savannah made her way around the deck, passing row after row of chairs, searching for Tammy, she nearly walked right by her.

Her friend was sitting with her feet drawn up to her hips and was hugging her shins. She had pulled a large, red blanket around her and over her face. If it hadn't been for the bright pink toenails sticking out from beneath the lower hem of the throw, Savannah wouldn't have recognized her.

No one in the history of the world had ever worn a shade of pink that bright on their toenails but Tammy. It matched her classic Volkswagen bug perfectly, so she had bought two dozen bottles. When it came to nail polish, she was set for life.

Unless, of course, she developed some taste.

Savannah reached down and tickled the toes. Instantly, Tammy's blond head popped up from inside the blanket.

"Hey, babycakes," Savannah said as she pulled a neighboring deck chair close to hers and sat down. "I'd ask if you're up here catching some rays, but not a chance of that happening with you doing your teepee impression there."

"It's cold," was her abrupt answer.

"Yes, it is a bit." Savannah took another blanket from her own chair and spread it lovingly around Tammy's shoulders. "I'm worried about you, puddin'," she said.

Tammy looked at her with sad, guilty eyes. "Don't worry about me. With all the Van Cleefs missing, you've got enough to worry about."

I've got a lot more than that to worry about, Savannah thought, but she figured it was best to keep the darker, more depressing circumstances to herself.

Her little friend, her Golden Sunshine Tammy, was obviously going through one of the worst times of her life. She didn't need any additional burdens

"I hear that you and Waycross have hit a rough patch, relationship-wise," she said.

Tammy shrugged. "Not exactly."

"Well, he's crying his eyes out there on the deck with Granny trying to comfort him. He thinks you want to be rid of him. Permanently."

Tammy's lower lip trembled. "I don't want to be rid of Waycross. I love him."

"He loves you, too. Somethin' fierce. But he must

have done something pretty bad for you to tell him, 'Just git away from me and leave me be.'"

Tammy gasped. "I *never* said that to him! I wouldn't! Think about it, Savannah. Does that sound like me or Waycross?"

"It *does* sound like Waycross. No doubt about it," Savannah agreed.

"What I said to him was, 'I need a few minutes to myself, honey. I need to think. Could you just give me a little space?' That's what I said."

Savannah nodded. "Sometimes, people hear what they *think* you're saying, what they're *afraid* you're saying, rather than your actual words."

"That's what he did. I'm telling you, I might be the woman carrying the baby, but during this pregnancy he's been the moody one, always asking me if I love him, if I'm going to stick with him, if I'm ever going to marry him."

There it was. The opening. Savannah jumped through with both feet. "Well? Are you? Going to marry him, that is."

Tears filled Tammy's eyes as she answered eagerly, "Oh, I hope so! I do."

"What?" Savannah shook her head, confused. "What do you mean you 'hope' so?"

"I hope I'm going to be able to. It's what I want more than anything in the world. More than I ever wanted anything in my whole *life*."

Savannah reached over and enclosed Tammy's hand between her own. She was surprised to feel how cold it was. "Tammy," she said, "if you want to get married, sweetheart, get married."

"It's not that easy."

"Actually, it is. You just do it."

"I can't just *do* it. If I could've just done it, I would've already done it, months ago."

"May I ask what's stopping you?"

"My mom. My dad. They made their feelings on the topic very, very clear. They won't allow it."

Savannah's mind raced, trying to absorb what she was hearing. "I'm sorry," she said. "I can't quite get my head around this. Where I come from, the parents of a girl who's . . . in a family way . . . they're the ones who usually insist on the young people getting married. Sometimes they insist with a shotgun in hand."

Tammy sniffed. "Maybe that's the way it is where you come from. Your people are more traditional in the way they see and handle these things. My parents are from the East Coast. They're traditional in some ways, too, but there are certain things that they aren't very flexible about."

"Like what?"

Crying even harder, Tammy could barely manage to speak the words between sobs: "Who . . . th-their . . . daughter marries."

"Whom you marry? But you want to marry a great guy, who loves you to pieces, whom you consider to be the love of your life, who's the father of your baby and wants to make a family with you. What's there for anybody to object to?"

"I—I just can't say it. It's so mean and . . ."

Tammy lost all control, dissolving into a puddle of tears.

Savannah pulled some tissues from her purse. Handing them to her distraught young friend, she said, "Stop crying, if you can, sugar. It's not good for you, getting all in an uproar like this. It's not good for the little one, either."

With what was obviously a great effort, Tammy attempted to compose herself. She wiped her tears away with the tissues, then blew her nose soundly.

"Atta girl," Savannah told her. "Now you just take your time and explain to me what's going on here. Don't pull any punches. Tell it like it is."

"I don't want to hurt your feelings, Savannah. That's why I haven't talked to you about it before. I haven't been able to talk to anybody about it. Especially Waycross. I couldn't break your hearts. I love you so much."

"We love you, too, honey. More than you could imagine. Don't you worry about how we're going to feel. Once the real truth is out in the open, everybody's going to feel better. Maybe not at first, but in the long run. Truth has that effect on people."

Savannah could see that Tammy was steeling herself to do as she was asked. She drew a deep breath, as deep as she could, considering the size of her tummy, and said, "My parents mean well. They really do. More than anything, they want me to be happy. They want what's best for me."

"Okay. But . . . ?"

"I'm their only child, and they've always had great hopes for me, for my future. My mom and dad are both very successful people. My father owns a Fortune 500 company. My mother's a world-renowned brain surgeon. They've worked very hard and accomplished a lot in their lives."

"That's wonderful."

Tammy's tears began again. "Yes, it is. I'm very

proud of them both. I always have been, even when I was a little kid. But they aren't proud of me."

"Oh, darlin'," Savannah said. "I'm sure that isn't true. Any mother or father would be honored to have you as a daughter. You are the most amazing, loving, loyal, and dedicated woman I have ever known in my life. I'm enormously proud just to say you're my friend. I can't imagine what it would be like to call you my daughter. I'm sure you're mistaken and they're very proud of you."

"I wish that was true, but they aren't the kind of people to hold back their opinions. And their opinion of me is that I've wasted my life."

"That's ridiculous. Even in the time that I've known you, you've accomplished a great deal. We may not have made a lot of money and we aren't brain surgeons, but we've saved lives."

"*You've* saved lives."

"Yes, I have. But in every instance that I can think of, I couldn't have done it without your help. We did it together. We're a great team, you and I and the rest of the Moonlight Magnolia gang. For every life we've saved, we've made ten lives better than they were before we came along. That's nothing to shake a stick at."

"I only wish my parents felt that way. They're always telling me what high hopes they had for me. They say that I was given the gifts of intelligence and beauty, but I threw them away to be a worthless hippie chick in California."

Savannah stifled a grin at the term "hippie chick." While the words might be applied to a nature-loving, free spirit gal like Tammy, the word "worthless" was miles from the truth.

"How did they want you to use your intelligence and beauty?"

Tammy shrugged. "I don't know for sure. They never really said. I was supposed to graduate from an Ivy League school, get some degrees, and find an occupation that they could brag about at cocktail parties. My daughter, the senator who will be running for president next election. My Tammy, who won the Nobel Prize for curing cancer. Something like that."

"That's not asking much. Every halfway decent parent expects that of their offspring."

Tammy caught Savannah's sarcastic tone and almost smiled.

Savannah continued. "How about, 'My daughter, who followed her heart and has become the World's Greatest Sleuth of All Time.'"

That gained her a full-fledged grin. "The second greatest," Tammy offered. "You'll always be number one as far as I'm concerned."

The two friends shared a silent, companionable moment. Then Savannah said, "Okay, so your folks wanted you to become rich and famous and don't think much of private detection. What does that have to do with my brother and the two of you getting married?"

Tammy hung her head. "That's the hurtful part. The part I can't tell Waycross or you or anybody."

Savannah nodded as understanding dawned on her. "He's not good enough for Mom and Pop."

Tammy simply nodded.

"He's a poor kid from a poor family from a wide-spot-in-the-road town in Georgia, and he wouldn't 'show' well at cocktail parties," Savannah offered.

"Something like that."

"Something *exactly* like that?"

"Yeah."

Savannah allowed the pain to wash through her. She really had no choice. It wasn't the first time that her family's nonpedigree had hurt her and those she loved.

But only for a moment. Then in the deepest part of her soul, she told the pain and the people who had caused it that she would have none of it or them.

"You're in love with my brother," Savannah told her. "He's as good a man as comes along in a lifetime. I'm pretty sure you told your parents that, right?"

"Of course I did. Over and over. But it made no difference."

"What do they expect you to do?"

"When I first told them, they wanted me to come back home and marry this other guy they picked out for me years ago. He's their best friends' son, and he just got a divorce. So they wanted me to have an abortion or give the baby up for adoption, move back home, and marry Franklin Dudley."

"But you don't want that."

"No! I can't stand Franklin Dudley. More important, I want this baby, to have it and raise it myself. I love Waycross, and I want to build a family with him. But when I told my parents that, they said I was being selfish. They said I should be more considerate of their feelings, that this is just killing them. They said they'll never attend a wedding, if I'm marrying someone like Waycross."

"You think there's a chance they'll change their minds?"

"No. Absolutely not. We had a big argument about it

last night and another one this morning. They made it clear that if I marry Waycross, they'll have nothing to do with me, or him, or the baby, for the rest of our lives."

As Tammy softly wept into her tissues, Savannah considered her next words thoughtfully. "I'm sorry to hear that, sweetheart."

"I know they're wrong. But I just can't bear to hurt anyone, let alone someone I love. Now, no matter what I do, I'll hurt some of the people I love most. How can I do the right thing when, no matter what I do, someone's going to be harmed?"

Anger, hot and all-consuming, poured through Savannah's veins, quickening her pulse and turning her cheeks red. At that moment, all she wanted was to give Mama and Poppa Hart an enormous piece of her mind.

"I understand the way my parents feel," Savannah heard Tammy saying. "Their parents had a lot of money, and my great-grandparents before them. People with a lot of money live in a different world. They're rich and—"

"No!" Savannah interjected. "It's not about that. 'Rich' has nothing to do with it. I've known plenty of people who probably have more wealth than your parents could dream of, but they respect their children's choices. They would want what's best for their sons and daughters, even if it meant that they married outside their social circles. Even if it meant they held a menial job, if that's what their hearts required to be joyful."

Savannah drew a deep breath and then dove back into the deep end. "This isn't because your parents are wealthy. This is because they're putting their prejudices ahead of their child's and grandchild's happiness. It's narrow-minded bigotry, plain and simple."

Tammy nodded thoughtfully. "That's true. If that's the way they choose to think, nothing I say is going to change their minds."

"Then that's their choice. Unfortunately, they've put you in the position where you have to choose, too. What is your choice, Tammy?"

"I don't know. What would you do?"

Shaking her head, Savannah replied, "I can't tell you what to do, Tammy. If I did, I would be no different than your parents. You aren't a fifteen-year-old girl. You're a woman. Soon you'll be a mother. You have to make your own choices and then live with them. That's the worst and the best part of being an adult."

Tammy thought for a long time. Savannah watched her, her heart in her throat, wondering if her words had helped or harmed.

Then, to her relief, Tammy lifted her chin, straightened her spine, and threw off her protective blankets. "I know what I'm going to do," she said with the determination of a queen readying her armies for war. "I'm going to make my choice based upon what's best for the one person who doesn't have a voice yet. My baby would want to be raised with the people who love it most, its mom and dad, and that's what's going to happen."

She rose from her chair, a bit awkwardly considering her added burden, and said, "Sorry, Savannah, but I have to leave you now. There's something important I have to do. Something I should've done about six and a half months ago, when I first realized I was pregnant."

As Savannah watched her friend hurry down the deck in the direction of her fiancé and her new, chosen future, she whispered to the bright blue sky, the dark crystal-clean waters, the emerald forests, and the mystic mountain range in the distance, "Ah, did you see that, Alaska? A gorgeous miracle, just like you. Our Tammy just became a woman."

Chapter 17

"**O**kay," Savannah said when she called Dirk from the ship's gangway. "We've got that particular family fire put out, it seems, and I'm now leaving the ship to come join you. Where are you?"

"I just left the service station," he told her. "The rest of the gang's out and about, scouring the town for Olive. I'm on my way to the taxi office. Want me to swing by the pier and pick you up?"

"Does Ben and Jerry's Chunky Monkey ice cream have nuts and chocolate?"

She heard him laugh. "Hurry on down to the road and stick out your thumb, babe. Your ride will be there in less than one minute."

True to his word, Dirk and the nasty old Bronco came sailing down the road in her direction fifty seconds later. As he drew near, she stuck out her hitchhiking thumb and one hip in a seductive pose. Early in life, she had discovered that particular gesture never failed to put a smirk on a man's face. Though she only used it on men she knew extremely well . . . like husbands.

As she jumped into the truck, he asked the predictable question. "Hey, good-lookin', where you headed?"

"Wherever you're going, darlin', is just fine with me."

They drove a block or two, then he said, "I'm really happy to see you feeling a little better, Van. I was worried about you."

"Tammy and I had a good talk," she replied. "I think it helped her, and I know it helped me."

"What'd you talk about?"

"Choices. How part of being an adult is making them and then living with them. I was feeling really bad about what happened to the Van Cleefs. I still do. But it was their choice to leave that suite, that ship, this morning without protection. So, whatever happened—"

"They have to live with it."

"Or, sadly . . . not."

The taxi "office" turned out to be little more than a lean-to shack nailed to the side of an old-fashioned saloon named Bottom of the Barrel. Inside Savannah and Dirk found a cranky middle-aged woman wearing a T-shirt with the image of a grizzly bear poised to bite a hunter in half. It read: Lunchtime in Alaska.

She was sitting at a rickety desk with a stack of rumpled papers, a badly chewed pencil, and a landline phone in front of her. She was gnawing on a plug of tobacco and spitting into an empty beer can.

At least, Savannah assumed and hoped it was empty.

Savannah had heard the saying, "Alaska women are

as tough as Alaska men." While she was sure that there were plenty of perfectly lovely, feminine, girlie-girl women in the state, this gal wasn't one of them.

"What?" punctuated by a spit, was the only greeting they received when walking into the room, filling the tiny space with their mere presence.

As always, when he felt he was being disrespected, Dirk reached for his badge. A gold detective shield impressed most folks and brought out their best behavior. With some others, it had the opposite effect.

This sweet damsel of the North was one of the "others."

"So what?" she said. "I don't know you, and you're not a state trooper. So that means you don't have any authority around here."

"Be that as it may, we're investigating a potential homicide," Dirk told her in his half-an-octave-lower-than-usual voice.

"And?" Another spit.

Savannah said, "We need to speak with one of your cabbies."

"Go stand on the queue down by the pier and hire one. That's how it's done around here."

"We have one particular driver in mind," Savannah told her, "His taxi is number 592."

"That's Jake. He's busy."

Dirk leaned over and pushed the landline phone toward her. "How's about you give busy Jake a call and tell him we need to speak to him."

"He's had a bad day. Got stuck in traffic up there by the glacier. Some stupid tourists ran themselves off the road. Again."

Savannah gave her a hard, blue, laser stare. But instead of being intimidated, Miss Tobacco Breath returned her glare and said, "What? Is that the so-called 'homicide' you're investigating? That wasn't murder. That was you forty-eighters coming here on vacation and being stupid. We don't go around killing folks up here, the way you fools do down there. We got grizzly bears, thin ice, airplane accidents, and the bitter cold to do that for us."

"I'm sure you do," Savannah said. For a moment, when the cantankerous woman had spoken the words "airplane accident," Savannah had seen a look of pain cross her wrinkled, weather-damaged face. Savannah wondered whom she had lost, and whether it was mechanical failure, poor climate conditions, or pilot error that had taken her loved one from her.

Not that it mattered.

Gone was gone.

"But, you see," Savannah continued, "we knew those stupid forty-eighters who died out there today, and we just want to make sure that it was their own error of judgment that cost them their lives and not somebody else's cruelty."

She paused for a moment, allowing her words to sink in. Then she said in her kindest, softest voice, "If you lost someone you cared for in an accident, you'd want to make sure it was an accident. Wouldn't you?"

For a moment the woman said nothing. She just sat still, not even chewing her tobacco. Then, abruptly, she reached for the telephone, picked up the receiver, and punched in some numbers. "Yeah, Jake. It's Myrtle. Come 'er."

She paused a moment and listened. Then shouted, "'Cause I told ya to!"

Slamming down the phone, she turned to Savannah and Dirk. "He'll be 'round in a minute. Wait outside. You're suckin' up all my air."

They quickly obliged, and before long, they were standing on the edge of the street, waiting, watching for a yellow cab, number 592, driven by a guy named Jake who was apparently pretty good at doing what he was told.

"Boy, she's a nasty bitch," Dirk observed.

"Naw, Myrtle's cool. I like her."

He gave her a look that suggested he doubted her sanity. "O-o-o-kay. I suppose there's no accountin' for taste."

Savannah spotted a cab coming toward them, then as it neared, saw the number on the front fender. "It's our guy," she said. "Let's hope he has more to say than his boss lady."

"And has better aim if he's spitting in a beer can."

"One can always hope."

The driver rolled down the passenger window and said, "Hey, are you the reason Myrtle yelled at me?"

"Yeah," Dirk told him.

"Actually, we just asked her if we could talk to you," Savannah clarified. "She chose to yell at you all on her own."

Jake sucked air through his teeth and nodded. "Yeah. Myrtle's like that." He pointed to the backseat. "You wanna get in and ride around while we chat, or you want me to get out and us go inside with Myrtle?"

It took five seconds for Savannah and Dirk to climb into the taxi, and another two seconds for him to spray gravel and get the car back onto the road.

Two minutes later, they were on the outskirts of town.

Jake pulled the cab onto a wide spot beside the road that overlooked a charming, rock-strewn brook, flowing through a dark, fog-shrouded valley. "This here is Copper Creek Road," he said. "That down there is Copper Creek."

"Yeah," Savannah said without enthusiasm. "We're familiar with it. Spent some time on it already today."

"Farther up though," Dirk added. "Near the glacier."

"Huh. Me too." Jake unbuckled his seat belt, reached over to a small cooler on the front passenger's floorboard, and opened it. "Want one?" he asked, pulling out a soda.

Dirk grabbed the can, but Savannah declined. She was already deeply regretting all the tea she'd had at the café. What went in had to come out. Eventually. She scolded herself for not remembering Stake-out Rule #1, about watching your fluid intake if bathrooms weren't plentiful. If they spent too much time out here in the wilderness, she might have to take a hike into the forest, find a secluded pine tree, and water it.

"What is it that you two wanted to talk to me about?" Jake wanted to know as he popped the top of his cola can. "You want an all day tour around town and the vicinity? I'll make you a deal. A lot cheaper than one of those bus tours and a lot more comfortable."

He shot them a wide grin that was missing a couple of teeth. "Plus you get the joy of my company."

"I'm sure that'd be great," Savannah said, "under different circumstances. Unfortunately, we don't have time to take any tours right now. In fact, we have a few questions to ask you. Important questions."

"Yeah." Dirk leaned forward and propped his forearms on the back of the front seat. "You said you were up by the glacier yourself earlier today?"

"Yes." Jake took a swig of his soda. "That was a fare I won't soon forget."

"How so?" Savannah asked.

"For one thing, she was a hottie. Not overly bright, but cute and friendly. Not like the usual grumpy old lady tourists I haul around every day."

For a moment, Savannah thought of the numerous "old ladies" that she knew and loved—their humor, their wisdom, their loyalty, their kindnesses. She decided that if Jake's elderly female patrons were "grumpy" it might have more to do with Jake than his fares. But since she wanted to stay on his good side, she decided to keep that particular observation to herself.

"We happen to know the young lady in question," Savannah told him. "We pretty much agree with your assessment of her. But right now, what we need to know is exactly what happened this morning from the moment you first had contact with her until she was out of your sight."

Suddenly, Jake seemed a bit wary. "Why should I tell you guys about one of my fares? Who are you people anyway?"

Once again, Dirk dragged out his badge and identified himself as police.

Jake looked at Savannah, evaluating. "Are you a cop, too?"

"Used to be," she replied.

"She's a private detective," Dirk snapped. "Close enough. Let's get on with this. How did you happen to pick this gal up? Did she call you?"

"Nope. I was driving by the pier and she flagged me down. I was on my way to get some breakfast, but one look at her, and I decided to stop."

"What time was that?" Savannah asked.

"I don't know for sure. Shortly after eight. That's usually when I get hungry and need some serious food."

Dirk was digging in his jacket pocket for his notebook and pen. "Sorry, buddy," he said, "but we need to know the exact time. You cabbies write that stuff down, don't you?"

"Yeah, I wrote it down. Myrtle would have my hide if I didn't." He searched among some paper litter on the passenger seat until he found his logbook. He looked it over and found the entry. "Picked her up at eight-ten."

"What did she say when she got in?" Savannah asked.

"She asked me if I could take her more than one place. If that was against taxicab rules. I laughed, 'cause that's kind of a dumb question, but she asked real cute. Like maybe she'd never taken a cab before in her whole life."

"Okay." Savannah was beginning to lose patience with Jake. If he said the word "cute" again, she might have to file a complaint with Myrtle. "Where did she say she wanted to go?"

"First she said she wanted to stop by a service station and buy a gas can and get it filled up. I asked her if her car was broke down somewhere and outta gas. She said, 'No, and don't ask me about it. I can't tell anybody what it's for.'"

Jake paused to drain half of his soda can. Then he wiped his mouth on his sleeve and continued. "So I took her over to Fred's service station, and Fred not only sold her a can, but he filled it up for her, too. And that shows you how hot she was. I went to school with Fred, and I've known him practically our whole lives. I've never known him to do anything for anybody. But he filled that can for her. Fred never would've done that for some cranky, ugly, old tourist lady."

Once again, Savannah's hackles rose a few notches, but, as before, she filed her indignation away for future reference. "After Fred filled the hottie's tank, what happened then?"

"She wanted to haul it back there on the floorboard next to her. That's just what I needed, a smelly gas can stinking up my interior. I told her if she wanted me to transport gas for her, it had to be in the trunk. She agreed, and I stuck it back there for her."

"All right," Dirk said. "Now we're getting to the good part. Where did she have you take her?"

"Up to the glacier."

Savannah's heart soared. She could almost hear that puzzle piece click into place. "You dropped her and her gas can at the glacier?"

"Not at the actual glacier. You have to hike on trails for a ways to see that. I dropped her at the Visitor Center."

"Didn't that seem a little odd to you?" Dirk asked. "Just a woman and her gas can, out there in the middle of nothin'?"

"Yeah, I guess. A little bit."

"You didn't think to ask her what she needed it for?" Savannah said.

Jake shrugged and looked a little sheepish. "No. Can't say that it crossed my mind. Like I said, she was really hot and cute. It was kinda distracting."

Dirk drew a deep breath and shook his head. Savannah could feel his impatience brewing like a thunderstorm on the horizon. "So that's it? That's all? She didn't say anything about what she was going to do with the gas?"

"Not a word."

"What time was it," Savannah asked, "when you dropped her off?"

Jake glanced again at his driver's log. "That was at eight twenty-eight."

"So, what you're telling me is," Dirk continued, "she just climbed out of your cab, you got out and handed her the gas can, and she went into the Visitor Center, carrying that thing like some kind of weird purse?"

Jake paused before answering, thinking it over. "Now that you mention it, that *was* a little weird."

"I reckon it was," Savannah said. "I'm pretty sure you're only supposed to carry gas can purses between Easter and Labor Day."

"No, that's not what I mean. The weird part was that she didn't go into the center at all. When I turned the cab around to leave, I saw her in my rearview mirror. She was walking away from the center, back down the road we had come, and I remember thinking right then, she might be as hot as a pistol, but that gal's a bit odd."

When Jake took them back to the taxi office to collect their Bronco, Savannah and Dirk got out of the cab, and Dirk pressed some money into his palm.

"Thanks, buddy," Dirk told him. "As it turns out, you're not as completely useless as I thought you were gonna be."

"Gee, thanks. I guess."

"There's just one thing," Savannah said, as she leaned inside the driver's open window and slapped him a wee bit too hard on his forearm. "The next time some of those old lady tourists get into your cab, I want you to think about something. A lot of those old ladies were *majorly* hot back in their day—the kind who would've caused your head to spin and would've set your undershorts afire if you'd been lucky enough to get your hands on one of them. Think about *that* the next time one of them climbs into your cab. You might treat her a little differently, and she might not be so cranky. Just try it on for size, huh?"

Jake gave her a wide-eyed, vacant stare.

Okay, by admonishing him, she hadn't changed his basic character, elevated social mores, or improved the planet. But what the heck? It was about time that somebody stood up for the Former Hotties and Still Pretty Damned Awesome Gals of the world.

Chapter 18

Just before Savannah and Dirk arrived at the Tongass Glacier Visitor Center, they passed the spot where the Van Cleefs had met their demise. As always, Savannah was struck by the strange difference in a locale once the debris of the traffic accident had been cleared away.

What had once been a scene of horror now looked mostly like any other stretch of road, any other curve, any other bit of forest.

Only the one tree they had struck bore signs of the event. Its bark was scuffed, its lower limbs burned. The needles and cones on the ground beneath it had been turned to ash, but the fire had spread no farther.

"It's a good thing this isn't the middle of their hot season," Dirk said, as though thinking the same thing she was.

"True. The whole forest could've been set on fire."

"That was a lucky break." Dirk's cheerful tone sounded pathetically false.

She gave him a look. "Here I thought that I was the family-appointed Pollyanna."

"You are. But lately, ever since you started this change-of-life business, you've been almost as grumpy as me. If you're not fulfilling your duties, being annoyingly cheerful and all that crap, somebody's got to do it."

She smiled and fluttered her eyelashes. "Do you mind?"

"Of course I mind. Who wants to act like they're happy when they're in a bad mood? It sucks." He reached over and tweaked one of her dark curls. "But what the hell, somebody has to do it. I guess it's only fair to take turns."

"It does have to be done, no doubt about it. Both of us can't be wallowing around in the abyss of depression. Not at the same time."

"That's for sure. It'd be war."

She noticed that he slowed the Bronco down a bit as they passed the actual crash site. She also noticed that his eyes, along with hers, were scanning the road on either side. It wasn't necessary to ask him what he was looking for.

A gas can.

Just as she was.

She wasn't surprised when she didn't spot one. Even Olive didn't seem foolish enough to set a car on fire with two people inside and then leave the gas tank in clear sight.

But then, while still a cop, Savannah had caught a guy robbing a convenience store that was right next door to the service station where he worked. He had been semi-cunning enough to wear a paper sack with eye holes cut out over his head. But since he was robbing the store on his lunch break, he was wearing his mechanics uniform with the name of the station and his own embroidered on the front.

As he often did, Dirk spoke her very thoughts, "Even she's not stupid enough to leave that can out here in plain sight. But then, you never know. Remember when that guy who wore his service station uniform to rob the—"

"Stop it! You're doing it again!"

"Reading your thoughts?"

"Yes, and it's creepy."

He laughed. "We're getting more alike every day, me and you. Two shall be one and all that."

"God forbid."

When they reached the Visitor Center, Savannah was surprised to see only one tour bus and a couple of taxis in the parking lot.

"Wow," she said, as they climbed out of the Bronco and headed up the path to the center. "You'd think a place like this would be more crowded."

"Remember, the trooper at the accident said that it's still early in the season. Not a lot of traffic up yet."

"True—unfortunately, for us. Otherwise a tour bus might have been passing by when the Van Cleefs crashed. That would've been nice."

She caught him giving her an odd look. "You know what I mean," she said. "It would've been bad for the people on the bus, obviously. Instead of having a nice, peaceful, Alaska vacation, they'd be waking up in their beds screaming from the memory. But at least we'd have a boatload of witnesses."

He gave her another, even odder, look.

She threw up her hands. "Okay! I'm an ex-cop, for heaven's sake. Not a humanist philosopher."

As they continued across the parking lot, he said, "I know what you meant, babe. You're just being practical."

"Yes, and I want to do a couple of things very badly. One: prove that this was a murder. Two: find out who did it."

"Me too, darlin'. At least we know that Fluff-Head Olive had something to do with it."

"Of course she did. What are the odds that some random somebody would leave a cruise ship, buy a can of gas, hire a cab to bring it up here within walking distance of the crash scene? A crash scene that reeked of gasoline."

"I find it hard to believe that she could have planned a murder on her own. But I agree that she is in on it, right up to those perky bosoms of hers that she's so proud of."

She looked up at him with a smirk and said, "They were *perky*? Really? I can't recall."

He shrugged. "Me either. When it comes to remembering things like boobs and the size of the fish we caught, we guys tend to embellish a bit."

"Get out. I never would've guessed."

He opened the center's door and they walked inside to find a state park ranger in the middle of the room giving a lecture to a group of tourists. The pretty female ranger's face bore the characteristics of her indigenous

Tlingit ancestors: exotic dark eyes, prominent cheek-bones, and smooth, bronzed skin.

She was comparing two large, framed photos on the wall. One showed a glacier as it had been many years ago. The second, more current picture revealed how much the ice had receded.

Any other time, Savannah might have been tempted to linger and listen, but today she couldn't afford to play the tourist. She and Dirk walked over to a concession stand where all sorts of souvenirs were sold. An older woman, who also appeared to have native heritage, was arranging hand-carved animals in a glass case.

She smiled when she saw Savannah and Dirk approach. "Good afternoon," she greeted them. "May I help you?"

"I certainly hope so," Savannah told her as she walked up to the counter and scrolled through the pictures on her cell phone. Finding the photo of Olive, she showed it to the clerk, at the same time that Dirk showed her his badge.

"Did you happen to see this lady here in the center this morning?" Savannah asked.

The woman didn't need to study the photo long before replying, "Yes, I did. Early this morning. Not long after we opened."

"When you saw her, what time was it?" Dirk asked.

"We opened at nine, and I saw her shortly after that. So maybe five after nine."

"What did she do?" Savannah wanted to know.

The clerk lowered her voice and leaned closer to Savannah. "She used the ladies room, and apparently she

really needed to. She rushed right inside and stayed
there for a long time."

"How long?"

"I'm not sure. Maybe ten minutes. Longer than
most people visit the restroom, I'd say."

Dirk scowled. "Do you have any idea what she was
doing in there?"

"Not really," the woman replied. "But when she
came out of the bathroom, she went straight out the
front door again. I was a little curious, I have to admit.
I've worked in this center for over twenty years, and
I've seen all kinds of things, weird stuff that's happened in those restrooms."

"I'll bet you have," Savannah said.

The clerk nodded vigorously and lowered her voice
even more. "I've caught people doing drugs, stealing
other people's belongings, beating each other to a pulp,
and, of course, having sex, in more different ways and
positions than you'd ever want to know about." Glancing at Dirk, she added, "Although you being a police-
man, you've probably seen it all yourself and more."

He gave her a twisted smile. "Let's just say that after
all I've seen, I'm forty-something going on ninety-
three."

"When you went into the restroom after she left,"
Savannah said, "did you see anything unusual?"

"No. Everything looked the same."

Savannah's mood plummeted. Apparently, she was
destined to be disappointed and deeply frustrated for
the umpteenth time in one afternoon.

"But there was something very unusual," the clerk
added.

Just as quickly Savannah's spirits rose to new heights.
"What was that?"

"The bathroom absolutely reeked of gasoline. It was
awful. I swear it smelled like she had taken a bath in it."

"You realize we're looking for a needle in a haystack,"
Dirk told Savannah after they had been searching the area
around the crash site for nearly an hour, looking for
Olive's now-infamous gas can.

"I'm still bummed out, so you're still on Pollyanna
duty," she told him. "That means you have to keep depressing thoughts like those to yourself."

For the first half hour of their search, Savannah had
been positively enchanted by the otherworldly beauty
of the ancient woods. The intoxicating, refreshing
scent of the evergreens, the crunch of the aromatic forest floor beneath her feet, the rocks and remains of
fallen trees covered by soft, damp moss—the natural
beauty of the land found a special place deep in her
heart.

Savannah knew that if she lived to be older than
Granny Reid, it would remain a part of her.

But as their search continued to yield nothing, Savannah tried to put the bewitching beauty of the place
aside and concentrate on the business at hand.

"Are you sure that gas can is red?" she called out to
Dirk, who was about twenty feet away, deeper into the
forest. "What if it's green? If it's green we're never
going to find the darn thing."

She could hear him sigh wearily, even from across
the distance. "Van, really? Have you ever in your life
seen a green gas can?"

"No. But—"

"No 'but.' There is no 'but.' It's like some kind of cosmic law that gas cans are red. Besides, the service station attendant told me he sold her a red one. He even showed me one that was just like it, and it was very red. I refuse to discuss this with you anymore."

But Savannah hadn't heard his last few sentences. Because she was looking at something a few feet away, well hidden under a thick fern cluster. A chunk of half-rotted tree bark had also been thrown over it.

"I got it," she yelled to Dirk.

"What?"

"I said, 'I got it.' It's over here, about six feet from the road."

She could hear him tromping loudly through the woods, headed in her direction.

"You sure?"

"Yeah, but it's green. Just like I told you."

"Huh? What?"

He burst through the bushes and looked where she was pointing. At a red gas can.

He chuckled. "You're a pistol, gal. One of these days I'm gonna have to take you over my knee and spank you."

"Yeah. Yeah. You might get the job done, darlin', but you'd be all bloody and bruised and crippled up somethin' fierce. It wouldn't be worth it, I guarantee you."

"Why do I believe that?"

They both rushed over to the gas can. Savannah found a stick and gingerly lifted one corner of the tree bark, giving them a better look.

"That's gotta be it," she said. "Not a speck of mud or even dust on it. Has to be fresh."

"It is. I can even smell the fumes from it."

"The lid's off," she said. "We should try to find that, too. That and the handle would be the most likely places for fingerprints."

"We'll look for it, but first I'm going to call that state trooper, Sergeant Bodin. He's gotta see this and process it."

"He's probably going to want to talk to our Little Miss Olive."

"If we can find her."

"Yes, *if* we can find her." She reached into her purse, pulled out her phone, and started to call Ryan. "I think we'd better put the rest of the team on that. With any luck she won't be standing in a forest, wearing a green dress."

Chapter 19

This time when dealing with Sergeant Bodin, Savannah detected a trace of humility, maybe even a bit of respect in the way he addressed her. Though all he'd said when they showed him the gas can was a simple, "Thanks. Good work."

His gratitude wasn't that important to her. What she wanted was his cooperation and willingness to help them figure out what had happened to Natasha and Colin Van Cleef.

Later, after the now-empty gas can had been carefully bagged and placed in the trunk of his cruiser, Bodin turned to her and Dirk and said, "You know, even before you called us, we'd changed our minds about this being an accident."

Savannah perked up. "Really. Why?"

"When we were helping Dr. Johnson remove the bodies from the car, that smell of gasoline that you noticed earlier . . . let's just say, it was overpowering. One of the mechanics who works for the towing company said that the two front seats had been soaked with gasoline. He said even after that hot fire, they're still deeply saturated."

"I guess that makes that gas can we found all the more important, huh?" Dirk said, practically glowing with self-importance.

Savannah decided not to mention that she had found the can, not "we." Embarrassing one's law enforcement husband in front of another law enforcer was a foolproof way of assuring that you were going to have a grumpy husband at least for an hour or two.

When she weighed the cost versus the benefit, she decided it wasn't worth it.

Bodin slammed his trunk shut and turned back to them. Brushing some dirt from his hands, he said, "I'm definitely going to have to interview that gal you spoke of, the personal assistant. What's her name?"

"Olive," Savannah told him. "Olive Kelly. We have our people looking for her right now, both on the ship and in town. We'll let you know the minute we find her."

He gave her a challenging little grin. "Unless, of course, I find her first."

"It doesn't really matter who finds her, does it, Sergeant?"

"No, I suppose not. But I am looking forward to asking a woman who's vacationing on a cruise ship what she was doing this morning, running around with a full gas can."

Savannah told him, "I will be very interested in watching you ask those questions. I can't wait to see what kind of explanation she's going to come up with. Especially since she didn't strike me as a particularly inventive gal."

Dirk chuckled. "Something tells me it'll involve a dog eating homework. Or she was holding the gas for a friend."

Savannah and Dirk had just arrived back in town, when Savannah's cell phone rang. She was delighted to see that it was Tammy calling. What a relief, to have her Princess of Sleuthdom back in business.

"Hello there, Miss Tamitha. What's shakin', puddin'?"

"I've got her! I've got her right here!"

"Who?"

"Olive Kelly. Waycross and I just stepped off the ship to walk around and see if we could find her. Boy, did we luck out! It wasn't five minutes until we saw her get out of an old van there by the pier."

"Are you following her?"

"No. I've got a hold of her arm, and I'm not letting go."

Savannah caught her breath. "Tammy, listen to me, girl. Let her go. Take your mitts off her right now and be very, very nice to her."

"But why?"

"Just do it."

"Okay, I let her go. But now she's going to get away."

"So, follow her. But whatever you do, don't put your hands on her again. Where are you exactly?"

"At the bottom of the gangway. She was trying to go up onto the ship."

"Then talk to her. See if you can get her to stay there. We'll be along in less than two minutes."

Savannah ended the call, turned to Dirk, and said, "Stomp that pedal, boy. We've gotta burn the wind and get to the ship as quick as we can."

"What's going on?" he asked. "What's that ding-a-ling done now?"

Savannah shrugged. "Um, nothing much."

"Come on, Van. Spill it."

"Okay, okay. Let's just say that, if she wanted to, I'm pretty sure that Olive Kelly could press charges against Miss Tammy for false arrest, false imprisonment, and kidnapping."

Dirk did exactly as Savannah suggested. While she made a quick phone call to Sergeant Bodin, he pressed the pedal to the metal and sent the old Bronco bouncing down the pothole-riddled road.

They arrived at the ship, not in two minutes, but in ninety seconds. Dirk stashed the Bronco in the first available parking space he could find, then they both jumped out of the vehicle and ran to the ship.

As they approached the gangway, they saw Tammy and Wayercross standing, side by side, blocking a very angry Olive Kelly from boarding the ship.

But, as Savannah had instructed her, neither Tammy nor Waycross were touching her.

"I don't know what you think you're doing," Olive was shouting. "You can't keep me from getting on my ship if I want to."

Olive stepped forward, placed her open palms on Waycross's broad chest, and gave him a hard shove.

Savannah watched, knowing that it would take a lot more than that to knock her brother off his feet. Waycross had been the only red-haired boy in the tiny town where they had been raised. More than once, Savannah had seen him taunted, bullied, and in some cases even attacked, because of his carrot top.

The abuse had never soured him. Waycross was as sweet as the day he was born.

But you couldn't knock him off his feet. No one could, and certainly not a petite blonde with a bad temper.

However, Savannah saw something else that concerned her far more. From the top of the gangway some of the ship's own security guards were watching the hostile exchange and obviously discussing it between themselves. Savannah had a feeling that it was only going to be another moment or two before they descended the gangway and took matters into their own hands.

"Uh-oh," she heard Dirk say, and they both redoubled their speed.

The guards were halfway down when Savannah and Dirk reached the quarreling trio. Dirk pulled out his badge and held it high for the guards to see. Apparently, they figured he had things in hand, because they turned and slowly made their way back into the ship.

"What is wrong with you people?" Olive said. "All I want is to get back on my ship and . . ." Her words trailed away as she recognized Savannah and Dirk. "Oh. It's you two."

"Yes, it's us," Savannah told her. "We need a few words with you."

Olive shook her head and stomped her foot like a two-year-old who had been denied her favorite sweet.

"No! I've had an absolutely awful day. My feet are killing me. I'm all dirty, and I'm not talking to anybody until I've had a shower."

Savannah had to agree with her there. The young woman did have a distinct smell about her—the odor of sweat, and plenty of it, mixed with the underlying pungency of gasoline, and yet another unpleasant scent that Savannah couldn't immediately identify.

Olive Kelly did need a shower, no doubt about it. But there were more important matters at hand. Especially since an Alaska State Trooper cruiser had just raced up to the pier with lights flashing.

It screeched to a stop, and in an instant, Sergeant Bodin and Corporal Riggs bailed out.

Savannah turned to Olive just in time to see the young woman's initial reaction when she spotted the troopers coming toward her. Beneath her toasty, perfect, copper tan, Olive Kelly turned pasty white.

Her knees seemed to buckle, and for a moment, Savannah thought she might faint.

Reaching out, she grabbed Olive's arm to steady her, and she could feel her body starting to shake violently.

"What is this?" Olive asked, her voice trembling as badly as her limbs. "What's going on?"

Dirk put out his hand and grabbed her by the other arm. "Miss Kelly, that awful day you've been having? It just got worse. Let's just say that you needing a shower . . . well, that just became the least of your problems."

"This is just plain stupid," Dirk whispered in Savannah's ear, as they watched Sergeant Bodin interrogate Olive Kelly. "You can't do a proper interview in a *bank*, for Pete's sake!"

"It's the only building in town with bars," Savannah replied in an equally hushed voice. "I heard they had a robbery fifty years ago, and that's when they installed them on the windows."

"Just in case there might be another one in the next half century?"

"I reckon."

"But where's the intimidation factor? How are you supposed to drum up any claustrophobia, or good, old-fashioned fear of the justice system?"

He had her there. Savannah looked around at the room, which was comfortably furnished with contemporary furniture in warm, earthy colors. Overall, the space was simply but tastefully decorated with framed black and white photos of Alaskan mountain beauty on the walls and a few tropical plants in each corner.

Someone was even taking the time and trouble to water the plants and dust the tables.

Savannah was impressed.

Olive Kelly, the detainee who was being "grilled," sat in a plush faux-leather chair as she was being questioned by Sergeant Bodin, who sat in a matching chair. Between the interviewer and the interviewee was a tasteful, oak end table, spread with numerous copies of *Architectural Digest* and *House Beautiful*.

Savannah and Dirk sat nearby on an equally cushy sofa. Their matching coffee table provided such selections as Forbes, *Consumer Reports*, and *Alaska* magazine.

Savannah surmised that this room was probably

used by people opening checking accounts and applying for loans.

She also strongly suspected it had never been used for a homicide investigation. Not even once.

Dirk glanced down at his watch and shook his head, disgusted. Again he leaned over and whispered in Savannah's ear, "If I had her back home in my sweat box, she'd have spilled her guts a long time ago."

"Sh-h-h," Savannah whispered when she saw Sergeant Bodin shoot them a warning look.

As Savannah watched Olive Kelly wipe the sweat off her forehead and cheeks with the sleeve of her sweater, it occurred to her that in this case, Dirk's so-called "sweat box" wasn't needed. This office, semi-luxurious at least by Saaxwoo standards, seemed to be doing the trick just fine.

Something told Savannah that Olive would fold like a flimsy cocktail umbrella if she were being questioned in the lobby of the Waldorf Astoria.

Although Savannah agreed with Dirk that if he had Olive in the tiny, claustrophobic, gray interrogation room back in the San Carmelita police station, this little song and dance would've been over long ago.

Even Sergeant Bodin seemed to be getting bored with the routine. For nearly an hour he had gone around the same circle with Olive.

She had a simple, straightforward story, and she was sticking with it. No matter how many times they had circumscribed her tale of woe, it always came back to the same thing.

"He told me to do it," she was saying, as she twisted the handful of tissues that she had been using to wipe her eyes and nose. "I never would have left the ship if he hadn't told me that I had to. It was life or death."

"It sure was," Sergeant Bodin agreed. "As it turned out, it was murder, and you're our only suspect."

Olive perked up slightly. "If it's another suspect you want, go find the guy who called me. The one who threatened me."

The sergeant groaned. "Right. The guy who told you to go buy some gas and leave it up by the glacier, and if you didn't, he'd kill you. That guy?"

"Not just me," Olive said, trying to wipe away the streaks of mascara that were streaming down her cheeks with her overused tissues. "He said he'd kill Mr. and Mrs. Van Cleef, too. All three of us."

"Unless you bought them some gas?"

"Yes! I swear to you, that's why I did it. Sneaking off the ship like that, buying the gas, and leaving it up there beside the road . . . Why else would I do all that stuff? It sure wasn't because it was fun. I did it to save our lives!"

She collapsed into tears, covering her eyes with her hands. "Now you're telling me that they're dead anyway. So I did all that for nothing!"

Savannah saw the sergeant's shoulders sagging with frustration and fatigue. Having been where he was many times, she knew what it was like to try to wring information from a suspect who was either too cunning or too stupid to provide any.

Then, there were the innocent ones. You could interrogate them for a month and they would give you nothing, because they had nothing to offer.

Savannah hadn't decided yet whether Olive Kelly

was cunning or stupid. She was quite sure that she wasn't innocent.

Savannah suspected that Sergeant Bodin wasn't sure about Olive either. From the weary look on his face, she had the feeling that he would prefer to be wrestling a grizzly or resisting a lust-besotted moose in rutting season.

She got the distinct impression that he was more of an "outdoor law enforcement" kinda guy.

Quietly, trying not to attract attention, Savannah reached into her purse and pulled out her cell phone. She crossed her left leg over her right and hid the phone in the crook of her knee. She felt Dirk lean against her, as he watched what she was doing.

She quickly texted Sergeant Bodin the message: **If you want to take a break, I'll have a go at her.**

Once his phone had dinged and he had read the message, it didn't take Bodin long to decide. He jumped up out of his chair as though someone had lit a string of firecrackers under his bottom.

"I've had quite enough of you, Miss Kelly," he told her as he walked to the door. "I'm going to go have a cup of coffee, and when I come back I'm arresting you for the murders of Natasha and Colin Van Cleef. It'll be first-degree, premeditated homicide, too. Nobody's going to kill two people in this area, my area, and get away with. So you better spend the next five minutes doing some real serious soul-searching."

Okay, Savannah thought. *It's going to be good cop– bad cop. No problem.*

Donning her very sweetest, most understanding, big

sister face, Savannah rose and sat down in the sergeant's recently vacated chair.

Looking across the end table at Olive Kelly, Savannah had to admit that it had been a long time since she had seen anyone that frightened.

Olive was shaking as violently as someone who had been left out in a blizzard on Christmas Eve, wearing nothing but their underwear.

She was crying so hard that Savannah glanced around the room and located the nearest trash can—beneath the end table next to them— just in case she started to throw up.

"Now, now, don't cry," Savannah told her as she reached into her purse and brought out a handful of clean tissues. "Here you go," she said, holding them out to Olive. "Looks like you could use a fresh supply."

When the young woman reached for them, her hand was filled with the dirty ones, and she didn't seem to have the presence of mind to get rid of them herself.

Gingerly, using only her thumb and forefinger, Savannah picked the soggy wad out of her hand and dropped it into the waste can. Then she pressed the new ones into her palm. "Come on now, sugar," she told Olive. "This ain't gonna cut it. Dry your eyes and blow your nose. He's going to be back soon, and you and I have to figure out what you're going to tell him."

"But I already told him the truth, and he didn't believe me," Olive wailed.

"Okay," Savannah said. "I believe you. I believe that what you've told him, so far, is true. But the problem is: you haven't told him the *whole* truth. Once you do, I think everything will be just fine."

Savannah glanced quickly over at Dirk and saw him give her "the sign." He lightly brushed his forefinger down the length of his nose and smiled.

It was the gesture they made when one knew that the other was telling a whopper of a lie. A sign that the fib-teller's nose was in danger of growing a foot or more.

Okay, so she knew that everything wasn't going to be peachy for Olive Kelly, no matter what she said. Being the one who dragged a gas can to a fatal vehicle crash, that wouldn't be easy to explain away.

But nowhere in the *Manual for Law Enforcement Investigation 101* did it say that an interrogator had to speak only the truth to a suspect. Soul-blackening, nose-growing lies, while perhaps a bit distasteful, were considered a "means" that was justified by the "end."

At least, that's what Savannah had told herself over the years when her Sunday school teachings collided with the reality of her job.

So it was only with the slightest quibbling of her conscience that Savannah intensified her "compassionate" smile, reached over, and patted Olive Kelly's trembling hand.

"Okay, sugar," she said. "Let's take it from the very beginning."

"All right." Olive took a deep breath, gathering herself and, Savannah hoped, her wits. "I got up this morning. I put on my robe. I went to the bathroom and peed."

Savannah heard Dirk groan.

"We can skip that part," Savannah told Olive. "Let's start with the moment you got your first communication from this mysterious man."

"He called me on my cell phone, and it really scared me, because he had a creepy voice."

"Creepy, as in how?"

"Like the creepy kind they use in creepy movies, when they really want to creep you out."

Savannah made a mental note to give Olive Kelly a thesaurus for Christmas.

"Okay. He had a creepy voice. Exactly what did he say?"

"I'm not really sure, because I had just woke up. I didn't even have my hair brushed yet. But he asked me if I wanted to save my own life and the Van Cleefs, too. Of course, I said, 'Sure.' I mean, who'd say no to a question like that?"

"Nobody at all," Savannah replied solemnly. "You did the right thing."

"Then he told me I had to get off the ship as soon as I could. He said to catch a taxi there by the pier, you know, where they line up."

Savannah nodded. "I'm familiar with the area. Go on."

"He said I should catch a cab and tell the driver that I wanted to go to the nearest service station. When I got there, I was supposed to buy a can and have them fill it up with gas. Then he said to tell the driver that I wanted to go to the Visitor Center up at the glacier. I wasn't sure what a glacier was, I'm still not, but I figured the driver would know, so I wasn't worried about it."

"Good thinking."

"Thank you."

"What happened then?"

"Then he told me that I was supposed to get out of the cab there at the Visitor Center and wait for the taxi to leave. Then I had to walk back down the road, carrying that big, heavy can, back the same way I had just come. That didn't make any sense to me at all."

"I can see why you were confused."

"But I did it anyway. I wanted to save the Van Cleefs' lives if I could. My own, too."

"You were very brave. I'm sure they would have appreciated it, if they'd known."

Olive's lower lip trembled. "I'd like to think so. I really would. Otherwise I went to all that trouble and ruined my best shoes for nothing."

Savannah glanced down at the expensive sandals that were now in tatters. With any luck, the lab would be able to get some gasoline droplets off them.

But, of course, she didn't bother to share that with Olive.

"What else did the creepy guy tell you to do?"

"He told me to walk two hundred steps away from the Visitor Center and put the gas can behind a tree on the side of the road."

"Any particular tree?"

"Yeah, the one with the red flag on it."

"Wow. A red flag and everything. I'm impressed."

"It made it easier. There are a lot of trees out there, and they all kinda look alike."

"That's true. Did you do that? Did you put the gas can behind the tree with the red flag?"

"Sure I did. It was a life-and-death situation, and after I put the can down, I did what he told me and started walking back toward town. It was a long walk, and my shoes were falling apart and giving me big, ugly blisters on my heels." She lifted her foot and

presented her evidence. Her heels were, indeed, badly
blistered. "I don't know what I would've done," she
continued, "if a nice lady hadn't come along in her van
and given me a ride. I think I would've been crippled
for life."

Olive was silent for a moment as she thought it over.
Then suddenly, her eyes flashed with indignation.
"You know, now that I think of it, that wasn't very considerate of that guy not to warn me about wearing
proper shoes to run that stupid errand of his. All he had
to say was, 'Wear some sneakers,' and I would've had
a lot easier day. He's really not a very nice person. If I
ever meet him, I'm going to tell him so, too."

Savannah sat for a while, studying the young assistant. So far, she believed every word Olive had spoken.
Every ridiculous word. But one aspect of the story was
very hard to believe.

"How did you remember all of those directions that
he gave you?" Savannah asked her. "Those are pretty
detailed. Especially things like walking two hundred
steps away from the center and the red flag on the tree.
Did you take notes when he called you?"

"No. I didn't have a paper and pencil. Remember, I
was still in my pajamas."

"Right. Then how did you recall all of his instructions?"

"I didn't remember them. I kept forgetting. I had to
call him a bunch of times and ask him what was next."

Savannah lit up. "You *called* him? You had his
phone number?"

"Sure. He called me. His number's in my phone."

Savannah mentally smacked herself on the forehead. Olive's phone. Of course!

Duh, Savannah, she mentally scolded herself. *You're losing it, girl.*

While she was reminding herself of her own shortcomings, Dirk was grabbing Olive's purse. He opened it, and Savannah expected him to reach inside immediately and pull out the cell phone.

Instead, he just sat there, staring rather wide eyed into the open pocketbook. Then he turned to Olive with a deeply suspicious look on his face.

"What is it?" Savannah asked him.

He handed the purse to her. "Look for yourself," he replied.

She did, and she was most surprised to see, not just Olive's cell phone, but a syringe as well. A large syringe that still held a bit of clear liquid that appeared to be tinged with blood.

It was no common junkie's syringe.

This gear was large enough to administer a very serious dosage of something to someone.

Possibly even two someones.

At that moment Sergeant Bodin reentered the room. "So? Have we come up with anything new?" he asked.

"I think so," Savannah said as she handed him the purse. "I think we might have found our answer as to why Colin Van Cleef didn't apply his brakes at any point going down that hill. And maybe why his wife didn't suggest it."

Chapter 20

Savannah and the rest of the Moonlight gang managed to find a game room aboard the ship that was unoccupied. Considering the sensitivity of the topics they would be discussing, they didn't want to have their tête-à-tête in the crowded casino, at poolside, or in the atrium lobby.

Everyone had assembled for the meeting except Tammy and Waycross, who were "out in the field." Whether that meant they were walking about town or strolling hand in-hand around the ship, Savannah didn't know or care, as long as they were getting along. If things were going well in Tammy & Waycross World, Savannah figured she could handle whatever was going on in hers.

She sat down at a table, shoved a chess set aside, and opened her notebook in front of her. The thing was getting thicker and thicker by the moment. Normally that would have pleased her. But now she felt like she had a thousand pieces of a puzzle but no clue how to put any of them together.

She and Dirk quickly informed the others of their most recent activities—finding the gas can, interviewing Olive, and discovering the syringe in her pocketbook.

"It's quite impressed I am with the two of you," John told them. "That's a fine afternoon's work."

"Maybe," Savannah replied. "But we're not an inch closer to finding our killer."

"Do we have any idea who Olive's mysterious, 'creepy' caller was?" Ryan asked.

"Not a clue."

"Were you able to get his phone number from her cell phone?" Richard wanted to know.

"Yes," Dirk told him. "But when Sergeant Bodin ran the number, it came back as one of those anonymous pay-as-you-go, throwaway phones. It could be anybody."

"I've heard tell of those kinda phones," Gran said. "Bad guys use 'em when they're up to no good, 'cause they can't be traced."

Dora piped up. "I used to have a second cousin who used those throwaway phones all the time. Called them 'burner' phones. Every time he turned around he was changing his number. He made a mess of my address book with all of that erasing and rewriting. I got to the point where I didn't bother to write down the numbers at all. I just waited for him to call me. Come to think of it, he was always moving a lot, too. Changed his address about every couple of months, and that made a mess of my address book, too. He got arrested for drug dealing last July." She turned to her husband. "Or was it August? I think it might've been August. Isn't that when we had to replace the refrigerator and it cost us an arm and a leg? You'd think I'd remember it better, considering how expensive that one appliance—"

"Has anyone else come up with anything?" Savannah interjected when Dora paused to take a breath.

Granny shook her head. "Nope. Sorry, sugar. I'm afraid I peaked early in the day with that service station and the gal with her gas can business."

"That's okay, Gran," Savannah told her. "That was a really important clue. You'll have bragging rights about that for years to come." She looked around the table. "Anybody else? Please?"

She could hear the pathetic tone in her own voice. She sounded as fragile and moody as a high school girl without a date for the prom.

It occurred to her that maybe she was in the wrong business. Maybe when she got back to San Carmelita, she should check the want ads to see if anybody was hiring workers to pet cats or eat chocolate for minimum wage.

"Actually, Dora and I uncovered something," Richard said. "It may be nothing, but—"

"Let's have it," Savannah told him. "We'll happily add it to all the 'nothing' we already have. Can't hurt."

"Okay then, here goes. . . ." Richard ran his fingers through his hair, then carefully rearranged it, making the most of every strand. "As you know, I've had my eye on Frank Bellissimo since we first spotted him in the dining room. If there's a man aboard this ship who's capable of cold-blooded murder, it's that guy."

"He's an evil one, for certain," John agreed.

Nodding, Ryan added, "You'll get no argument there."

"Today, just for fun," Richard continued, "we went up and down the taxi queue out by the pier, showing cabbies his picture and asking if they'd seen him today. We found one who drove him around for several hours this morning. Bright and early. Before we spotted him in the afternoon, shopping for rings."

"Wow, Dad. Good work," Dirk said. "Where did the driver take him?"

"Apparently, everywhere. Said he was looking for somebody and wanted to drive around until he found the person."

"Did he say who this 'somebody' was?"

"No. But the driver said that he would perk up every time he saw a woman with long blond hair walking down the street."

Savannah felt a surge of optimism. "Really? Long blond hair like Olive Kelly's?"

"Maybe," Richard continued. "And according to the cabbie, every time the woman turned out to be the wrong one, old Frankie boy would throw a tantrum. He'd curse and punch the back of the driver's seat."

"How lovely for the cabbie," Savannah observed.

"I don't think I've ever heard Frank Bellissimo's voice," said Ryan. "Have you, Richard?"

"Yes. I heard him testify in court. For the better part of the day, in fact."

"Does he sound 'creepy'?" Savannah wanted to know.

Richard nodded thoughtfully. "As a matter of fact, he does. He has a deep voice and a Jersey accent. He's straight out of Central Casting for the part of Gangster Thug."

Dora jumped in. "If he's a criminal, then he probably knows all about those burner phones like my cousin's.

You know, my cousin spent some time in New Jersey. They might know each other. Now wouldn't that just be the strangest coincidence?"

"It would, honey," Richard said. He reached over and squeezed her hand. "I think it's pretty safe to say they don't know each other. But all the same, I'm wondering if he called Olive Kelly, gave her those instructions, and then tried to find her. Maybe to check and see if she was following his orders."

"Come to think of it," Ryan said to John, "this might go along with what you and I were discussing earlier. The thing about the threatening letters."

"What about them?" Savannah asked.

"John and I were reading over the copies that Tammy made for us of those letters. Did you notice that Natasha Van Cleef is never addressed directly? She assumed they were meant for her, but she wasn't specifically mentioned."

"What did y'all make of that?" Granny asked.

"We wondered," John said, "if perhaps the letters were meant for Colin Van Cleef and not his wife. If Van Cleef's an out-of-control gambler, and we have a mob enforcer aboard who's known for collecting debts the hard way, maybe those threats were sent to him and not her."

Savannah glanced down at her notebook, then began to thumb through the pages. She studied her own copies of the threats.

Be warned. Your time is short. Soon you will die a terrible death.

Count the hours. Hours. Minutes. Count them and enjoy them. That's all you have left.

*I have her. She's alive. For now. Meet me and
I'll let her live. Don't, she dies.*

John and Ryan were correct. There was nothing in
the words to suggest that they had been written to a
woman and not a man.

Savannah had assumed that the third letter was written to Natasha and referred to the capture and holding
of her personal assistant, Olive Kelly. She assumed it
was a ruse to lure the Van Cleefs off the ship, where
they could be murdered more easily. But since Olive
was known by both Natasha and Colin, the letter could
have been meant for him as well as his wife.

Savannah thought it over. "It makes about as much
sense as anything else we've come up with so far."

Dirk nodded. "That's true. Maybe we need to have a
little chat with Frank Bellissimo, see whom he was
looking for out there on the streets today and why."

No one at the table looked excited.

No one at the table held up their hand to offer assistance.

"Don't everybody volunteer at once," Dirk grumbled.

"That Bellissimo fella is a mountain of flesh, and
most of it is pure muscle," John observed. "We've had
problems in the past with those extra-large lads. I recall sitting on an ice pack for a week or more after
going fisticuffs with one of their number."

"Maybe we could all surround him," Dirk said, "and
then, if he acts up, we'll tackle him and take him to the
ground."

"I'm pretty sure that was our original plan when we

went after the bloke who brought me to such sorrow before," John replied dryly.

Ryan nodded. "I know John. He's a guy who prefers to learn from his mistakes of the past."

Dora had an idea. "Richard, you and Dirk could slap cuffs on him first. Surely that'd slow him down a bit."

Richard gave his wife an affectionate grin. "Easier said than done, honey. One of the worst things you can do is get a single cuff on one of those guys; then he starts swinging around and clocks you with your own cuffs. Now *that's* a bad scene."

The present and former law enforcement personnel sitting at the table all nodded vigorously in agreement, having seen it happen at least once in the course of their careers.

"I have an idea," said a soft, sweet voice.

They all turned to Granny.

"What's that, Gran?" Savannah asked.

"What if we just try to talk to this fellow, all nice and calm like? You know, the way we'd talk to anybody else on the street or in our homes. Butter won't melt in our mouths. We'll be just as nice as can be. But if he gets his dander up and turns all ugly and nasty on us, we'll just walk away and leave him be."

They all sat in stunned silence for a while, absorbing her words.

Finally, it was John who said, "Now, there's a radical idea. Unique in the annals of law enforcement."

Dirk gave Granny a playful grin. "We can't go starting any new trends, Gran. If we were nice to bad guys, they might get used to it, and then where'd we be?"

"It's worth a try," Savannah added, "since I'd bet

that none of us thought to pack a Taser among our toiletries."

"But who's gonna do it?" Dirk asked. "We all know it can't be me. I'm not exactly known for my people skills."

"I don't think it should be John or me," Ryan said. "Those mob-affiliated guys can smell a fed, even ex-feds like us, a mile off."

As excuses went, those sounded a little thin to Savannah, but she decided not to call them on it. She also recalled how poor John had looked, sitting on that ice pack, nursing a major hernia. For a while there, the Gibson family jewels had been in serious jeopardy.

She couldn't judge him for being reluctant to step into a similar situation.

"I took a class on hostage negotiation, years ago," Richard offered.

Everyone looked excited until he added, "But I'm pretty sure I got a D. Maybe even a D minus. I recall the instructor mentioning that I ran out of patience far too quickly to deal with delicate situations."

"Apparently, not knowing how to talk to folks and play well with others runs in the family," Dirk mumbled, with a quick glance at Savannah.

"Lord, help us," she said, casting her eyes heavenward. "We have Dirk, who has the people skills of a badger, a guy who nearly flunked Negotiation Class, and a couple of feds whom a mobster could smell a mile off. I guess I could do it, but guys like that frequently have less than healthy attitudes toward women. I'm not sure how far I'd get."

"I'll do it," Granny said, raising her hand. "It was my idea, and I wanna try it. I'm officially volunteering."

"No, no, no," were the cries that rounded the table.

"We can't let you do something like that, Granny," Savannah told her.

Gran bristled. "Why not? I'll do it right out in the open where there's lots of people around. Do you really think that big galoot is so stupid he'd beat up an old lady right there in front of God and everybody?"

"Um . . ." Savannah thought it over. "Probably not."

"If he did, y'all could just jump in and do what you said you'd do. Tackle him, throw him to the ground, cuff him, and if necessary, beat the puddin' outta him. Whatever it took, right?"

After a long silence, eventually, reluctant nods of semiapproval began to go around the table.

"Then it's settled," Gran said, rising from her chair. "Let's go get 'im."

When they had all stood, she added, "Just one thing. Before we go out that door, I think we should join hands and say a little prayer."

The Moonlight Magnolia members traded doubtful glances, then reluctantly joined hands, making sure it was male/female all the way around, except for Ryan and John.

Gran bowed her head and said, "Dear Lord, we're embarking on a harrowing mission right now. We're putting our lives on the line for Truth and Justice and the American Way. We ask that your hand be upon us. We pray that you keep us safe from harm. If that oversized peckerwood should start to act up, would you please help us kick his rear end into next Thursday? Amen."

More than one hearty "Amen!" echoed around the circle.

Savannah laughed as they headed for the door, proceeding under the protective hand of the Almighty.

Yes, they would be fine. Her granny had always been the Queen of Prayers Most Practical.

Chapter 21

The Moonlight Magnolia crew found Frank Bellissimo in the atrium lobby. He was sitting alone on a love seat near the grand piano, looking most forlorn and watching his fellow passengers pass back and forth through the security check.

Savannah couldn't recall ever seeing a more miserable fellow. The anger he had exhibited the night before as he had stomped through the dining room appeared to have dissipated. Now he seemed deflated, somehow smaller, and far less scary than he had before.

That fact caused Savannah to feel a little less anxious about walking her vulnerable grandmother virtually into the lion's maw.

From their hiding place, behind some potted palms, she and Gran watched Frank watch the other passengers. "I think he's doing the same thing that Tammy and Waycross were earlier," Granny said. "He's trying to see if that blond gal he was looking for all day is getting back on the ship."

"I'll bet you're right," Savannah said as she observed Richard and Dora enter a coffee shop on the other side of the atrium to her right. She nudged Granny and nodded in their direction as they took seats at the small round tables with marble tops and wrought-iron chairs.

Granny saw and smiled. "Okay," she said. "We've got Mama and Poppa Bear in place."

Savannah saw Dirk, Ryan, and John stroll into the atrium, as well. They sidled over to a quaint little shop that was selling gelato and slid into a booth that had easy access to the piano area where moping Franky B. sat and pouted.

"Okay," Granny said. "The gang's all here. Let's get this shindig rollin'."

Savannah gave the guys in the gelato shop and Dirk's parents in the coffee bar a brief nod, which they returned.

For better or for worse, it was showtime.

Savannah placed her hand on her grandmother's shoulder. "Are you sure about this, Granny? I keep telling you, you don't have to do it."

"Of course I don't have to do it. I know that. I *want* to do it."

"You don't have to prove anything to us, Gran. I want you to know that."

Granny gave an impatient sniff. "Of course I know that. I'm not tryin' to prove nothin' to nobody. It's just that I'm sure I can do this better than any of the rest of you, so it oughta be my job."

"Okay. But if you run into any trouble at all—"

"I know. I know. Just holler and y'all will come

runnin' and do that throwin' down, slappin' the cuffs on thing."

"In a heartbeat. As a matter of fact, if I see you do anything, like even scratch your nose lopsided, I'll come running to rescue you."

"I know you will, sugar. It won't come to that, but I'm grateful for the thought anyway."

She stood on tiptoe and kissed her granddaughter's cheek. "Besides, he don't look all that mean to me. In fact, he looks like a sad sack who could use a little bit o' company."

Casually, Gran left Savannah and meandered over to the piano. A good-looking gentleman in a formal black suit, stiff white shirt, and black bow tie was playing an old-fashioned love song with remarkable skill and passion.

Gran stood next to his stool for a time and listened to him play. When his song was finished, Savannah watched her grandmother tap the pianist on the shoulder and say something to him that brought a sweet smile to his face.

That was her Granny Reid. Everywhere she went she seemed to bring out the best in people.

Savannah only hoped that her contact with Frank Bellissimo would render the same result.

She held her breath as Granny sauntered over to the love seat where Bellissimo sat. Would she be able to strike up a conversation with him? Or would he tell her in typical tough guy fashion to get lost?

So intently was Samantha focusing on the two of them that she didn't even notice her own husband when he left Ryan and John in the gelato shop. She didn't see him until he walked up and stood beside her.

"I've always loved your granny," he said softly in her ear. "But I don't think I've ever been as proud of her as I am right now."

"Can you imagine having that much moxie when you're in your eighties?" Savannah asked.

"No, but I can certainly imagine her granddaughter having that much when she hits eighty. In fact I'd say it's a done deal."

Savannah laughed. "I wish I could hear what they're saying to each other. Gran sat down beside him, and he didn't kick her off the seat. I'd say that's a good start."

"It sure is. Look, he's talking to her. I'd say he's telling her what he's doing sitting there. Why he's watching the security checkpoint."

Savannah thought the same thing. Big, ugly, tough guy Frank Bellissimo and the sweet little lady from down in Dixie were having a most pleasant and quite animated conversation. Frank's hands were waving around with wild abandon as he stated his case, and Granny was leaning toward him, her eyes intent upon his face. She was nodding vigorously at the end of each of his sentences, as though he had just said the most interesting thing she'd ever heard.

Suddenly, Savannah felt someone poke her in the ribs.

"Boo!" said a cheerful female voice in her right ear.

Savannah turned to see Tammy and Waycross grinning at her and Dirk.

"Whatcha doin' hiding here behind these palm trees?" her brother asked. "Are we spying on someone?"

Savannah nodded toward the piano and the love seat.

Tammy caught her breath. "Good heavens! What is Granny doing talking to that awful man?"

"She's treating him like a nice human being, whether he is or not. She was sure that was the best plan for interrogating him. Since the only other plans that we could come up with involved bloodshed, severe bruising, and probably stitches, we decided to let her try her way first."

"Good idea," Waycross said with a thoughtful nod. "Granny's always been the very best at weaseling information out of people. Usually without them even knowing she's doing it."

They all watched as Frank seemed to experience some sort of emotional breakdown. Leaning forward, he put his elbows on his knees and covered his eyes with his hands.

"What's wrong with him?" Savannah asked.

"I don't know," Dirk replied. "If I didn't know better I'd think he was crying."

"No way."

Granny reached over, placed her hand on Frank's broad back, and began patting him like a baby who needed to burp.

"Actually," Tammy said, "he might be crying, considering what we found out."

"What *you* found out?" Savannah turned to Tammy. "What did you find out?"

"He's got woman problems," Waycross said, shaking his head sadly.

"He's going through menopause, too?" Dirk asked.

Savannah wanted to smack him. But that would have given away their position. Overt violence was seldom a good idea when surveilling a subject from behind potted palms.

"No," Tammy responded, tittering. "Of course not."

"His fiancée's gone and ditched him," Waycross told them. "She won't even talk to him. Slept in a deck chair last night just to avoid him."

"How do you know that?" Savannah asked.

"She told us all about it, not an hour ago." Tammy looked extremely satisfied with herself. Savannah might have even found it mildly annoying, except that what she was saying was so informative.

"How did you find out that he has a fiancée?" Dirk asked.

"Social media." Tammy gave him a smug grin. "You should try it sometime. Most people leave their information wide open. You can find out a lot about anybody in two minutes."

"Like that they have a pretty blond fiancée named Desiree Haddrill," Waycross said. "Then you can look on the passenger manifest and—lookie there!—find out that she's aboard. Sharing a stateroom with him, in fact."

Tammy nodded. "Except that she isn't sharing it with him, because she's mad at him."

"Do you happen to know why?" Savannah asked. "Was that on social media, too?"

Tammy gave Waycross a funny look, and he blushed bright red. Savannah knew that scarlet-cheeked flush all too well. Waycross had done something naughty. Or Tammy had, and he knew about it.

"No," Tammy admitted reluctantly, "it wasn't on the Internet. I had to get . . . um . . . creative to find out the nitty-gritty stuff."

Savannah was afraid to ask, but she had to. "Okay. What did you do?"

"You don't wanna know," Waycross said, turning even redder. "I'm pretty sure that would make you an accomplice or something."

"What the hell did you do? Fess up," Dirk demanded.

Savannah gave a quick glance over toward Granny and Frank. But they hadn't heard Dirk's outburst. Now Gran had her arm completely wrapped across Frank's shoulders, and she was leaning on him, practically cuddling him.

"I stole her purse," Savannah heard Tammy say.

She whipped around and locked eyes with her best friend. "You didn't!"

Waycross nodded. "She did. We went looking for Desiree and found her there in the casino, playing one of those slot machines. No sooner did we see her than she walked over to a bar to get herself a drink, and she left her purse right there by the machine."

"That's right," Tammy said. "When you think about it, she was practically asking for it."

"She was not asking for anything," Savannah told her. "She was an innocent victim and you're a purse snatcher. Good Lord, Tammy. What's wrong with you?"

Dirk shook his head. "It's women problems. I'm telling you—menopause, pregnancy, it's all the same thing. Messes up the way a woman thinks."

Savannah fixed him with a baleful stare. "You know, an unsuspecting guy could get 'messed up,' saying stupid stuff like that around women who aren't thinking straight." She turned back to Tammy. "Give her back her purse, right now, before anybody realizes you've got it."

"I already did. What do you think I am, a purse snatcher?"

Dirk threw up his hands and said to Savannah, "See? Messed up."

Savannah laid her hands on Tammy's shoulders and looked deep into her eyes. "I just want to make sure I've got this straight. You stole her purse, and then you gave it back to her?"

Tammy grinned. "I did. I picked it up and dropped it into my tote. She went back to her slot machine and played for a little while. Then when she got up to go, she reached for her purse and it wasn't there. I let her look for a while. Then once she got good and frustrated, I snuck the purse out of my tote, walked over, and asked her if that was what she was looking for. I said I'd found it on the floor. I know that was a fib, but—"

"Well, hell," Dirk said, "if you've taken up purse snatching for a hobby, what's a little fib here and there?"

"What possessed you to do such a thing?" Savannah asked.

"I needed to bond with her. Really quick," Tammy explained. "What better way than that, giving a woman back her purse that she thought she'd lost?"

"I probably could've thought of one or two better ways," Savannah said. "But what's done is done. Did you find out anything else other than that she's engaged to Frank and it's not going well?"

"She found out what the fight was all about," Waycross said. "Turns out he wasn't the least bit romantic when he proposed. He kinda asked her on the fly, all matter-of-fact like, when they were walking down the hallway to their room."

"That's true," Tammy said sadly. "No dropping down on one knee. No ring. No speech about love. Just 'Whaddaya say we get hitched?'"

Even Dirk groaned. "Oh, man. He screwed up big. Even I did the knee and the ring thing."

"Exactly," Tammy said. "And everybody knows you're the least romantic guy on the planet."

"Hey!"

"Now, now," Savannah interjected before the drama could escalate. "It looks like Granny and Frank are bringing it to a close. Heads up, everybody."

"I can see why," Tammy said, pointing to a pretty blond woman who was just coming through the security checkpoint, shopping bags in hand. "There's Desiree now."

To their astonishment Frank jumped to his feet, pulled Granny to hers, and gave her an enormous bear hug and an enthusiastic, if brief, kiss on the lips. Then he released Gran and rushed over to his fiancée.

"Come on now, Desi," Savannah heard Tammy whisper. "Take my advice. Be sweet the next time you see him and things will go better."

As suggested, Desiree gave him a friendly, if luke-warm, smile. He grabbed the packages out of her arms with one hand and gently stroked her cheek with the other.

Granny left the love seat area and slowly made her way back toward the group behind the palm trees. When she joined them, she said, "He was just a bit misguided in the romance department. In need of a bit of Granny Reid's advice for the lovelorn. Let's see if he takes it now."

They all watched breathlessly as Frank deposited the packages on the love seat. Then he plucked a pink rose from a bouquet that was decorating a nearby table and handed it to his companion. She ducked her head and giggled sweetly.

Taking her by the hand, he led her to the piano. He leaned over and made a request, and a moment later the musician was playing a lovely rendition of Elvis's "Can't Help Falling in Love."

Big, clunky Frank Bellissimo wrapped his arms around the woman he loved and began dancing her across the atrium floor, whirling her with surprising skill around the fountain and back to the piano, much to the delight of onlookers. By the end of the song, twenty or more people had stopped to watch the couple. Even Ryan and John, Dora and Richard, and the Moonlight Magnolia gang who had been hiding behind the palms had mingled with the audience.

The moment the song ended, those watching clapped and cheered uproariously. Amid the applause, Frank dropped to one knee, reached into his pocket, and produced an engagement ring with a stone the size of a doorknob. He held it up to her and said in a loud voice, dripping with attitude and a strong Jersey accent, "Desiree Haddrill, I love you. I never loved a woman in my whole life the way I love you. If you'll marry me, I'll never do anything wrong again in my life. I swear it."

She snatched the ring from his hand, slipped it on her finger, and dissolved into a fit of ecstatic tears.

Frank picked her up, his arms around her waist, kissed her, then swung her wildly in circles around and around the room, like she was a limp, understuffed doll. If anyone had been standing too close, her feet would have taken them out, knocked them down like bowling pins.

But the audience gave the lovers a wide berth and all ended well.

Granny gave a sniff and wiped her eyes with the back of her hand. "I've seen chickens get their necks wrung with more grace than that. But at least his heart's in the right place."

"What did you two talk about over there on the love seat?" Savannah asked.

"He told me how bad his life is going. I told him that if he wants his life to go well he's gotta do good stuff and lay off the leg-breakin' junk. He swore he was turning over a new leaf, then and there."

Dirk looked doubtful. "Come on, Granny. Have you ever in your life seen a bad guy go good?"

"No. I can't say as I have," she admitted. "But the day that I lose faith that it's possible is the day that I give up on this world and everybody in it. I don't intend to ever do that."

Chapter 22

Once Frank and Desiree had left the atrium, Savannah looked at her watch and realized it was rapidly approaching dinnertime.

She turned to her family and friends and said, "We should all go back to our rooms, freshen up a little, and then get ready for dinner."

"I feel bad, us takin' a break," Gran said, "since our best suspect just got cleared."

"Frank wasn't our best," Dirk chimed in. "Olive is. Don't forget that Sergeant Bodin's still got her locked up at the bank."

Savannah shook her head. "That just sounds too weird. You don't think he'll keep her overnight, do you? I think the ship sails tonight around nine o'clock. If she's not aboard . . ."

That was the moment when she realized they had a major issue. They all realized it at once.

"What are we going to do?" Dora said. "How are

you guys going to solve this case if you've sailed away on a ship?"

Savannah turned to Dirk, a sick feeling growing in the pit of her belly. "We can't," she said, incredulous that she could even be thinking of abandoning ship, let alone saying it.

"But we can't stay here in Saaxwoo," Tammy said. "Waycross and I walked from one end of it to the other and didn't see a single hotel or boardinghouse. We'd have no place to sleep."

Savannah looked at Tammy with her swollen tummy, then turned to her brother, whose eyes were wide with concern. "Don't worry, sugar," she said. "We don't all have to leave the ship, and for sure you don't."

Ryan spoke up. "If you two are staying, so are we."

"Me too," Granny said.

"You're *all* going ashore. Now!"

Savannah spun around to see who it was behind her who had said such a thing, and found herself face to face with Chief Security Guard Poole. Behind him stood four of his guards, dressed in black uniforms, their arms crossed over their chests and stern looks on their faces.

"What the hell?" Dirk said, taking a step toward Poole. "What's that supposed to mean?"

"Exactly what I said," Poole replied. "The captain has asked me to escort your entire party ashore."

Savannah fought to keep her temper under control. Whatever was wrong, she was pretty sure it wouldn't improve the situation if she were to soundly box Poole's ears or give him a bloody nose. "May I ask," she said with a slightly sarcastic tone, "what we've done to deserve this great honor?"

"You're disturbing the peace and upsetting many of the passengers."

"What passengers have we disturbed?" Savannah asked. "We've hardly even had a chance to rub elbows with any of them, let alone ruffle anybody's feathers."

Poole turned to Tammy and produced a pair of handcuffs. "You, Miss Hart, are under arrest."

In an instant, Savannah stepped between Poole and her friend. "Under arrest for what?" she asked, although she had a sinking feeling that she knew what he was going to say next.

"Stealing another passenger's purse."

Yes. That was it. Bingo.

Holy cow, she thought. *What now?*

Poole was moving around Savannah, closer to Tammy, and opening one of the cuffs.

"No!" Dirk blocked Poole and laid his open hand on his chest. "You won't be putting cuffs on her. It won't happen. She's no threat whatsoever to anyone. Whatever you think she's done, we'll discuss it. But without restraints."

The two men glared at each other, neither moving nor saying a word for what seemed like forever. Poole had an angry, determined look on his face, but Dirk's expression was that of outraged indignation. He was also considerably taller than the chief, with a lot more bulk.

Savannah would have bet on her husband in a boxing or wrestling match against Poole any day.

Apparently, the ship's chief security guard came to the same conclusion, because he reluctantly slipped the cuffs back into his pants pocket.

He glanced beyond them to the security checkpoint,

where they saw a familiar face passing through, boarding the ship.

"You have ten minutes," Poole told the group, "to prepare to go ashore. My guards will escort you to your staterooms to pack your things. Then they will bring you back here to the atrium, and you, Miss Hart, will be delivered into Sergeant Bodin's custody."

Savannah watched the blood drain from her friend's face. Tammy's golden California tan quickly became a pasty gray.

Savannah moved closer to Poole, and in a quiet but menacing tone, she said, "Tammy has done *nothing* wrong. If you speak to the woman whose purse was supposedly stolen, you'll see that, as a matter of fact, she *has* her purse. She had misplaced it, was looking for it, and thanks to Tammy, it was restored to her."

"We know exactly what happened, Miss Reid. The entire incident was recorded with the casino CCTV."

"If you watched the entire 'incident,' as you call it, then you know that no harm has been done here today on your ship. As anyone with two eyes can see, this young woman is very much in a family way. She doesn't need to be distressed by any foolishness on your part. If anything happens to her, I'll hold you personally responsible."

"That's right," said Granny as she moved to stand beside Savannah. "You're playing with fire here, boy. I'm in my eighties. I've got one foot in the grave and the other on a stick of hot butter. I could kick off at any minute. This girl that you're accusing is very dear to me, a precious part of my family. If I was to see something bad happen to her, I'm sure it would push me right over the edge. What are all those cruising fans gonna think of you and your ship when they read that story in the pages of *Adventurous Cruising* or *Everybody on Deck* magazines?"

John moved to the fore, as well. It was beginning to get crowded in Chief Security Guard Poole's personal space. "What she says is true, lad," he told Poole. "Don't be a clot. Use your bonce. You can't kick an expectant mother and an octogenarian off a ship."

"Watch me." Poole snapped his fingers and his security team instantly divided themselves among the group. One guard per cabin.

Savannah shot Dirk a helpless look, which he returned.

Poole's guards were efficient. Three seconds later, they were all on their way out of the atrium, marching toward their rooms, with a guy with a black uniform and an even darker disposition following close behind.

"So much for our free, dream trip to Alaska," Savannah grumbled when they reached their stateroom.

"We'll see plenty of Alaska," Dirk replied. "Up close and personal. It's the loss of that all-night buffet that I'll be mourning."

The entire Moonlight gang, plus Dora, Richard, and Patricia Chumley, stood on the pier amid the mountain of their luggage and souvenir shopping bags.

They were all upset, but Patricia even more than the others. "I didn't do anything wrong," she said for the third time in the past five minutes. "I was shopping all day. Then I went back to my room and had a shower and a nap. Why would I get kicked off the ship for that?"

Savannah wanted to be a source of comfort and re-assurance for the highly annoyed editor. But she was exhausted and had very little to offer.

"I'm sorry, Patricia," she told her. "I really am. If I had my way, we would all be sitting down to dinner right now in that big fancy dining room. But right now we have bigger fish to fry. Before sundown we have to find—"

Dora interrupted her. "We may not have fish to fry, but if anybody gets hungry I do have some peanut butter and jelly sandwiches in my overnight bag."

Savannah stared at her mother-in-law for a long moment, then shook her head and continued. "As I was saying, we have to find overnight lodging for ten people in a town that I'm pretty sure doesn't have a hotel."

Savannah marched over to Sergeant Bodin, who was assuring the weeping Tammy that she was not going to be arrested for purse snatching or any other felonious activities.

"Please don't cry, Miss Hart," he was telling her. "I wouldn't lock you up in a bank overnight with a sus-pected murderess. I promise you. Olive Kelly isn't even in the bank right now. I let her go."

"You what?" Savannah demanded. "You turned her loose?"

He nodded. "I did. I had nothing to hold her on. Last time I checked, it wasn't illegal to carry a can of gas around the woods, as long as you don't light it. We don't have any solid proof that she did."

"Where is she?" Savannah wanted to know.

"Probably the Honey Bear Motel. That's where I told her to go when she asked me where she could spend the night."

A motel? A motel? Savannah thought. She felt like the sun had suddenly burst from behind the clouds and shone its warm, vitamin D–giving rays upon her face.

John joined them just in time to hear the sergeant's last remark. "A motel! Savannah, isn't that a fine thing? It appears we'll have lodging after all!" He turned to the trooper. "This Honey Bear establishment that you spoke of, you recommend it?"

"With all my heart."

"It's that good?" John asked.

"It's the only one in town. It beats sleeping out in the woods. At least the bear's on a chain."

"Good grief, there really is a bear." Savannah couldn't believe her eyes. A fully grown brown bear was chained to the porch of the motel, near the office door.

Fortunately for those wishing to do business with the innkeeper, the chain was too short for the bear to reach them when they were entering and exiting the building.

Unfortunately for the bear, he had very little freedom, and Savannah's heart ached for him when they walked by and saw how limited his movements were.

The animal had no bed, per se, only a pile of hay that had been tossed against the building. A large dog's water dish was his only possession.

An old-fashioned refrigerator with a soft drink logo on its door stood between the bear and the front door. A cardboard sign had been fastened to the refrigerator with a strip of duct tape. It read: FEED THE BEAR A SODA—$5.00.

"I don't know who owns this motel," Savannah said. "But I hate them already."

Dirk pointed to the padlock that secured the chain around the animal's neck. "If I had a key or a hacksaw, I'd set that guy free in a heartbeat. Let him run around the woods, the way a bear's supposed to."

Savannah shook her head sadly. "He can't be set free. Not anywhere near human beings anyway. They've ruined him by keeping him here and feeding him."

As they passed through the front door, Dirk said in a low voice, "You'd better keep your opinions to yourself for the time being, Van. Remember, we can't all sleep in the Bronco."

If Savannah had hated the innkeeper before she laid eyes on him, she loathed him once she actually saw him.

Hearing the bell above the door ring when they had entered, he had emerged from a room in the back and greeted them with a grunt.

"No way!" she said to Dirk. "Kenny Bates has a brother."

She looked over the motel owner, mentally comparing him to her least favorite police officer in the world, Kenny Bates. Back in San Carmelita, Kenny made Savannah's life miserable every time she had the unpleasant task of visiting the county morgue.

Kenny was madly in lust with her. She wanted to stomp a mud hole in Kenny's backside and toss him off the end of the town pier.

Theirs was a relationship made in hell, and here, two thousand miles away, was a guy who was the spitting image of him.

He wore an old, dingy undershirt with holes in it that revealed far more of his belly than she would ever want to see. His baggy khakis were unzipped. He shuffled across the floor in house slippers that were bound together with swaths of duct tape.

Savannah tried not to be overly judgmental of her fellow man. So she decided she didn't mind the smell of tuna fish from the sandwich that he was eating. With his mouth wide open.

She did mind the overpowering stench of body odor though. She minded it a lot.

She was glad that Granny had stayed with the others outside and waited for her and Dirk to conduct the group's business. Granny didn't abide what she called "rank filthiness."

Many times Savannah had heard her say, "Even the poorest among us can afford the price of one bar of soap. There's no excuse for being dirty. None a'tall."

"What can I do ya for?" the guy asked Savannah, giving her a long, lecherous look up and down her figure.

"You can put your eyeballs back in your head," Dirk said, "'cause that's my wife you're talking to and gawking at."

Savannah stifled a snicker. So much for watching one's mouth and not saying anything offensive that might jeopardize their prospects of having a roof over their heads for the night.

But the innkeeper didn't appear to take offense. Something told Savannah that people spoke offensive things to him frequently. Probably on an hourly basis.

"We need some rooms for the night," Dirk told him.

"Rooms?" He gave them a smarmy little grin. "I figured you two would be sharing one."

"We will," Dirk snapped. "Like I said, she's my wife.

But we've got a bunch of friends and relatives waiting outside. We're gonna need five rooms, at least. Six if you've got 'em."

"I got four."

Savannah's mind raced through the possible combinations of people inhabiting the same bedroom.

"No-o-o!"

She hadn't meant to scream the word, but she was sure she could hear it echo around the office walls for a full minute afterward.

She drew a deep breath and regrouped. "What I mean is, we have a party of ten adults, and we really, really do need a minimum of five rooms. If there's any way you can accommodate us, we'd be most obliged."

Kenny's twin brother wasn't moved. He dug at some tuna stuck between his teeth with a long, dirty pinky nail.

"Four. Take 'em or leave 'em."

One quick, sideways look at her husband told Savannah that he was about to snap.

"Do you have extra roll-away beds?" she asked.

"Yep. One."

Savannah turned to Dirk. "Your folks are sleeping with us, and we get the roll-away."

He gave her a look of horror that gradually faded into numbed resignation. "Whatever. Let's just do it." He turned to Kenny B. of the North. "How much will that be?"

The innkeeper named a sum that was so exorbitant that Savannah and Dirk thought he was joking. But after several moments of stony silence, they realized he was serious.

"That's ridiculous!" Dirk shouted. "Hell's bells! We could stay at the Ritz for that!"

He shrugged. "Then go stay at the Ritz."

A few minutes later, when Savannah and Dirk walked out of the office, keys in hand and hardly any money at all in Dirk's pockets or Savannah's purse, they had to pass by the bear.

"Tell ya what, fella," Dirk told the poor creature. "If I can swing it, I'll find a way to feed you a really big dinner before I leave. It'll stink like sweat and taste a little like tuna, but something tells me you won't mind."

Chapter 23

Dora Jones talked in her sleep, too.

Savannah could hardly believe it. But no sooner had her mother-in-law dozed off than she began chattering away. Unfortunately, the topics of the woman's nocturnal mutterings were no more interesting than her daytime subjects.

Dirk rolled toward Savannah, and the simple movement produced a cacophony of creaks and moans from the flimsy roll-away bed.

"This wasn't the worst day of my life," he said, "but I think it's in the top ten."

"I hear ya."

"Close the door, Richard," Dora said from the other side of the dark room. "You left that screen door open again. I can hear it squeaking. I asked you to oil the hinges. Remember? Yes. Last week. Might have been last month when I asked you to clean the air conditioner."

Richard replied with a roof-rattling snore.

"I'm sorry, sweetie," Dirk said, pulling her close.

"You always say you're sorry," Dora replied. "But that doesn't get the hinges oiled, now does it?"

Suddenly, Savannah started to laugh.

Yes, it was a laugh that bordered on hysteria. But it was either that or cry, and crying would just give her a headache, which she didn't need on top of everything else.

Dirk nudged her. "You're laughing, right?"

"Yes. Might as well," she said. "On this bed, with your parents five feet away, we certainly can't fool around."

He chuckled and kissed the top of her head. "After the day you've had, I'm touched that you even considered it."

She moved her palm over his bare chest, delighting in the smoothness of his skin and the bristly roughness of his chest hair.

"I almost always think about it," she told him, her voice deep and throaty. "But sometimes it's a case of 'the spirit is willing but the flesh is weak.'"

"I hear ya. Right now I don't think I could even—"

"Eeeeeeeeee! Oh! Oh! Oh! Oh! Eeeeeeeeeeeee!"

Savannah shot straight up and out of bed like a circus performer being fired from a giant cannon.

In the middle of the floor, she gyrated violently, performing a strange, highly vigorous, nonrhythmic dance.

Dirk leaped out of bed, too, and tried to grab her, but she was flailing her arms in the air so wildly that she caught him in the eye with a vicious right cross.

Holding his eye, he began to dance up and down and yell, too.

"What the hell's going on?" shouted Richard as he flipped on the table light. He jumped out of bed and hurried to his son and daughter-in-law. "What's the matter with you two? What happened? Are you hurt?"

"Hell yes, I'm hurt!" Dirk said, his hand over his eye. "My wife just slugged me, and for no damned good reason!"

Dora slept on, but commented on the event. "Richard, those cats are making a racket in the back alley again. Could you do something about that?"

Richard grabbed Savannah by her shoulders and shook her. "Savannah! Honey, what's wrong with you? Why did you hit Dirk?"

She could hardly breathe, let alone speak, her teeth were chattering so hard.

But finally, she eked out one word. "Sp-sp-spi . . . der."

"Spiders are good for us," Dora muttered, rolling onto her stomach. "They catch and kill harmful bugs."

Savannah froze, then whirled toward the bed.

Suddenly, her mind cleared, her thoughts began to actually form sentences again. "There *are* no bugs that are more harmful than spiders," she told her sleeping mother-in-law through gritted teeth, "They are little monsters. That's all they are. Hideous beasts! The only thing they're good for is squashing. Squashing them until they are nothing but a tiny, wet spot on the floor or sidewalk or pavement. Squash, squash, squash!"

Someone knocked on the door, and they heard Ryan ask, "Is everybody okay in there?"

Richard walked over to the door and opened it a crack. "No," he said. "My son and his wife are having a domestic dispute."

"Oh?"

Savannah could hear a world of disbelief and amazement in Ryan's one syllable.

"Has . . . has anyone been harmed?" John asked.

"Yes. Dirk has a black eye."

"Oh, dear."

She could tell that John was equally amazed by this strange turn of events.

"Can we offer any sort of first aid?" John wanted to know.

Richard turned and looked back at his son, whose eye was growing blacker by the moment. "If you can lay your hands on some ice, that'd probably be a good idea."

"Straightaway."

Savannah walked back to the roll-away bed and with thumb and forefinger, delicately lifted the pillow by its corner. She peered beneath it.

Nothing.

Peeling one blanket and sheet back at a time, she gradually stripped the bed. But she found not one hairy leg of the offender who had dropped down from the ceiling and landed on her bare arm.

She went into the bathroom, took off her nightgown, and shook it vigorously.

Still nothing.

She slipped the gown back on and returned to the bedroom. She was just in time to see John's arm, handing an ice bucket through the partially open door.

"Hope all is well," she heard him say. "Let us know if you need us to help . . . to intervene . . . or whatever."

Richard just nodded, then closed the door and handed the bucket to Dirk.

It was when Dirk lowered his hand from his eye to accept the ice, that Savannah realized the extent of the damage she had done to her beloved.

His eye was not only black, but nearly swollen closed.

"Oh, sugar!" she said. "I really got you a good one there! I'm so, so sorry."

Distraught and guilt-ridden, she ducked back into the bathroom and hurried out with a hand towel. She wrapped some of the ice in the towel and started to move toward Dirk with it.

"No!" he said. "Stay away from me. You and your damned spiders. Sheez, woman. I never saw anybody go as nuts as you do over a helpless, little bug. You need some of that aversion therapy that Dr. Phil talks about. God knows you need *help*!"

"I do not! A lot of people are afraid of spiders. They aren't helpless at all. They bite, you know. Some of them are venomous."

"Very few. For the most part, they're a lot more afraid of you than you are of them."

"That isn't possible. I nearly had a heart attack."

"You have a stupid, unnatural fear of them."

"Do not."

Dirk grumbled under his breath as he applied the ice pack to his ever-increasing bruise.

She ventured back to the bed and began her search again. She knew she wasn't going to find the cursed thing. Once the cursed creatures landed on you, they always just evaporated.

Until, of course, you turned the lights back off, and then they would rematerialize and bite you with their murderous venom and kill you in the most painful, horrible way possible.

She picked up her pillow from the bed, inspected every inch of it, and then beat the daylights out of it. Tucking it under her arm, she walked over to her wounded husband and placed a loving kiss on his cheek.

"I apologize for injuring you, darlin'. I hope you feel better soon. I forgive you for suggesting that I have a psychiatric disorder and need professional help."

Her indignant little speech delivered, she marched to the door.

When she opened it, Dirk said, "Savannah, it's dark out there. Where do you think you're going?"

"To sleep in the Bronco, of course. Heaven knows I can never sleep in *that* bed again." She headed out the door. "Irrational fear, my butt."

Eventually, Savannah figured out how to lower the seats in the Bronco to provide a hard but flat sleeping surface. The space was far from roomy. She managed to find a halfway comfortable position, lying on her side. She couldn't even think about stretching out, but as long as she was in a tight, fetal position, it worked.

As tired as she was, she figured that as long as she was horizontal she'd be able to sleep.

But it was cold, and she could practically feel the temperature dropping by the minute. She wished she'd brought a blanket, but of course that would have defeated the whole purpose, since the spider would have been lurking in its folds.

Waiting. Fangs bared.

In spite of the cold, she was so tired that she was about to drop off, when she heard it.

A unique, spine-tingling, bloodcurdling, ancient sound. A sound that had struck fear in the hearts of mankind since the dawn of time.

A wolf's howl.

It was soon followed by another and another, until the dark woods behind the motel rang with it.

Savannah shivered as the sound went through her, colder and more chilling than the cold of the Alaskan night.

That was when Dirk knocked on the Bronco's window and scared her half to death.

In a heartbeat, she flung the door open, welcoming him inside.

As he crawled in next to her and wrapped his warm arms around her, he said, "Wow, it's sure snug in here."

"Especially for full-sized folks like you and me."

"It's cold, too. Babe, is there any way I can talk you into coming back inside?"

"No," she said, her voice quivering.

"I didn't think so."

Before she knew what he was doing, he had enfolded her in a blanket, wrapping her tightly.

"No!" she objected. "That's not one off our bed, is it? That spider could still be—"

"Sh-h-h," he said. "It's from my parents' bed."

"Really? You wouldn't lie to me about something like that, would you?"

He laughed. "I might. But I'm not. Dad offered. Said we'd freeze out here without a blanket, and you'd never stand for using one of yours."

She snuggled into the blanket and against him. "I love your dad."

"He loves you. So does his son."

"Obviously."

They cuddled for a while, enjoying the warmth of each other's bodies, listening to the wolves howl, an owl hoot, an eagle scream, and the wind blow around them.

"Alaska's kinda cool," he said.

"That's what I was just thinking myself. Now that you're out here with me, that is. By myself it was spooky, but now that you're here, it's like we're part of it all. Part of nature."

His lips traced a line of kisses from her mouth down to her throat. His hands moved slowly beneath the blanket, then under her nightgown, exploring her softness, enjoying her warmth.

"Since we're all alone out here," he whispered, "and becoming one with nature . . . whatcha say we do the ol' Grizzly Bear Hump?"

"Gr-r-r-r . . ."

Chapter 24

"**I** won't ask you what happened between you and your husband last night, Savannah girl."

"Thank you, Granny. I do appreciate your self-restraint."

"Though I can't say it's easy. It's been a long time since I've seen a man sporting a shiner like the one he's got today."

"I'm sure that not knowing is just about eating you alive."

"It is. But far be it from me to pry into a family member's private affairs."

Savannah sighed and looked across the picnic table at her grandmother, whose blue eyes were bright with curiosity and humor.

There was a fine line between wanting to remain informed about the important aspects of a loved one's life and pure nosiness. Granny Reid had a tendency to dance lightly back and forth across that line.

Of course, she didn't "pry" into your personal business. She didn't use medieval torture devices, and she seldom resorted to blackmail, extortion, or threats of physical violence.

Mostly, she would just relentlessly pester you with questions, day and night, until you finally caved and spilled your secrets.

Savannah was there—at the breaking point.

As soon as the men had piled into the Bronco and left the motel in search of fresh coffee and something that would serve as breakfast food, Granny had begun her interrogation.

Considering that Savannah was still exhausted from her previous day's trials and a night of "communing with nature," she wasn't able to hold out long.

"Okay, Gran," she said. "It was a spider issue. That's all I'm going to say about it."

Glancing over Granny's shoulder, Savannah could see Tammy strolling toward them on a trail leading out of the forest. She had a Styrofoam cup in her hand and a big grin on her face.

Granny shook her head and gave Savannah a sympathetic smile. "You and your spiders. I swear you'd tackle a rabid tiger if you needed to, and I've seen you tie into criminals twice your size, but one teensy weensy spider, and you're a mess."

Savannah grinned, considering the odds of having to wrangle a tiger with rabies in the greater Los Angeles area. The chances were slightly less than her having to wrestle a perpetrator who was literally twice her size. Fortunately, very few bad guys were that large.

Tammy hurried up to them and sat down on the picnic table bench beside Granny. "Look what I found," she said, excitedly holding out the cup so they could see the contents. "Wild strawberries! There was a big patch of them in a meadow just beyond those trees. I even saw a mother deer and her fawn, eating the berries. I think it was the most beautiful sight I've ever seen."

Tammy looked around them at the decrepit motel, the shabby, badly littered picnic area, the splintery, rickety table where they were seated . . . and the glory of the Alaskan wilderness only feet away. "I'm just so glad we're here," she said, breathing in the fragrant, evergreen-scented air.

Savannah smiled, thinking how much she loved this young woman. Tammy lived her life by being present every moment and every place and appreciating all it had to offer.

Reaching into the cup, Savannah nabbed one of the strawberries and popped it into her mouth. Okay, so it wasn't washed. But if eating unwashed fruit hadn't killed the mother deer and the fawn, she figured she'd probably survive. Sometimes you just had to walk on the wild side.

"Thank you for bringing those back," Savannah told Tammy as she reached for another.

Tammy swatted her hand away. "No! Those aren't for you. They're for my new friend. He needs them a lot worse than you do."

Savannah and Granny watched as Tammy trotted over to the porch where the bear was chained. Tammy talked to the animal in soft, gentle tones, then quickly placed the cup within his reach and backed away.

The bear's nose began to twitch. His ears perked. With surprising speed, he crossed the small distance and nabbed the cup. In seconds he devoured the berries and the cup.

Then for a long time, he cleaned his face and licked his paws, savoring every remaining molecule of his treat, while Tammy stood nearby telling him what a beautiful, wonderful boy he was.

"She'll make a great mama," Gran said. "And our Waycross is going to be the best daddy you ever saw."

A few, brief thoughts of regret passed through Savannah's mind and heart. Now that menopause had arrived, she and Dirk would be having no children of their own. She had no doubt that if he had kids, her husband would be the best father she had ever known.

But she put the thoughts aside. They interfered with the joy she felt for her friend, and she wouldn't allow it. Like Tammy, she was determined to enjoy every moment that life gave her and accept those moments for what they were.

When Tammy rejoined them at the table, the conversation turned to the case at hand.

"Olive's still in her room," Tammy said. "I listened at the door just to make sure she's still alive, and I heard her crying."

Gran lifted one eyebrow. "As long as she doesn't fly the coop. I'm surprised that trooper guy let her go. What if she takes off?"

"Where would she go?" Savannah pointed to the mountains behind them. "This little town is cut off from the rest of the world, ocean on one side and wilderness on the other. I guess she could hike back into the woods, but something tells me she's no survivalist."

"That's true," Gran said thoughtfully. "I have to tell you, it was mighty interesting, sharing a room and a bed with that Patricia gal. I never knew a real live book editor before. She's even from New York City. Lives in a part of town called 'the Village.' Can you imagine a little village inside a big city like that? I can't imagine living in such a place."

"Me either," Tammy said. "I'm sure New York is very glamorous with the shops and the restaurants, the museums and the theaters. But I need to have real, honest-to-goodness nature around me. Not just steel and cement."

Granny nodded. "I do believe it does something to people, living in a big city. Changes them, and not in a good way. That Patricia is a nice enough girl in most respects, but she's got a heap of anger brewing down inside her. I think it's from having people around you all the time. I love mankind, but I'm not that fond of people, and I sure as shootin' don't want 'em crowdin' all around me like that."

"Patricia is angry?" Savannah was instantly alert. "How so?"

"Once the lights were out, and we were just lyin' there, she started talkin' about Natasha Van Cleef. She didn't seem overly fond of her, to say the least. Said she was a difficult author to deal with."

"In what way?" Tammy asked.

"Patricia said that she wasn't as good a writer as everybody gives her credit for. She said that the last three books Natasha turned in were awful, not even publishable. Patricia herself had to work them over somethin' fierce before they could even go to print. That's what she said. 'Go to print.' That's one of those publishing expressions."

"Did she resent having to do the author's work for her?" Savannah asked.

"I didn't get the idea that she hated doing the actual work. In fact, I think Patricia would like to be an author herself, more than anything in the world. I think she enjoyed the work. But one of the main critics from a big newspaper reviewed the last book and said it was the best work that Natasha Van Cleef had ever done. That really bothered Patricia, 'cause the good stuff that he was bragging on, that was hers, not Natasha's."

The three women fell silent as they considered the implications of this new insight into the editor's personality. Possibly an insight into motive?

"In your best estimation, Granny, just how angry was Patricia about all this stuff?" Savannah asked.

"You're asking me if she was mad enough to kill somebody, right?"

Savannah nodded. "You've been around a long time, Granny. You're very good at figuring out what people are capable of, or not."

"Savannah darlin', I'll teach you, here and now, what the years have taught me. I've learned that you *never* know what anybody's capable of. You're doing better than most if you even know what *you're* capable of."

Tapping her fingers on the worn, gray tabletop, Tammy had a thoughtful, troubled expression on her usually peaceful face. "Where is Patricia right now?" she asked.

"Out for a nature walk, like you were," Savannah told her. "Why?"

Instead of answering Savannah's question, Tammy turned to Granny. "Does she have any kind of computer with her? Or a big, electronic tablet of some sort?"

"Yes, sugar, she does. I saw her writing some letters or something last night when I got out of the shower."

"Do you happen to know where it is now?"

"I believe I saw her stick it in the side of that red leather bag she was carrying."

"Wait a minute," Savannah interjected. "I don't like the sound of this. Remember, Miss Tamitha, you're unofficially, strictly on probation right now. You need to watch your step and keep your nose clean."

Tammy gave her a sly smile that did nothing to alleviate her fears. "Don't worry. I'm not going to do anything morally wrong." She turned to Granny. "Did Patricia happen to mention if she has a pet?"

"Yes," Granny replied. "She said last night that she's really missing her cat."

"What's its name?"

"Pookie."

Tammy held out her hand. "Lemme have your room key, Gran."

As Gran placed the key into Tammy's open palm, she said, "You better watch your p's and q's, girlie, or you could wind up in a heap of trouble."

"No!" Savannah tried to snatch the key away from Tammy, but her friend was too quick. "Tammy, I know what you're up to," Savannah said, "and I absolutely forbid you to do it."

"Yeah. Okay. Whatever." Tammy rose from the table.

"It's illegal. A felony . . . probably," Savannah told her. "You only get to commit one felony per week, and you've already reached your quota."

"Okay. I'll keep that in mind." She snickered. "But you know, it's only illegal if you get caught."

As Tammy strolled away, she threw one parting remark over her shoulder. "If you happen to see Patricia, be sure to send me a quick text. I'll be in Granny's room, getting her a sweater. I wouldn't want her to catch a chill out here in this morning air."

When Dirk, Ryan, John, Waycross, and Richard returned with breakfast, they brought enough to feed General Sherman's army, and even that wasn't enough.

"Mercy, but this crowd can put away the grub," Gran said as she surveyed the carnage of empty bags, wrapping papers, soiled napkins, and dirty paper plates. "I'm glad I don't have to feed y'all every day. You'd eat a body outta house and home."

The only person who had eaten lightly was Patricia Chumley. Apparently, she wasn't that interested in socializing. When the guys had returned, bringing donuts and muffins, as well as bagels stuffed with eggs, cheese, bacon, or sausage, she had taken a bran muffin and retired to a rusty lounge chair on the other side of the motel. Sitting there, within sight but out of earshot, she had a large electronic tablet on her lap and was typing away on it.

"Okay, everybody," Savannah said when she was sure Patricia wasn't watching them. "Now that you've got some food in your bellies and your brains are hopefully working, we have some news."

Instantly, she had their full attention. Even the still-drowsy Dora, who had just rolled out of bed, set the remains of her peanut butter and jelly sandwich aside to listen.

"While you boys were off hunting game to feed the clan here, Gran gave us a heads-up about Patricia over there. She said she wasn't that fond of our dearly departed author."

Once Savannah had filled them in on the particulars of the frustrated editor with the heart of a thwarted author, Savannah shared the more spectacular finding.

"Someone among us, and I won't mention any names, Tammy, discovered an amazing fact that we will know, but can't legally prove."

"Because my girl would probably be arrested?" Waycross said, reaching over and tugging a lock of Tammy's long hair.

"Precisely." Savannah drew a deep breath and cast a quick look over at Patricia. The editor was still typing away, totally absorbed. "That tablet that she's working on, let's just say it holds a fascinating document."

"What is that, love?" John asked.

"The very first threatening letter that Natasha received the first week of March."

Dirk shrugged. "So? We all have that letter on our tablets or phones or whatever device we use."

"Yes. But the one on Patricia's tablet was written with that device on February nineteenth."

"Holy sh—" Dirk looked at his mom, then Gran. "Sorry. Holy cow! That's for sure?"

Tammy nodded. "No doubt about it. She'd deleted it, but as we say in the computer hacking biz, 'Deleted ain't gone.'"

"You guys say that?" Richard asked.

Giggling, Tammy said, "I don't know if everybody says it. But it's still true."

"Too bad we can't take that to Sergeant Bodin," Ryan said. "I think he's convinced that Olive's our culprit."

"Could they both be in on it?" Dora asked. "You said yesterday that Olive wasn't smart enough to do it on her own. But Patricia's very intelligent. You'd have to be to do the job of an editor. Why, I once knew this girl in college who was very smart, and she wanted to be a big-time editor in New York, like that Patricia is. But even though she majored in English . . . or was it English literature? It might have been—"

"So, what's our next move?" Dirk said, placing his hand over his mother's and giving it a squeeze. "Should we confront Patricia?"

"Not about the letter," Savannah said. "We can't, since there's no legal way we'd know about it."

"What if you just question her about what she was doing yesterday?" Dora offered. "See if she has an alibi for the time of the accident."

Everyone stared at her for a moment, expecting more. But she was finished.

How refreshing and sensible, Savannah thought.

"Good idea," she told Dora. "Thank you."

"Whether she has an alibi or not," Dirk said, "she'll still have to answer for that letter sooner or later. We'll just have to work out a way to tell Sergeant Bodin that he needs to check that tablet of hers."

"One step at a time." Savannah rose from the table. "I think it's time for me to have a chat with Ms. Chumley."

"Keep in mind how smart she is," Dora warned her. "Geniuses, they're very different from us regular folks, you know. Contrary to popular belief, they don't tend to be those guys with the Coke bottle glasses and all nerdy, shy, and frail. The majority of them are taller and healthier and better socially adjusted than the rest. . . ."

Savannah could hear Dora droning almost the entire way as she walked across the property to where Patricia was sitting. But when she glanced back over her shoulder she saw that, even though everyone else was ignoring her soliloquy and talking among themselves, Richard Jones was listening to his wife with rapt attention. He looked as though he was totally fascinated with every word that fell from her lips.

Love came in many forms, and *that* was love.

Chapter 25

"**I** don't understand," Patricia said, her eyes blazing, her hands on her hips. "Why are you asking me my whereabouts yesterday? Do you and your little half-ass security detail consider me a suspect?"

Savannah swallowed the insult to her agency and held Patricia's gaze, her own eyes intense and searching. Since the moment Savannah had asked the woman to have a chat with her in the privacy of her room, Patricia had been difficult. She had taken Savannah to the unit she shared with Granny, and offered her a seat in the room's one chair beside the dresser. But that had been the extent of her hospitality.

Once Savannah had asked the first hard question, the woman had gone from neutral to overdrive in a heartbeat.

"We consider everyone a suspect until we can prove that they aren't," Savannah told her. "We're just naturally suspicious people. Comes in handy for PIs."

Patricia stomped over to the stack of suitcases and shopping bags. She began tossing the bags onto the bed. "Yes, I have an alibi. Yesterday, I had a lovely day shopping," she said. "I bought Alaska stuff for my sister, my nieces and nephews, and everybody back at the office. That's what I did with my day. I didn't spend it murdering anybody."

She sat down abruptly on the foot of the bed, as though she had just run out of fuel. Tears filled her eyes. "I didn't even hear about what had happened until I got back to the ship."

"How were you informed?"

"I went to the cafeteria to get a soft serve ice-cream cone, and I overheard two little old ladies discussing it as they raided the cookie bar. They were very upset because they'd booked the cruise just to see Natasha. They had signed up for an onboard writing class with her and everything. They were heartbroken."

She sniffed and wiped away the tears that were spilling down her cheeks. "I didn't like Natasha, okay? Your grandma probably told you that I said that. She was a pompous diva who treated the people beneath her badly. Between you and me, she was highly overrated as a talent. But I wouldn't kill her."

Savannah hesitated, wondering whether or not to play her ace.

She decided that she might as well slap it on the table, and whatever happened, so be it. If push came to shove and Tammy was accused of something, Savannah was ready to confess to it herself.

"You wouldn't kill her," Savannah said softly. "But you would threaten to."

Patricia's breath left her in one, huge gasp, as though

a heavyweight boxer had just punched her in the diaphragm. "What?" she said.

Savannah kept her own face as neutral as possible, though her heart was pounding. "You heard me. We know you wrote the letters, Patricia. There's no use in denying it."

"No! No, I wouldn't! I didn't!"

She had her hand over her chest, clutching the front of her shirt. For a moment, Savannah thought she might be having a heart attack.

"Yes, Patricia. You *did*. We have absolute, irrefutable proof. So let's move on to *why*."

Suddenly, the editor's entire body sagged, as though her last bit of strength had deserted her. "It was a stupid, stupid thing to do, and I regretted it the moment I dropped the letter into the slot there in the post office wall."

"Then why did you do it?"

"I was exhausted. I had been working, day and night for a month, doing a complete rewrite on a horrible manuscript that she'd turned in. It was awful. The worst book ever written in the history of the world. Obviously, she hadn't even tried to produce a novel that was coherent, let alone entertaining."

Patricia looked out the window, but her eyes seemed vacant, as though she was gazing into a most troubling chapter of her past. "She was late with the book, too, which played havoc with Production's schedule. They needed it. I had to get it done."

She looked down at her hands, folded in her lap. "I was drinking more than I should. Wine instead of food is never a good idea. I finished the book, sent it in, and then drank myself stupid. I thought about how she sat out there in her mansion on the beach in sunny California while I was stuck in the New York slush and snow, writing her book for her."

She drew a shuddering breath. "So I wrote her a little something else to read. Something I hoped would ruin her day, sitting there on her sun-drenched patio overlooking the Pacific, and I stuck it in the mail."

"When did she tell you that she'd gotten it?"

"Three days later. As soon as she received it. She was beside herself. So worried. So upset. She said things had been really bad for her lately anyway, what with Colin messing around with Olive."

"Colin was messing with Olive?"

"Colin was an absolute whore. He messed with anybody he could get his hands on."

That's worth knowing, Savannah told herself.

"Anyway," Patricia continued, "after hearing how awful her life was, I realized why she'd had such a hard time with the book. I felt like a total jerk for adding to her problems."

Savannah thought of all the enjoyable hours her favorite author had given her over the years. Such great books with intricately woven plots, sympathetic characters, all interspersed with bits of humor and wise observations on life.

She couldn't imagine how difficult it would be to produce something wonderful like that if your personal life was in a shambles.

"If you felt so bad about writing that letter," Savannah said, "why did you keep writing them?"

Of course, she didn't know for sure that Patricia had written the second and third one, but a stab in the dark frequently hit its target.

"I didn't! I swear to you, I did not write those. I don't know who did. I'm serious when I tell you that I felt awful that I'd written one. I was horrified to hear that someone else was keeping it going."

"Then why do all three letters look exactly the same?"

"I don't know! I wondered about that myself. But they're on standard copy paper sold by a well-known chain of office supply stores. They were written with the default font of a common word-processing program. You can't get more generic than that. It might just be a coincidence."

Savannah said nothing, just quietly studied the woman before her with the predatory eyes of a former police detective. From the way the woman bit her lower lip to the way she was twisting the large turquoise ring on her finger around and around. From Patricia's tearstained cheeks to her slumped shoulders, Savannah could see she was a broken woman, haunted by what she had done.

The problem was: Savannah wasn't sure what, exactly, she had and hadn't done.

"You said you shopped all day yesterday," Savannah finally said. "From the time you left the ship until you returned."

"That's right."

"Okay, then start opening up those bags of souvenirs, the ones you bought for your nieces and nephews and everybody back at the office. Let's have a look at your receipts. Every last one of them. We're going to see if you really do have an alibi or not."

* * *

"She had nothing to do with it," Savannah told Waycross and Tammy as Dirk drove the four of them to the coroner's office. "I'm well acquainted with the shopping habits of females, and I assure you, no woman can buy that many things in one day and still have time to commit murder. Patricia's innocent."

"But she wrote the threatening letter," Tammy insisted. "No nice person does something like that."

"A nice person with a drinking problem might if they were stuck on Stupid," Waycross said. "If they were as tired and mad as she told Savannah she was."

"Then who wrote the others?" Dirk asked.

"Yeah," Tammy said, "that really narrows down the list. It had to be someone who knew about the first letter. Someone who actually saw it. Otherwise, how could they duplicate it?"

"That's a good point," Dirk said, getting excited. "Let's think about who's on that list."

Savannah got far less excited. "Okay, here we go. Natasha, Patricia, Olive, Colin, her publisher, and anyone there at the publishing house that he might've shown it to. I would've passed a thing like that around to my closest friends. Wouldn't you? Then there are the people on the ship. Natasha told me that she had to inform the security staff and the cruise director. And of course the captain had to know. She probably told her best friends and closest relatives. Oh, and the butler was there when she received a letter, and you know what they say about butlers."

"That they did it," Tammy supplied.

"Okay," Dirk said, far less excited. "So the short list is actually a very long list. Which puts us back at square one."

Savannah turned halfway in her seat to look back at Waycross. "I'm glad Dr. Johnson invited us over today, and that he's going to let you take a look at the car. I'm keeping my fingers crossed that you'll be able to find something."

Waycross looked doubtful. "You might as well uncross your fingers, Sis. I've seen insurance jobs, cars that were burnt to a crisp. You can't tell much about them. But I'll sure give it a try."

"I'm sure you will, darlin'. If there's anything there to find, I know you'll spot it."

They passed through the town and out the other side, then turned inland on a small side road. Since there were only three buildings on the one-block long street, it wasn't difficult to figure out which was the doctor's.

There was also the telltale sign stuck in the front lawn.

Tammy read it aloud: **Dr. Arthur Johnson, Veterinarian.**

"He's a vet?" Dirk was mortified. "We have a coroner who's a veterinarian?"

"Hey!" Tammy shouted, springing to the defense of vets everywhere. "It just so happens that animal doctors have to know as much as human doctors do, only about all the different species."

"Dirk has a lot of respect for vets," Savannah said. "But we were hoping for a medical doctor, the kind who is accustomed to examining human bodies. I guess it was too much to hope that they might have a bit of forensic schooling, too."

"At least in little ol' wide-spot-in-the-road McGill,

the coroner's an undertaker," Waycross observed. "He's used to messing with dead bodies."

Dirk parked the Bronco, and they all started to climb out.

"Maybe we shouldn't judge this fellow till we talk to him," Savannah suggested. "We have to be fair and give him a chance."

"Eh," Dirk mumbled, "fair's overrated."

The moment they entered the veterinarian's office, Savannah was overwhelmed by the pungent odor of wet fur. One of her memory bells chimed. She had smelled that same odor recently, but she couldn't recall when or the circumstances.

Doctor Johnson came out of the back room, wiping his hands on a large, white cloth. Savannah could see that the rag was stained with gray and black ash.

Oh, no, she thought, *he's still working on them.*

She had somehow hoped he had finished with the bodies. But if he had been working on them since yesterday, she was grateful that he was taking his time.

Dirk didn't wait to exchange pleasantries. "How's it going, Doc?" he asked. "Are these worse than the ones you've seen before?"

"I've never seen a burnt body before," the doctor replied.

Dirk shot Savannah a quick "I-told-you-so" look.

"Having seen these," the coroner continued, "I hope never to again."

"How are the autopsies coming?" Tammy asked.

"I just finished." He walked over to the benches where patients and their owners usually sat, waiting to be seen. Sitting down, he gave a long, weary sigh. "I feel bad that I couldn't do a proper postmortem on them. There's just, frankly, not much left to work with."

He waved to them to be seated and peeled off his soiled jacket, which had once been white but now, like the cloth, was dingy gray.

As they chose seats and sat down, he said, "You may or may not be relieved to hear that it was, indeed, the Van Cleefs. I just made a positive identification from the dental records."

"You got their dental records this quick?" Savannah was flabbergasted. For some reason, she assumed that the postal service only delivered mail to this remote village once a month. Weekly at best.

He smiled, as though reading her thoughts. "When we need to, we can get an overnight express service to bring us something from the lower forty-eight. They fly it to Ketchikan and then they bring it to us by boat. It costs a fortune, but if you need it, what can you do?" He shrugged. "We're in a remote region, to be sure, but technology's been building inroads into even our little niche in the world."

"The dental records that you got from California," Savannah said, "they match without a doubt?"

"No doubt at all. It was them."

Savannah had assumed it was from the very beginning. Yet, actually hearing the words hurt her heart more than she had anticipated it would.

Looking over at her brother, Savannah could see that he was antsy to get his hands on the vehicle. He'd talked of nothing else since Dr. Johnson had called him that morning and made the offer.

"Would you mind, Doctor," she said, "if my brother got started on the SUV?"

"No, of course not. It's out back in my garage. Help yourself. If you need any tools, just look around on my walls and take whatever you want. If you take something apart, please put it back to the way it was. Other investigators might need to look at it."

"I won't take anything apart," Waycross said as he shot to his feet and started toward the door.

"Wait a minute," Tammy called out, hurrying after him. "I want to come with."

"Are you sure, sugar?" Waycross looked doubtful.

"Of course. I'll be your assistant."

When the two of them had gone, Savannah turned back to the vet. "Did you get a chance to analyze the stuff that was in the syringe we found in Olive Kelly's purse?"

"That was an easy one because of its unpleasant odor," he said. "I'd know that smell a mile off. It's pentocholine."

"That's a liquid you're familiar with, Doc?" Dirk asked.

"Sadly, very." He paused to wipe the sweat off his brow with his shirt sleeve. "We vets use it all the time when we have to euthanize animals. It's very humane. Quick. Even for larger animals."

"Who has access to that drug in this area?" Dirk wanted to know.

"Anyone who raises animals might have it. Farmers, dairymen. We do have a few in the area. Some put down their own animals when the time comes. Others call on me to do it for them."

"Where do they get this pento . . . ?" Savannah asked.

"Pento*choline*. It can be purchased online from companies who sell pet supplies."

"Something that powerful?" Dirk looked doubtful. "Isn't that dangerous?"

"It's intended to be used only on animals. There are a lot of drugs that require a prescription when you're buying them for humans, but not if they're for pets or livestock."

"That liquid in the syringe," Savannah said, "is it strong enough to kill a human being?"

"If that syringe was full," Dr. Johnson said, "there's no doubt that it would be enough to kill two."

When they had concluded their conversation, Dr. Johnson led Savannah and Dirk around the house to a large garage in the rear of the property. Inside he had placed the burned Chevy.

Tammy was standing in the doorway and Waycross was just inside, putting his shirt back on and running a bottle of water over his hands to clean them.

"Did you find anything interesting?" the vet asked him as he walked out of the garage.

"Only that the gas tank is in one piece," Waycross replied. "It wasn't punctured at all. Also, the gear shift's in Drive, not Neutral. They didn't coast to the bottom of that mountain."

"Unless somebody allowed it to coast down in Neutral and then shifted it into Drive after the accident," Savannah suggested.

Waycross nodded. "Yes. I reckon if they had a mind to, there'd be nothing to stop 'em."

Savannah walked over to the garage door and glanced inside. She had already seen more than she wanted to of the wrecked car the day before. Yet, she seemed drawn to look at it one more time.

Once her eyes adjusted to the gloom of the interior, she noticed some rough wooden shelves lining one wall of the building. On the shelves sat all different sizes of boxes. Some as small as a foot long. Others were four feet or more.

The boxes didn't look like storage containers. To Savannah, they looked like small coffins.

"What are those?" she asked Dr. Johnson.

He gave her a funny look and said, "Those are pets who passed in the winter when the ground was too hard to bury them. Around Memorial Day, the ground will be thawed enough for us to start putting them in the ground."

When she looked surprised, he shrugged and said, "I know. We have to do a lot of things differently up here. It's a different world."

Savannah looked at the line of little coffins and thought of all the town's kids waiting until spring thawed to bury poor Fluffy and Rover. "You're right about that," she said. "Alaska is beautiful and wild and wonderful, and it's strange. A very different world, indeed."

Chapter 26

The Moonlight Magnolia members who had been left at the motel for lack of space in the Bronco caught cabs and met Savannah, Dirk, Tammy, and Waycross at the pier.

A possible eatery for lunch was discussed. Dora wanted to return to the hot dog joint because of the low prices. Most of the others wanted to try the Red Moose Tail Saloon, but Gran wouldn't be caught dead in such a "den of iniquity," as she called it.

Since no burger joints were to be found, they wound up settling for fish and chips from a nearby stand and eating it in a small park near Myrtle's taxi office.

No sooner had they started eating than Dora mentioned something that nearly killed their appetites. "Once your case is solved, has anybody thought about how we're going to get out of this place?" she asked.

They glanced over to the place where their ship had

been docked. The *Arctic Queen* had flown the coop during the night, leaving a depressingly large and empty space.

"There's no airport here," Ryan said. "John and I checked this morning."

"'Tis true," John agreed. "A gloomy situation, for sure."

"We could hire some sort of boat to take us to Ketchikan and catch a flight home from there," Richard suggested.

Dora gouged him in the ribs. "Do you have any idea how expensive that would be? Don't even think about it."

"What else are we gonna do?" Richard asked. "Unless you want to relocate and live here for the rest of our lives or swim home, we don't have much of a choice."

Savannah's spirits sank as she realized that Dora was absolutely right. Now that her client was dead, who was paying the bills? It looked like the Moonlight Magnolia gang had been left to fend for themselves.

"I can't think about that now," Dirk said. "If any of the rest of you want to go home, we'll do what we can to get you there. But for me and Van, we have to solve this case before we can think about going anywhere."

"John and I are here as long as you are," Ryan assured Dirk.

"Us too," Tammy said.

"Patricia and Olive aren't going anywhere until we get this figured out," Savannah said. "Especially now that we know Patricia wrote the first threatening letter and Olive had that syringe in her purse with a lethal drug in it."

"We'll stay, too," Richard said. "We came along for the fun; we'll stick in there with you when the times are bad, too."

Dirk dunked several fries into a puddle of ketchup. "Then let's solve this stupid case so we can get back home. I need to see a palm tree pretty quick before my nerves snap."

"Okay," Savannah said. "Here's what's bothering me about the case. First of all, where were Natasha and Colin for those two and a half hours when they were unaccounted for? They rented the Chevy from Larry just before nine o'clock and asked him how to get to the glacier. Then they're found at the bottom of the hill around one-thirty p.m."

"How long do the state troopers think the car had been burning when they arrived?" Richard asked.

"They didn't know or even have a great guess," Dirk told his dad. "But they said the fire was really roaring. They didn't think it had been too long."

Richard nodded. "I've seen car fires before. Even without an accelerant, they can go from a small flame to fully engulfed in no time."

"Where were they?" Savannah asked again. "Where were they from nine o'clock until they were discovered? We should have asked about them, too, when we were at the Visitor Center."

"John and I can grab a taxi and run up there," Ryan said. "We'll find out if they were ever actually there and, if so, when they left."

"Thanks, buddy," Dirk told him. "Appreciate it."

Granny had been uncharacteristically quiet throughout lunch. But finally, she spoke up. "I've been thinking how it was done and I think I've got it."

"Do tell," Savannah said.

"They were dead when they were put into the car. Somebody drove the car up there to the top of that hill with their bodies for company. Then at the top of the hill, the murderer put them in their proper seats, put the car in Neutral, and let it roll to the bottom and crash."

"Okay, that works so far. Go on."

"Then the killer went to the crashed car, put the gear shift in Drive, doused poor Natasha and her unfaithful old man with gas, and set the whole thing on fire."

One by one, the others sitting at the table nodded their heads in agreement.

"That would explain the gas and the syringe in Olive's purse," Savannah mused. "But how do you suppose she got that medication and the needle? The ship security never would have let her bring that aboard. They're very thorough. Airline security either, and she had to fly to Seattle from Los Angeles."

"She must have bought it here," Tammy said. She had already taken her tablet from her purse and was searching Internet sites. "I'm just wondering what sort of establishment might be raising animals out there near the crash site." She scrolled, typed, scrolled some more. "There's a little farm out there, about two miles from the Tongass Glacier Visitor Center. Looks like they have a barn, so they might have livestock. Also there's a . . . hmmm . . . What is this?" She glanced up from her screen, all smiles. "This is so cool. Half a mile before you get to the center, there's a musher's camp where they raise huskies and train them, and they give sled rides, too."

Savannah looked at Dirk. "Now that's interesting.

Right location, and they might keep that pento-whatever it is around, in case a dog needs to be put down."

"They might have sold that stuff to Olive," he replied. "Wanna go out there and ask them about it?"

"Sure." She looked around the table. "How about you, Dora? Will you and Richard be okay on your own this afternoon?"

Dora nodded enthusiastically. "I saw a thrift store down by that old church on the edge of town. I've never been to an Alaskan thrift store. They're bound to have interesting treasures in there."

Richard smiled, though it looked more like he was gritting his teeth. "That's what we'll be doing, all right. All afternoon."

Waycross gathered up the table's trash and threw it into a nearby garbage bin. He tossed a few leftover fries to some squawking seagulls. "If y'all don't need us, we'll be wanderin' around this area here, soakin' in the sights."

"Be sure to call us if you need anything," Tammy added. "Anything at all."

"Okay." Savannah picked up her purse and slung the strap over her shoulder. "Let's get crackin'. We've gotta get this case wrapped up. If I have to stay too many more nights at the Honey Bear Motel, I might just cut my strings and go straight up."

Chapter 27

Savannah and Dirk had a bit of trouble finding the musher's camp on Copper Creek Road near the glacier. They passed it twice, and it was only on the third time searching the area that they spotted the sign, mostly hidden among the brush on the side of the road.

"There it is!" Savannah exclaimed, pointing to the faded marker that was leaning so far to the side that it touched the ground. "It says Yager's Champion Huskies. This has to be the place."

As Dirk drove the Bronco off the pavement onto the dirt road, he said, "Yager must not be too interested in new business, or he'd spruce up that sign a bit and cut down the weeds around it."

"Maybe Yager and his business have passed their prime. Look at the size of the potholes in this road. I can't imagine anybody taking a ride through here, pulled by a husky team or not."

Savannah heard them, even before she saw them. The high-pitched yipping and yapping of the huskies. It was a sound not that far removed from the wild howling of wolves she had heard the night before. It sent a chill through her, and yet thrilled her soul at the same time.

As they drove down the road, they could see ahead to their right several rows of small, blue doghouses. There was nothing charming or architecturally pleasing about the structures. They were strictly utilitarian with arched, roughly cut out doors and flat roofs. On top of more than half of those roofs were full-grown huskies in all of their glory. Some of the dogs were napping, while others sat and surveyed their surroundings attentively, their ears perked, noses sniffing the air.

All of the dogs were tethered with chains, but appeared to have space to move about and interact without becoming entangled with their neighbors.

Several yowled as the Bronco drove by. Savannah could see them watching the truck closely, with quizzical looks on their beautiful black and white faces.

"Wow, what gorgeous animals! I wish I had one," she said. "Like a wolf, only much prettier."

"One that, hopefully, wouldn't eat you or the girls."

As Savannah studied the faces of the dogs they were passing, she thought of how Diamante and Cleopatra had soundly defeated the Colonel. She had a feeling they might lose the battle with some of these canines, who appeared to be much closer to their wolf ancestors than the Colonel, by far.

"Maybe if the cats were introduced when the husky was still a pup," she mused. "That way the girlies could smack him around if necessary and get their bluff in on him."

"It worked with you and me." He chuckled and drove on past the kennel and toward a house trailer parked deeper into the property.

Beside the trailer was an area, enclosed by a high hurricane fence. The ground inside was covered with straw, the occasional blanket, and three more dog-houses. Lying on the bedding were three of the most beautiful animals Savannah had ever seen. A pure white husky with dark eyes, a large one with a full black mask and bright blue eyes, and a third dog with a red mask and pale blue eyes. Their coats were far more lush, their markings more distinct than the animals tethered in the kennel.

"Why do you suppose these three get the royal treat-ment?" Dirk asked as he parked the Bronco near the trailer.

"Call it a hunch," Savannah replied, "but I suspect these might be Mr. Yager's champions mentioned on the sign on the road. As in, his breeding stock."

They got out of the Bronco and looked around for the owner. When they saw no one about, they headed for the trailer, intending to knock on the door.

Before they reached it, the door flew open and someone stepped out wearing tattered jeans and a red flannel shirt.

Savannah was about to say, "Hello. Are you Mr. Yager?" when she realized that, in spite of her ex-tremely short red hair, the person was female.

Savannah quickly reevaluated her greeting. "Good afternoon. My name is Savannah Reid, and this is my husband, Detective Sergeant Dirk Coulter. We were just enjoying your beautiful animals. You have so many of them."

"I only have three," the woman said. "These three." She pointed to the ones in the fenced enclosure. Then she waved an arm in the direction of the kennel with its tiny houses and tethered dogs. "Those are sled dogs. I just watch them for their owners during off-season."

"Then you breed huskies?"

"Used to. But my two dams are getting old now. I've decided they deserve to retire. Like me."

"Some days that's a tempting prospect," Savannah said. She walked over to the woman and held out her hand. "I'm sorry, I didn't catch your name."

"Edith Yager."

When they shook hands, Savannah was surprised to feel the roughness of her skin, the calluses that could only be created by hard manual labor.

Something about Edith Yager told Savannah that the woman hadn't lived one soft day in her life.

"If you two came up here, hoping for a sled ride, I'm afraid you'll be disappointed. We don't do that around here anymore. We used to, years ago, when my daddy ran the place. After he died my sister and me tried to keep it going. But then she got sick and, well, everything's been going downhill since then."

"We didn't come here for a sled ride," Dirk said. He pulled his badge from his jacket and showed it to her briefly.

Savannah couldn't help noticing how Edith's friendly, open demeanor seemed to disappear in an instant. Suddenly, her face was guarded, hostile even, as she crossed her arms over her chest and backed away a few steps.

"I guess you know what happened down the road yesterday," he said.

"I heard about it," was the curt reply.

"We're investigating that."

"Why?" She looked genuinely frightened and confused. "I hear it was an accident."

"That's what we're trying to determine," Savannah said softly, trying to regain some of their previous rapport. But it was not to be found.

Edith walked back to her trailer door. Savannah thought she was going to disappear inside, so she hurried after her.

Taking her phone from her purse, Savannah said, "I just want to ask you if you've seen the people in these pictures."

Savannah quickly found the photo of Natasha and held it out for Edith to see. "This is the famous author Natasha Van Cleef. She was killed in that car crash. But we were wondering if maybe you saw her yesterday morning before the wreck."

"No. No, I didn't see anybody."

"Would you please just look at the picture?"

Edith ventured a quick glance. "No, don't know her. Never saw her. Never heard of her."

"Okay." Savannah located Colin's picture and showed it to her, as well. "How about this gentleman? He was her husband, and he died in that crash yesterday, too."

"No! Never saw him either. Never heard of him."

Savannah didn't believe her. On the job she had been lied to hourly, if not more frequently, so she was well acquainted with what liars looked like.

They looked like Edith Yager did right now: avoid-

ing the other person's eyes, shifting their feet, breathing irregularly, and looking like they'd rather be anywhere else on earth.

"Are you sure, Edith?" Savannah asked her gently.
"They were driving a bright red Chevy HHR."

"I didn't see anybody yesterday. I was here all day,
taking care of the dogs."

"Can anybody verify that?" Dirk asked, less kindly
than Savannah.

"Not unless you speak Husky," was the equally
abrupt reply.

Unable to think of anything else to say, Savannah
was ready to end the conversation when, for the first
time, she noticed that the place had a distinct smell
about it. The predictable smell of a dog kennel.

Yager's champions smelled like dogs. Dog fur. Dog
urine. Dog waste. Dogs.

It smelled like Dr. Arthur Johnson's veterinary
clinic.

More important, it smelled the way Olive Kelly had
smelled yesterday.

The realization hit Savannah hard.

She liked Edith Yager, tough gal that she was.
She'd hate to think she was involved in anything she
shouldn't be.

Savannah searched her phone once more and brought
up the picture of Olive. Holding it out to Edith, she said,
"How about this young woman?" she asked. "Did you
happen to see her yesterday, Ms. Yager?"

"No. I told you, I didn't see anybody."

"May I ask what sort of vehicle you drive, Ms.
Yager?"

Edith ran her shaking hand over her short bristle of red hair. "I drive an old van. It was my dad's."

"What color?"

"White. Why?"

Quickly, before Edith had time to protest, Savannah held her camera up, pointed it at the woman, and snapped a photo of her.

"Hey, what did you do?" Edith went from wary to outraged in a heartbeat. "Did you just take my picture? Why did you do that?"

Savannah turned and said to Dirk, "I think we can go now. We've got what we need. For the time being anyway."

As they walked back to the Bronco, they could hear Edith yelling, "You leave and don't come back. I don't want you on my property anymore. You come back here, I might just sic my dogs on you!"

On their way back to the road, when they passed the kennel, even the huskies seemed disenchanted with them. They raised their noses to the sky and howled an unsettling good-bye . . . or was it a warning?

Savannah couldn't be sure.

Chapter 28

The moment Savannah and Dirk left Edith Yager's property, they headed back to town, to the Honey Bear Motel.

"Let me talk to her," Savannah told him as they crawled out of the Bronco and headed toward the far end of the building, where Olive Kelly was staying.

"I'll call Dr. Johnson," Dirk said, "and ask him if he was able to lift any prints off that syringe."

"Gotcha. Meet me by the picnic area."

"You don't wanna go in our room? Maybe stretch out on the bed for a moment."

She pinched his cheek. "Aren't you just the funniest feller? A real knee-slapper, that's you."

He laughed, bent down, and gave her a peck on the lips. "Go talk to the ding-a-ling. I'll call the doc."

They parted ways, and Savannah headed for room number 12.

When she knocked on the door, it took so long for Olive to answer that Savannah was afraid she might have left. But eventually the door opened a crack and a badly bedraggled blonde stuck her nose out.

"What?" she said.

"You and I need to talk," Savannah told her.

"I've got nothing to say to you. Thanks to you people, my life is ruined."

"Come on now. It can't be all that—"

"It is that bad! My bosses are dead. I don't have a job anymore, and I can't even leave this stupid little nothing town and go home because the cops won't let me, and I wouldn't have any money to get back home even if they did."

"But surely you could—"

"No! I *couldn't*! I'm never going to get out of this place, and who's gonna give me a job? Do you think anybody around here needs a personal assistant? Of course not. I'll probably wind up having to turn tricks down there by the pier and—"

"Just *stop*!" Savannah reached out and pushed the door wide open.

At first, she was sorry she had. She didn't realize that Olive was in her underwear, "barely there" panties and a "hardly anything" bra that looked like they had been purchased in a porn shop.

"Put on some clothes, Olive," she told the nearly hysterical blonde. "Get a hold of yourself. You'll be able to go home again, one way or the other. Stop with the drama crap. It only makes things worse."

Olive shuffled over to the rumpled bed and picked an even more rumpled T-shirt. She slipped it on, then plopped herself onto the foot of the bed.

The shirt did precious little to cover her assets, but

Savannah decided to let it go. In situations like this, you had to pick your battles.

"I have something to show you that might make your problems a bit better," Savannah told her, taking her phone from her purse.

Olive brushed a handful of hair back from her forehead and out of her eyes. "What?"

Savannah searched for the picture of Edith and showed it to her. "Do you recognize this woman?"

Olive leaned forward and squinted at the screen. She lit up in an instant. "Sure! That's the woman I told you about. The one who gave me a ride in her van."

"The van that smelled like dogs?"

"It reeked! She had five dogs in the back and some of them were still wet from having a bath." She shuddered. "I can still smell it. Yuck."

Pausing, she reconsidered. "But it could have smelled ten times worse and I still would have taken that ride. My feet were killing me!"

Savannah couldn't help smiling, in spite of Olive's lament. She just loved it when a piece finally fit into a puzzle.

"Okay, good," she said. "Now, I'm going to ask you something else and I want you to think really hard before you answer. All right?"

Olive screwed her face into a "thoughtful" expression. "Okay. What is it?"

"From the moment you got into that van, until the moment she dropped you off at the pier, did you get out of the vehicle for any reason?"

She thought hard, then her eyes lit up. "Yeah. We were going down the road and she said that she heard something bumping under the van, like maybe she'd run over a branch, and it got stuck or something. She pulled off the road and asked me if I'd get out and look."

Savannah grinned. "You did."

"I did, but I couldn't see anything."

"Now, one more question. When you got out to look under the van, where was your purse?"

"Why?"

Savannah sighed and ordered her eyeballs not to roll. "Just think about it, Olive. Try to remember. It might be important."

Again, Olive's forehead furrowed with the effort of getting ready to think. "Okay." Finally, she answered, "On the floorboard. It was on the floorboard the whole time."

Savannah loved it when she got the answer she wanted. "Where is your purse now?"

"That trooper guy took it. He put it in a brown grocery bag and wrote something on it." The blonde's eyes blazed. "Boy, he's got a lot of nerve doing that. My mascara's in there! I've been running around with *no eyelashes* because of him!"

Hmmm, a natural blonde, Savannah thought as she left the room. *Wonders never cease!*

As planned, Savannah and Dirk rendezvoused in the picnic area.

Patricia Chumley was still reading. She ignored them, and they returned the favor.

They sat down at a table and watched for a moment as some children purchased a five-dollar soda from the innkeeper, who then allowed them to give it to the eager bear.

He sat back on his haunches, lifted the bottle like a baby taking its formula, and downed it in a few seconds.

The children pealed with laughter, and the innkeeper looked pleased, too, as he shoved the five dollars into his pants pocket.

"That bear's going to get diabetes," Savannah said. "How many of those things a day do you reckon he drinks?"

"Let's just say, I'll betcha that old coot makes more money off the bear than he does this flea-bag motel."

"This spider-ridden, flea-bag motel."

He rubbed his hand over his eyes and it occurred to her that he was probably exhausted. Sleeping scrunched in the back of the Bronco hadn't helped.

Just to keep his arachno-whacked-out wife company.

How sweet. No wonder she loved him.

"Did she identify Edith?" he asked her.

"Bingo. She said Edith asked her to get out of the van to check something that turned out to be bogus. Olive left her purse in the vehicle when she did."

"Good. Dr. Johnson said he found prints on the syringe and the purse that weren't Olive's. I told him to compare them to Edith's."

"Her DMV thumbprint?"

"Better. He's got her full set. Years ago, she and her sister used to do some courier work back and forth from Ketchikan. They had to be bonded."

"Good."

"He shared another juicy tidbit. Turns out that the syringe had human blood in it, mixed with the pento-whatcha-ma-call-it."

"Wow, that's great! Can we get a DNA?"

"He sent it off. Who knows when it'll be back."

Savannah's phone rang. She looked at it and said, "Ryan. Good. Maybe they found out something up at the glacier center." She answered it, "Hi, sugar. What's shakin'?"

"Not sure how this shakes out," was his reply. "Don't know if you'll be glad or distressed to hear our news."

"Let's hear it."

"The Van Cleefs weren't at the Tongass Glacier Visitor Center yesterday. We showed their picture to everyone and then, just to be absolutely sure, we watched the security video of the entrance from when the center opened until after the accident. Nary a Van Cleef."

"Your eyes must be tired."

He laughed. "Yes, that much fast-forwarding can make you a bit dizzy, but we'd do anything for you, kiddo."

"Don't think I don't appreciate it."

Savannah looked across the table and saw Dirk grimace.

He didn't really mind if she flirted with Ryan, since there was no threat of it ever going anywhere. But he seemed to feel the need to register at least a modicum of disgust when it occurred. It was the macho thing to do.

"There's another reason that you're going to appreciate us even more," Ryan was saying. "We heard about your little, um, domestic dispute last night. We've arranged to change rooms with you. We didn't see anything in our number ten that had more than two legs. So, we'll swap with you. Okay?"

Gratitude flowed through her soul like the Hoover Dam floodgates opening. "Really? Are you kidding?

You'd do that for me?" Then she paused, considering the ramifications. "Are you telling me that you're willing to sleep with Dirk's parents?"

"No," was the firm reply. "They're great people, and we like them a lot. But we talked to them about this already. They're definitely moving with *you*."

Savannah had another call coming through, so she said good-bye, along with some more slobbery sweet expressions of undying gratitude.

Switching modes, she answered the new call with her most professional hello.

It was Dr. Johnson with still more news.

"I'm shocked to say it, but you and your husband were right," he said. "Those were Edith Yager's fingerprints on the syringe. Also on the clasp of the purse that belongs to Ms. Kelly."

Savannah gave Dirk a thumbs-up. "That's great news, Doctor. But why would you say you're shocked?"

"Because Edith Yager is one of the best people I've ever known in my life," he said. "Yes, she's a bit rough around the edges, and maybe not everybody's cup of tea. But I always figured that anybody who loves animals can't be all bad. I've been her vet for twenty years, and her father's before her. The Yagers have always been good people."

Savannah considered his words, then stacked them against the evidence. "Then tell me this, Doc. What's a good person doing with a syringe containing a lethal concoction mixed with human blood?"

While Dirk met with Sergeant Bodin and the magistrate to obtain a warrant to search Edith Yager's trailer and property, Savannah decided to take a short walk down the street to Myrtle's taxi office.

She figured if anybody was expert on the town's gossip, it would be the owner/dispatcher of the local taxi service.

When she opened the door to the office, she could hear Myrtle raging at Jake yet again.

"How many times have I told you to check in with me before you leave the center, huh? You drop off a fare, you call me and see if there's somebody there who wants a ride back. This ain't that hard, lame brain! Now here you are, back in town, and you've gotta turn around and drive back up there. You're burning twice as much gas, and your fare's waiting half an hour!"

She slammed down the phone and spit loudly into the soda can on her desk.

Seeing a dark brown streak run down the woman's chin, Savannah knew she would never again be able to drink from a soft drink can for the rest of her life.

Myrtle looked up, saw Savannah, and accidentally allowed a smile to play across her lips before squelching it.

"What do you want?" she snapped.

Savannah shrugged and stepped farther into the dark, tiny office. "I just wanted to pop in for a minute and say hi."

"I doubt that," Myrtle replied. "Nobody drops by here just to see me."

"Okay. I have an ulterior motive. I want to gossip, too."

Myrtle's eyes gleamed, but like her smile, the glimmer was fleeting.

"Then sit down," she said, pushing a metal folding

chair in Savannah's direction. "Take a load off. Want a soda?"

"No, thanks. I'm on a diet." Savannah reached up to make sure her nose wasn't growing.

Heaven knows, girl, she told herself. *That's the biggest whopper of a lie you ever told!*

"Who you wanna gossip about?" Myrtle said, almost looking excited.

"Edith Yager," Savannah replied. "Do you know her very well?"

"Know her? All my life."

"What's your impression of her? If you don't mind me asking."

Myrtle considered her answer a long time before answering, which pleased Savannah. It was rare to have someone give a thoughtful reply to such a question.

"I'm fond of Edith," she said finally. "Though I don't care to be around her much the way I once did."

"Why is that?"

"Because she used to be nicer. Back when her father and her sister were alive. She used to be happy and that made her easier to be around."

Savannah nodded. "The same could be said of most of us, I reckon."

Myrtle's eyes bored into Savannah's with such intensity that Savannah had a hard time not looking away. The dispatcher reminded Savannah of Dirk when he was interrogating a very difficult, potentially violent suspect.

Finally, Myrtle said, "Have you ever lost somebody you loved, Savannah Reid? Somebody you loved with all your heart."

"Yes, I have. I lost my grandfather, and he was very, very dear to me."

"Then you know that it changes you. You don't get over it. You don't 'find closure,' whatever the hell that's supposed to mean. You don't reach the end of your grief and 'go on' with your life. Your life will never be the same once they're gone, and neither will you. That's the truth about grief."

She stopped to spit in one can and then take a swig of soda from the other. "That's a little secret we humans keep from each other. We don't talk about how some losses kill a part of you, and you never get it back. Grief ain't the Iditarod. You can't pass over a finish line and be done with it."

"Whom did you lose, Myrtle?" Savannah asked, afraid she might have ventured too far.

But Myrtle smiled as tears filled her eyes. "I lost my husband five years ago. He was a pilot, the best anywhere around. But the storm was a big one and it came on fast."

She paused, pulled in a shaky breath, and finally continued. "Part of me died that day along with him. Just like part of Edith died six months ago with her sister."

"What was her cause of death?"

"Cancer. It's the one that takes all the truly good people, ain't it?"

Savannah nodded. "Seems it does, yes."

"Edith nursed her sister up until the day she passed. Never complained to anybody about it neither. I respect that in a person."

"Me too."

"But once Mary Beth was gone, Edith just closed

herself up there in that trailer with her dogs and none of us heard from her. Not until that business with the author, her so-called best friend forever."

Savannah sat up straight in her chair and held her breath. "An author? Her best friend?"

"Yeah. I guess it was that one who was killed up by the glacier."

"She was Edith's best friend?"

Myrtle shook her head and sniffed. "In Edith's mind, I guess. Edith said that author contacted her about buying a husky puppy. According to Edith, they e-mailed back and forth a lot about all the different markings on huskies and colors and how to raise them. Really bonded, they did."

Savannah's mind was already racing forward to the time when she would try to get the authorities to let Tammy search Edith's computer for those correspondences.

"Then Edith found out that Natasha gal was coming here, getting off a cruise ship and spending a day here in little ol' Saaxwoo. Edith went crazy, telling everybody in town that her very best friend was coming to see her. She bought paint and re-did the inside of that old trailer. She sewed new curtains for the windows. She couldn't wait for her author friend to come visit her."

"Did she? Go visit her, that is."

Myrtle leaned back in her chair and propped her feet on her desk. "Don't know. But something's wrong. Once a week, like clockwork, Edith drives into town to pick up dog food. Normally, she would've come in today. But she didn't."

"Is that a big deal?"

"To Edith it is."

"If you had to guess about what happened between Edith and Natasha, what would you reckon it was?"

"I'd say, if that famous author gal didn't take the time to go to see Edith, she would have been mighty disappointed. More disappointed than you or me's ever been in our lives. Devastated. Not to mention humiliated, since she told everybody in town that gal was coming to visit her. On the other hand, if the author gal *did* go see Edith, and then she wound up dead a stone's throw from Edith's house, I'd say that was a strange occurrence. Wouldn't you?"

"I would."

Savannah's phone jingled. She glanced down and read the simple text from Dirk: **Got warrant. Coming to get you.**

"I have to go, Myrtle," she said, rising from her chair. "But I want to thank you for taking time to talk to me."

"No big deal. I didn't mind."

Savannah reached for Myrtle's hand and shook it, then enclosed it in both of hers. "I have to tell you," she said, "I don't know what I'd do if I lost my husband. I'm so sorry that you lost yours. That you lost part of your life. That you lost a precious part of yourself that you won't get back."

Once again, Myrtle's eyes filled with tears. She gave an abrupt nod and said, "Thanks."

Savannah left quickly, because she could tell that Myrtle was about to cry. Even though she'd known her less than twenty-four hours, Savannah knew that Myrtle wouldn't want anyone to see her cry.

Chapter 29

Savannah and Dirk stood beside the Bronco, near the YAGER'S CHAMPION HUSKIES sign, listening to Sergeant Bodin instruct Corporal Riggs as they prepared to execute the search warrant on Edith Yager. He warned Riggs that, while she was a seemingly gentle woman, she was also a murder suspect and they should exercise caution at all times.

Finally, he turned to Dirk and said, "Since you're outside your jurisdiction, Detective, you won't be acting in an official capacity. But all the same, I'm glad you're along, and I'll appreciate any help you can offer." A look of humility crossed his face. "I'm sure you've done this sort of thing more often than we have."

"No problem," Dirk said. "But if she's got a grizzly in that trailer, he's all yours."

"Deal." Bodin turned to Savannah. "The same goes for you, Ms. Reid. You and the members of your agency have brought us this far in the investigation. Please feel free to assist any way you can, as long as, well . . . you know . . ."

"As long as I don't touch any of your evidence with my dirty civilian hands and bungle the chain of custody."

He grinned good-naturedly. "Something like that."

With a wide wave of his arm, he said, "Okay, let's go get 'er done."

Ten minutes later, they were all four inside Edith Yager's trailer. It was an extremely cozy fit.

Edith stood quietly in the corner, her head down, staring at the soiled, fur-matted carpet. Savannah thought she'd never seen a suspect looking so sad.

Not nervous. Not frightened. Not anxious.

Just sad.

Corporal Riggs was sticking close to her side, watching her, a wary look on his face, as though he expected her to fly into a frenzy of violence at any moment.

Bodin, Dirk, and Savannah were trying to search the trailer, but it wasn't a simple task. Obviously, there had been efforts made to improve the place: the fresh paint, badly applied, on the walls and some new gingham curtains over the windows. There were signs that it had been in bad shape before those renovations.

The carpet bore the stains and smells of dogs who weren't house-trained. The furniture was almost as thickly covered with the shed fur as the carpet.

The stench was overpowering and made Savannah's eyes water.

In the course of her law enforcement career, she had

seen as bad as this. Maybe even worse. But it had been a long, long time.

She reminded herself that she wasn't there to judge Edith Yager's housekeeping skills. Myrtle had said that she was depressed. Sometimes depressed people found it difficult to do even simple tasks in the interest of basic sanitation.

She was here to determine whether or not Edith was a killer who had taken two people's lives in a horrible way.

The first thing she had noticed when she'd walked through the door was a long bookshelf, suspended over the sofa. From one end to another, it held mystery books. Savannah recognized them all, because she had the same books on her shelf in her living room.

They had all been written by Natasha Van Cleef.

Edith had collected the hardcovers, paperbacks, and large-print editions of each release. French, German, Spanish, and Japanese versions were also scattered among the collection.

"I thought you said you didn't know Natasha Van Cleef," Savannah said to her. "You said you'd never heard of her."

Edith said nothing, but just kept staring at the floor.

At the end of the shelf was a picture frame and inside was one of Natasha's author headshots. It had been autographed: *To Edith, with best wishes, Natasha.*

Sergeant Bodin was searching through a tiny desk in the corner. An ancient laptop computer took up most of the desk writing surface. On the floor beneath it sat an antiquated printer.

Bodin opened the desk's one drawer, and almost immediately he found several things of interest.

The first was a stack of letters, all written to or received from Natasha Van Cleef. The ones sent by the
author were still tucked in their envelopes. The letters
from Edith to Natasha were printed on computer paper.

To Savannah's delight, Edith appeared to print and
save a copy of any letters she wrote.

Bodin handed Savannah a stack of the papers and she
began to skim through them. At first, the correspondence
seemed to be typical fan letters from a reader to a beloved
author, with Edith extolling Natasha's talent and thank-
ing her for hours of reading pleasure. Then Natasha had
responded with a couple of brief notes, acknowledging
the fan mail.

Soon, the women had begun to discuss the prospect
of Natasha purchasing a husky puppy from Edith.
More letters followed, arranging the payments and
making transportation plans. Pictures were sent of the
available litter mates, and a deal had been struck.

"You and Natasha had quite a pen pal thing going
on here," Savannah told Edith. "Until you found out
she was coming through on a cruise ship. Looks like
you invited her to come visit you, but she declined."

Edith shrugged, looked up for a moment, then lowered her eyes again. "She said she was busy. Had a lot
going on. No big deal."

"But it was a big deal, wasn't it?" Savannah said.
"You told everyone in Saaxwoo that she was coming to
visit you. You cleaned, and painted, and sewed new
curtains. You must have been pretty mad when she
wouldn't at least drop by and meet you."

"No. She was busy. I understood."

Savannah had worked her way through the stack all

the way to the bottom. There she saw three letters that were all too familiar to her.

With gloved hands, she pulled them out and walked over to Edith. Holding them up so that her suspect could see, she said, "I've seen these before, Edith. Or at least, copies of them. These are the letters you wrote to threaten Ms. Van Cleef. Including the one you wrote on the day you killed her and her husband."

Edith glanced up, took a look at the letters, then quickly cast her eyes downward again.

Dirk and Bodin were watching the exchange carefully. Bodin said, "If she was your good buddy, why would you threaten her life?"

"I didn't threaten Ms. Van Cleef."

"Then what are these?" Savannah said. "They sure aren't love letters."

"I don't know. I never saw those before."

"Right," Dirk said. "They're in your desk with your letters, but you know nothing about them."

At that moment, Corporal Riggs spoke up. "Hey, look up there on top of the refrigerator. I know what that is."

They all turned to see where he was pointing. It was an electronic device of some sort, a small, black apparatus with a headset microphone attached.

"What is it?" asked his sergeant.

"That's a voice changer. You use it to alter the sound of your voice. My brother and I had one just like it. We used it on Halloween to make our voices sound spooky and freak out the trick-or-treaters."

Savannah turned to Edith. "Why would a woman who raises and boards huskies need something like that?"

When Edith didn't reply, Dirk said, "Maybe to call a silly blond girl and have her fetch gasoline for you, but make her think you're a guy?"

"Why did you do that, Edith?" Bodin asked. "You could have bought some gas yourself. No one would have thought anything of it. Wouldn't it have been easier to just bring your own?"

Savannah stepped closer to Edith. "You had her buy the gas and deliver it for the same reason that you stuck that syringe in her purse. You wanted to frame her for the murders you committed."

For the first time since they had knocked on her door and served the warrant, Edith looked genuinely frightened as she lifted her head and stared into Savannah's eyes. But she said nothing, offered no defense.

Savannah continued. "I think I know how you did it, Edith. Somehow you found out about the letter Patricia Chumley wrote to Natasha. When she told you she didn't have time for you, couldn't be bothered stopping by your humble home, you got mad and wrote her two more."

Dirk stepped forward and picked up her train of thought. "Then, once you lured Olive off the ship, you sent Natasha another letter, threatening to hurt Olive if she didn't come to you."

"Once she and Colin got here, you somehow injected them with that drug," Savannah said. "You put their bodies in the car and drove it to the hill. You sent it down the incline in Neutral, crashed it, then shifted it back into Drive."

"You poured the gas on it," Bodin said, "to burn the evidence. Then you drove down the road toward town, picked up Olive, and planted the syringe on her."

"I didn't hurt Natasha," Edith said softly, her voice trembling. "She was my friend. I wouldn't hurt her."

"Well, I think you did." Sergeant Bodin took his cuffs from his pocket and said in a voice most official, "Edith Yager, I'm arresting you for the murders of Natasha and Colin Van Cleef. You have the right to remain silent. Anything you say can and will be used . . ."

Once the suspect was Mirandized, she was led outside. Savannah and Dirk watched the troopers stash her in the back of their cruiser. But a moment later, Sergeant Bodin motioned them over. "She wants to talk to Savannah," he said.

Savannah leaned down at the passenger's door and looked at the frightened woman inside.

"Yes?" she said, wondering how on earth this woman had committed such a heinous crime, how she could have inflicted such horror upon someone like Natasha, simply because she felt rejected, neglected.

"I have a favor to ask you," Edith said, her voice and manner so humble that Savannah didn't give in to the temptation to tell her that she would do no favors for a woman who had murdered her favorite author and client.

"What do you want me to do?" she asked.

"Would you please, please call Doc Johnson and ask him to find someone to come out here and take care of the dogs. Not just feed and water them. I talk to them, every one of them, several times a day. They need the human contact. They need—"

Her voice broke and she started to cry. Ugly, wracking sobs.

"I will," Savannah said. "I'll do that right now.

Don't worry. I'm sure he'll make certain they're cared for."

As Savannah backed away from the car, Corporal Riggs closed the door and both troopers got into the cruiser.

"Thank you," Sergeant Bodin called out through his open window as he drove away.

"You're welcome." Savannah mouthed the words, but she didn't feel them.

Usually, when she solved a case, she had a good feeling deep inside. She felt satisfied that justice had been served, the scales had been balanced, and all that good stuff.

Dirk slid his arm around her shoulders and pulled her to his side. "You okay, Van?" he asked.

"Not really."

"We got the bad guy. Or, in this case, the bad girl."

"I know. But she just doesn't seem that bad," Savannah said.

"A lot of 'em don't. That's one reason why our jobs suck."

"I don't like that. Bad people should look bad and act bad all the time. Then you could spot them right away in a crowd, and you wouldn't feel awful when you bust them and make them go off to jail for the rest of their lives and leave their doggies behind."

"Let's go find the rest of the gang and celebrate with a nice dinner."

"Celebrate?"

"Yes. Celebrate. We took a killer off the street, babe. It's a good thing."

"Okay. As soon as I call Dr. Johnson."

"Sure. No problem. Make your call. But don't dawdle. I've got a date with a long-legged Alaskan snow crab beauty."

She shook her head, and as she dialed the phone she thought how different she and her husband were.

She was worried about things like justice, good and evil, and weighing the evidence thereof.

He was fretting about his crab leg dinner.

Chapter 30

Savannah and Dirk sat in the Bronco, enjoying a bit of privacy and watching the sun as it began to set among the forest trees. Sunset came late in Alaska, they had observed, but when it did, the density of the darkness was startling and a bit unsettling.

But, in other ways, Savannah found that she liked nighttime in America's last frontier. Without all the man-made illumination, nature's lights sparkled all the brighter. Overhead more stars than she had ever seen in the sky were already beginning to twinkle. The full moon was rising and appeared so close that she felt the urge to reach up and touch it.

"You were awfully quiet tonight, Van," Dirk told her. "I know my girl. When she gets quiet, that's never a good sign."

"I might just be tired," she replied.

"You might be, but that's not all that's wrong with

you. What's going on in that head of yours, darlin'? Tell ol' Dirk about it."

"Something's not right," she admitted. "I've got a voice screaming inside me that there's more to this than what we've got."

"Okay. So you think we missed something. What?"

"I'm not sure. I just got this strong inkling that something's wrong. It's like a really bad itch deep inside that won't go away."

She glanced at her watch. It was nine thirty-eight. "I guess it's too late to call Dr. Johnson. He might be in bed already."

"He might be, but I doubt it. Why do you need to talk to him?"

"I just want to ask him one question. Just one itty-bitty question, and if he answers it right, I'll sleep a lot better tonight."

Dirk chuckled. "Call him. Anything that leads to a good night's sleep for us is worth waking him up in the middle of his."

Savannah quickly took out her phone and punched in Dr. Johnson's number. He answered on the second ring.

"Hello, Savannah. It's good to hear from you always, but if you're calling about the dogs, we got them all squared away. They're well taken care of and will be until some sort of arrangements can be made for them, depending on what happens with Edith."

"That's wonderful. Thank you, Doc. But that's not why I'm calling."

"Oh, all right. Then how can I help you?"

"I have a question about the dental records. Can you tell me again how you received them?"

"Sure. They were delivered here to our office."

"By whom?"

"A service called Alaskan Express Parcel Service. I believe I told you before, the packages are flown to Ketchikan and then AEPS brings them to Saaxwoo by boat."

"Once they've docked here in Saaxwoo, someone actually brings your package to you, or you have to go get it?"

"They hand deliver it."

"Did the courier place the records in *your* hand?"

"No. My office assistant received them. I was out on a call."

"Did she mention anything about the delivery?"

"Not that I remember. Is there something you need to know about the delivery, Savannah?"

She paused, then decided to plunge ahead. Once your foot's wet, she told herself, you might as well go for a swim.

"You mentioned that you were able to obtain a full set of Edith Yager's fingerprints because she and her sister worked for a courier company some years back."

"Yes. They did."

"Did they happen to work for AEPS?"

There was a long pause on the other end. "Yes."

"I know it's late," Savannah said, "and I hate to ask you. But would you mind calling your office assistant and asking if she knew the person who actually delivered those records?"

"I don't mind, Savannah," he said, though he didn't sound thrilled. "If you think it would be helpful. I'll call you right back."

"Thank you, Doctor."

As they ended the call, Savannah turned in her seat and saw that her husband was watching her closely. She knew he had been following every word of the phone conversation.

"You think Edith delivered that package?" he asked.

"It's a long shot, but we have to turn over every rock."

"She doesn't work for that service anymore, babe."

"No. But how hard would it be for her to get her hands on that package? Think about how loosey goosey they are around here about stuff. Everybody knows everybody. If she was there when the boat docked and saw someone she knew getting off with that package in hand, it would be so easy to say, 'Hey, I'm on my way up to the doc's place right now. I'll drop it off for you. The paperwork? I'll give it to you next time I see you. Have a good day.'"

"It's a long shot."

"That's what the doctor just said. But how many long shots have paid off for us, big boy?"

He reached over, took her hand, and toyed with her wedding ring. "All the most important ones," he said.

Her phone rang.

"It's Doc Johnson. That was quick." She answered it, her pulse pounding. "Yes, Doctor?"

"You're not going to believe this." He sounded breathless, excited.

"Try me."

"It was Edith! She told my office girl that she ran into the courier at the dock and told him she'd bring it up here for him. They're old buddies from back in the day. Apparently, she does that a lot."

"Damn," Savannah whispered. "I'm good."

"What was that?" Dr. Johnson asked.

"Nothing. Just thinking out loud."

She looked over and saw that Dirk was grinning broadly and shaking his head.

"That kinda compromises your evidence there, Doctor," she said, "if the primary suspect had it in her possession."

"Yes, I'm afraid it does."

"I have something else to ask you."

"Okay."

"Those pets that you've got in cold storage there in your garage, because the ground's too hard to bury them . . ."

"Yes."

"Do they do that for people, too?"

"Cemeteries creep me out," Dirk said when they got out of the Bronco and began to walk around the ancient graveyard. "Especially after sunset. I want you to know, Van, I wouldn't be out here running around in the dark, visiting dead people, for just anybody."

"I know, sugar, and I appreciate it very much."

"How much?"

"You'll never know." She reconsidered. "At least, not as long as we're still sleeping in the same room as your parents."

"Yeah. Right." He shifted the tire iron that he was carrying to the other hand. The tire iron that Savannah had requested he bring, but hadn't explained why.

She headed toward the right rear of the graveyard, as instructed by Dr. Johnson. Even though both she and Dirk were equipped with large, powerful flashlights, the beams did little to dispel the gloom of the place.

The full moon had decided to slip behind thick clouds only a moment after they had arrived.

Bad timing.

"Don't tell me this doesn't bother you," Dirk said, trudging along at her heels. "This is a spooky and depressing place, and most people wouldn't be caught dead out here."

"Ha, ha," she said dryly. "Dirk made a funny."

"Seriously, doesn't it bother you at least a little?"

"No," she said, picking her way among the old stones. Some had moss growing on them. Some were leaning. Some had even fallen. Here and there sat one that looked relatively new.

"I believe that cemeteries," she said, "are peaceful, gentle places. There's no one to hurt you in a place like this. Just folks taking a long rest—"

"A dirt nap?"

"Whatever, after their weary journeys. God bless 'em. Some lived a long time. Some had short lives, but went through a lot. They've earned their rest."

He tripped over a leaning stone and nearly fell. "Still gives me the willies."

Savannah was trying to remember something she had read once that had changed her outlook on graveyards. "A cemetery—a place of perfect repose where, at last, every wound is healed, every problem resolved, every burden laid aside, and every task completed," she said, quoting the passage as best she could recall it.

"Is that it up there?" Dirk said, pointing his flashlight at a small wooden building approximately twelve feet square.

"Must be," she said. "It's the only building out here."

"Not very fancy," he observed as they walked up to the structure and saw that it had no windows and only one door.

"In tiny, isolated towns like this, I don't suppose 'fancy' has a very high priority."

"Let me guess," Dirk said, studying the large padlock on the door. "That's why you wanted me to bring the tire iron."

She nodded, giving him her sweetest smile. "Would you mind, please?"

"What if you don't find whatever the heck you think you'll find in there?"

"Then we owe the fine city of Saaxwoo a padlock. We'll send them one when we get back home. Anonymously. We'll mail it from a Los Angeles post office."

"Okay."

He stuck the pry end of the iron through the lock and gave it a twist. It crumbled.

"O-o-o-o, well done," she told him. "So manly."

"Yeah, yeah. Whatever. Let's get this over with. It's getting cold out here . . . colder than one of those, you know, one of them gals who wears a metal bra thing and Viking horns on her head and sings opera."

She gave him a long, blank look. "There's no saying like that. You just made that up, didn't you?"

"Yeah."

"I thought so, because it doesn't make any sense. Why would Brünnhilde be any colder than anyone else?"

"'Cause she's wearing a metal bra, okay? I was trying to avoid saying, 'Colder than a witch's tit.' Most women don't like that. But now I'm sorry I started it. Sheez."

Savannah reached for the door and swung it open. "I'm glad you're with me, darlin'," she said when she looked inside and saw the same sort of shelves as the ones in Dr. Johnson's garage, only larger. The sight of the coffins, four of them, sitting on the shelves was unnerving.

Especially in the darkness of night. Especially in the cold.

Especially with the sound of wolves starting to howl in the not so distant distance.

"Thanks, babe," he said, all annoyances and insults put aside. "Let's just get this chore done so we can go back to the motel and snuggle."

Reluctantly, she walked inside. He followed, and they played their flashlight beams over one coffin after another, until they found the one that bore a tiny metal plaque that read: MARY BETH YAGER.

"That's it," Savannah said, turning to Dirk. "Ready to do it?"

He lifted his tire iron. "Ready to sink to the lowest level of my law enforcement career? Yeah, sure. Why not?"

He stuck the pointed end of the tire iron beneath the lid of the casket. It pried open with surprisingly little effort.

The space between the coffin lid and the shelf above it was at least ten inches, giving them room to lift it high enough to see inside.

"Sorry, Mary Beth," Dirk muttered. "This wasn't my idea. It's just that I've got this half-whacked wife who gets weird ideas about . . ."

But Savannah wasn't hearing him. She was shining her light inside the casket, preparing herself to see the remains of Edith's beloved sister, who had died of cancer six months past.

Savannah could hardly breathe as she listened to her own pulse pounding in her ears.

There was, indeed, a corpse inside, but it wasn't Mary Beth Yager.

It wasn't Natasha Van Cleef.

It was the body of an enormous husky.

Chapter 31

"What the hell do we do now?" Dirk asked when they were, once again, outside the storage building.

"I think you need to make a phone call to Sergeant Bodin. Tell him what's in there."

"Tell him we broke in, you mean."

"Broke in?" Savannah picked up the shattered lock from the ground and hurled it into the bushes. "Who had to break in?"

"I pried open a coffin."

"You lifted a lid and looked inside. Semantics, big boy. Choose your words judiciously, and ditch that tire iron before he gets here."

"Then you call him, Miss Smartie Pants, since I don't know how to talk to people."

But Savannah was looking around, beyond the cemetery, through the trees, deep into the nearby forest.

Fortunately, the moon had come out from behind the clouds and was flooding the cemetery and its surroundings with silver light.

But it wasn't silver light she was looking for. It was golden light.

"You make the call, huh, sugar?" she said. "I've got something to do."

"What?" He looked moderately alarmed. "What next? Haven't we had enough creepy excitement for one night?"

"Tell Sergeant Bodin to come on out here now. We might have something else to show him."

"Something besides a dead husky in a human being's coffin?"

"Yes," she mumbled absentmindedly as she walked away from him, heading toward the back of the cemetery and the beginning of a small path.

"Don't go out there in the dark by yourself," he called after her. "Savannah, come back here."

But she didn't hear his warning, didn't hear him following her, talking on his phone.

She was focused on what she was pretty sure was the glow of a chimney top ahead, through the trees. Sparks floating upward on a cloud of smoke.

"Ah, that I had a humble cottage," she whispered as she neared what turned out to be, indeed, a lovely little log cabin, tucked among the trees, and beyond it, a charming, moonlit meadow.

Golden lantern light, man-made light, illuminated the cabin's few windows. Occasionally, a shadow crossed one of them.

Someone was home.

Dirk ended his brief phone conversation and hurried

to her side. "What's going on, Van?" he asked, sounding worried.

"I need to have a conversation with the person inside that cabin. Now."

"Okay—are you going to tell me why, or am I just
supposed to guess?"

"I need you to wait out here, darlin'."

"Wait? Why?"

"Because this is something I want to do myself. I
need to."

"What if you need help?"

"I'll holler."

She passed in front of him and made her way quickly
but quietly up to the door of the cabin. She tried the
knob, thinking that maybe . . . just maybe . . .

It was unlocked.

Slowly she pushed it open and stepped inside.

A woman stood at a cast iron woodstove, stirring a
pot of something that smelled divine, its aroma min-
gling with the scent of home-baked bread.

Her long silver curls were pulled back in a ponytail.
She wore old, baggy jeans and a man's wool shirt. On
her feet were beaded, leather moccasins.

When she turned from the stove, she saw Savannah
and dropped her wooden spoon.

"Hello, Natasha," Savannah said.

"How?" The woman leaned against a counter, as
though unable to stand without support. "How did you
find me?" she asked, her face a study in defeat.

Savannah gave her a sad smile. "*Ah, that I had a
humble cottage near such a place,*" she recited. "*Perhaps there I, a still living being, could rest as they do.
The perfect and complete rest of the dead.*"

Savannah paused and then added, "From a novel called *The Deepest Sleep*, by Natasha Van Cleef—one of my favorite books. I believe you're familiar with it."

Finally, Natasha found her voice. "I wish *you* weren't. How many times have you read it?"

"Five, I believe."

"That's four times more than I have."

"That's too bad. It's a good book. Well worth rereading."

Natasha pointed to a fully stocked bookcase. The top shelf was lined with her own novels. "Would you believe that was one of the things I was looking forward to most? Getting to read all the stuff I've written over the years. Also, to have time to read the classics again and see how much more meaningful they are now than when they were a professor's required reading."

"Now you'll have to read them in a jail cell. That's sad. But not as sad as what you and Edith did to your husband."

"He deserved it."

"He would probably disagree with you. If you hadn't shot him full of a lethal drug and then burned his body to a crisp."

"He didn't feel a thing. That's more compassion than he deserved, the filthy, rotten womanizer."

"He was having an affair with Olive?"

"She was just one of many. But he was going to actually leave me for her. You met her. She's an idiot, but then he always did like them stupid. They made him feel smarter. I wanted to retire, live out the rest of my life in peace. Do you think I'd divide the fortune that I alone made with a man like that?"

"Guess not."

"Damn right."

"Why Edith?"

Natasha reached down and picked up the wooden spoon from the floor. She tossed it into the sink. "Edith loves me. I don't know why. From the moment we first corresponded, she considered me some kind of soul sister. It was actually her idea."

"Not the whole thing. I recognize a Natasha Van Cleef plot when I see one."

"No, not the whole thing. The part about using her sister's body was Edith's. She said Mary Beth wouldn't mind, that she'd wanted to be cremated anyway, but there's no crematorium nearby."

"Switching the dental records?"

"That was her, too. She used to work for a courier service. But you probably already know that now."

"Yes. I do." Savannah searched her favorite author's eyes, trying to see into the soul of the woman she'd thought she knew so well from her writing. "I understand why and how you set up Olive. But what I don't understand is how you could frame a woman like Edith, who was so loyal to you. Misguided loyalty, no doubt, but a devoted friend, nevertheless."

On unsteady legs, Natasha walked over to a chair and sank down upon it. She looked old and so very tired, Savannah thought. Not at all like the vibrant woman who sat under her wisteria arbor and pretended to be terrified. Not like the author putting on makeup in her ship suite, getting ready for her adoring fans.

"I didn't intend to frame Edith in the beginning. It never crossed my mind, until I could see you were getting close. Much too close."

"That's when you put the copies of the threatening letters in Edith's trailer."

"Yes. I did it that day when you came to visit her, while you were there and she was outside talking to you."

"You're all heart," Savannah said coldly.

"I used to be. People change. Usually not for the best." She stared down at her hands, now void of rings or nail polish. The hands, not of a busy celebrity, but of a simple woman leading a simple life.

But hands that committed murder, Savannah reminded herself.

"Did you inject your husband yourself, Natasha?" Savannah asked, her face grim. "Or did you have Edith do it?"

"I did it myself. He was my problem, mine to deal with."

"Was she there when you did it? Did she help?"

Natasha looked down at the floor, and for the first time looked as though she felt a bit guilty. "I'd rather not say. Let's just assume that she had very little to do with any of it. The actual killing anyway."

"Why did you hire me?" Savannah wanted to know. "If you're going to murder your husband, why on earth would you take a full detective agency along with you? Didn't you think we'd figure it out?"

Natasha laughed, but the sound was bitter. "I was afraid that these knucklehead troopers wouldn't see that it was murder."

"Because you wanted them to know it was homicide, but think Olive did it. You weren't happy with just killing your husband; you had to get the other woman, too."

"Wouldn't you want to kill your husband if he was unfaithful, if he made a fool of you?"

"Probably. I'd fantasize about it, but I wouldn't actually do it."

"I'm a woman of action. I've always worked hard to make my dreams come true."

"This dream was more of a nightmare."

"It's certainly turning out to be. Thanks to you. I really didn't think you'd find out about Edith. I thought you'd stop at Olive."

"Then you should have hired a different detective. I work hard to reach my goals, too."

Natasha gave Savannah a genuine smile, and for a moment something akin to camaraderie passed between the women. "Maybe I wanted a worthy adversary," Natasha said. "I've been writing about cops and private detectives for years. You're both rolled into one. Maybe I wanted to see if I was as good as the real thing."

Natasha glanced over to the nearest window and added, "Your husband has been watching us out there since you came inside. You might as well invite him in. It's cold out there."

Savannah looked out the window and, sure enough, there was Dirk, with his nose pressed to the glass. She motioned him to come in.

"How long until the troopers arrive?" Natasha asked.

"Anytime now. By the way, you grossly underestimated the Alaska State Troopers. They're a million miles away from 'knuckleheads.' If you hadn't brought me along on the trip, they absolutely would have figured out it was murder. And sooner or later, they'd have nailed you."

"Then I was doomed either way," Natasha said, looking like she wanted to be in that neighboring cemetery, sleeping the deepest sleep.

"You were doomed," Savannah told her, "the moment you decided to take the life of another human being, Natasha. We make choices. We have to live with the consequences. You'll probably be in jail for the rest of your life, and you'll have nobody to blame but yourself."

The next morning, the Moonlight gang and guests, Olive and Patricia, sat at the picnic tables, consuming yet another mountain of goodies.

The food was good, the morning air crisp and fresh, some killers had been caught, and everyone's mood was considerably lighter.

Except Granny's.

Granny began to complain. "I can't believe that you let us just sleep through all the excitement," she said. "I would've given an arm and a leg to have been there and seen the look on that awful Natasha's face when she turned around and saw you standing there."

Savannah smiled. "It was one of the more satisfying moments of my professional careers, I must admit. She was quite smug, that one, thinking she could manipulate us into busting the wrong person."

"Now that the case is solved and Natasha and Edith are in custody," Patricia said, "I suppose we can leave this place and go back home, as long as we return for the trial, of course."

"Go home how?" Olive said. "Hop on a whale as it swims by?"

Savannah and Dirk grinned at each other. Dirk winked at her, though it was difficult with his still swollen and black eye.

"Should we tell them?" Savannah asked him, looking around the table at her family and friends.

"Sure. Go ahead. There's no time like the present to share a little good news."

"What good news?" Dora asked. "Did you find a good deal on a boat to take us to Ketchikan?"

"Or you just discovered a heliport nearby?" John suggested with a grin.

"The Alaska State Troopers are going to give us an escort out?" Richard offered.

Savannah held up her phone. "It just so happens that I received a very special phone call this morning. One that has lovely implications for all of us."

Instantly, the chattering along the tables hushed. It was so quiet they could hear the bear snoring on the nearby porch.

"It was the cruise line. Apparently, we made this morning's national news, and it was reported that they threw a pregnant woman and elderly lady off the ship. Then that mother-to-be and senior citizen helped solve the murder of one of their passengers. They'd like to make it up to us."

"Make it up to us? Make it up to us?" Tammy began bouncing on her seat.

"They are most welcome to make it up to us!" John said. "That sounds perfectly lovely!"

"As long as they don't charge us for whatever it is," Dora added.

Savannah laughed. "Another ship, the *Northern Lights*, will be docking this afternoon at four p.m., and they said it would be their pleasure to welcome us all aboard, so that we can resume our cruising adventure. They said they would provide us with . . ."

The rest of Savannah's news was lost in the tumult of cheers, screams of joy, raucous shouts, and even a baritone duet from Ryan and John. As a result, they didn't hear that they would be receiving staterooms with private balconies or that they were invited to dine at the captain's table that very evening.

The pandemonium continued until Tammy spotted a large pickup truck pulling in front of the motel office. On the truck's door was the logo for Alaska Fish and Game.

"Hey, everybody," Tammy shouted. "Quiet! I've got a little surprise of my own. We aren't the only ones getting sprung from this joint today. Watch."

Two rangers, a male and a female, stepped out of the truck and walked up the motel office steps. They paused near the bear for a long time, looking him over, obviously discussing him.

They started to open the door, but before they could, the innkeeper stepped outside. He was wearing the same dirty khakis, still unzipped, and dingy undershirt.

When Savannah noticed the woman ranger recoil from him in horror, she chuckled, thinking how she, herself, had reacted when she'd caught a sniff of him.

A heated argument continued for quite a while. But in the end, the bear's owner retreated angrily into his office and left the rangers to get on with their mission of relocating the bear.

The gang gathered nearby and offered their help, which the rangers gladly accepted, when the bear was tranquilized and needed to be loaded into the truck.

"You're going to take him far away, right?" Tammy said, once she had been identified as the person who had called and asked the state to intervene on the animal's behalf.

"Very far away. We have to," the female ranger said. "He's far too familiar with humans and would go to them for food the first chance he got. We'll make sure he's relocated well away from people and will remain so."

"You did a good thing, Miss Hart," the other ranger replied. "This bear will get to be a bear again, instead of that jerk's circus performer. Thank you."

Tammy leaned down and petted the unconscious animal's ears, then lovingly stroked his face. "You have a good time wherever you're going," she told him. "Find a pretty girl bear and have some sweet little cubs."

As the rangers drove away with their sleeping cargo, Tammy stood, tears streaming down her pretty face.

"What's the matter, sugar?" Waycross said, giving her a kiss on the cheek. "I thought you'd be happy seeing him on his way to freedom."

"I am. But I'm just imagining the sugar and caffeine withdrawal he's going to have. Poor boy. It's a crime what was done to him."

Dirk leaned over and whispered in Savannah's ear, "Women and their hormones. Good grief. She's bawling 'cause that bear's goin' on a diet."

"These are the fun days. Wait till the postpartum blues hit. Then the terrible twos and potty training. You're gonna have to hide in your man cave until the kid starts kindergarten."

Chapter 32

"**W**ow! Dinner at the captain's table is wonderful!" Tammy whispered in Savannah's ear as yet another amazing course was set in front of them, a halibut medallion in a lime-crabmeat beurre blanc.

"This fish is the best I've ever had," Granny announced. "Better than the fresh-caught catfish that Sketter Malden serves at her summer shindigs down by the river." She took another bite and rolled her eyes. "I sure wish I knew the recipe for this white gravy that's on it. I never ate gravy this good in my life."

"John makes beurre blanc," Ryan told her. "He'll show you how sometime if you like."

Savannah wished the evening could go on forever. To go from stress, worry, and sleeping curled up in the back of an old Bronco, to dining in high style on a ship even more luxurious than the *Arctic Queen*—she was in heaven.

Captain Mitchell was now in an animated conversation with an actress sitting to his right. But before he had been gracious and attentive as they regaled the table with a much abbreviated and sanitized account of the case they had solved. He seemed anxious to leave them with an excellent opinion of the cruise line.

Savannah could have told him that he didn't need to try so hard. She would be delighted to just live at sea if she were allowed.

Across the table from her sat her long-suffering hubby with his black eye. When asked by the other guests how he'd received it, he had looked at her, grinned, and said, "Spider attack."

He had received a ton of sympathy, and her reputation as a basically sane woman had remained intact.

She loved him to pieces. Couldn't help it. Even if he was sopping his beurre blanc with a chunk of bread and licking a bit of the residue off his pinky.

"I am so full," Tammy said. "My belly is really complaining." She rose from her seat and whispered to Savannah, "Darn. I'm going to have to go to the bathroom again."

That was the fourth time in less than an hour. "Are you okay?" Savannah asked, rising to go with her.

"Yes, I just have a little problem," Tammy said as she shuffled along to the ladies room with Savannah close behind.

Once inside, Tammy remained in the stall so long that Savannah was beginning to get seriously concerned. When she finally exited, her face a delicate shade of pink, rather than its usual golden, Savannah said, "What's the matter, sugar? A case of what Granny calls the 'green apple quick-step'?"

"Heaven's no. I wish I *did* have a bit of that. I've got the opposite problem. Savannah, I have never been so constipated in my life! It's awful. I've been needing to go every ten minutes or so, but I can't. It's been going on for hours."

Another woman walked in, washed her hands, and fussed with her hair. Tammy waited until she left to continue. "It's so embarrassing. I just sit there and try and try to go, but nothing comes out except"—her cheeks reddened even more—"except a little pee."

Savannah listened with ever-growing concern. "Are you telling me that for the past few hours, you've been coming in here every ten minutes or so, sitting down and pushing, and water's been coming out?"

"Yes. It's getting worse and worse, too. Oh, I think I have to go back in there again."

"Tammy." Savannah caught her by the arm. "Honey, I don't think you're constipated. I think you're in labor."

"But I can't be. It doesn't hurt horrible like they say labor does. I just really need to— Oh . . . oh . . . This feels really weird. Look, my stomach is like tightening up. How strange. It's never done that before. Feel, Savannah. It's like a rock."

She tried to place Savannah's hand on her abdomen, but Savannah was too busy making a phone call to Dirk. "Ask Captain Mitchell to alert sick bay. We've got a lady in late-stage labor coming down."

Tammy grabbed Savannah's sleeve. "Wait! Wait! Tell the captain to please come down there, too! Waycross and I, we aren't married yet! We want to be married when the baby comes!"

Savannah stared at her, incredulous for a moment, then snapped to attention. "And something else, babe," she told Dirk. "Bring the captain with you, kicking and screaming if necessary. Apparently, Tammy wants to get married."

As Savannah sat on the edge of her best friend's bed, rubbed her back, and timed her contractions, she thought, *I've seen some unusual things in my life, but this here takes the cake.*

Of course, there would be no cake, no bride's bouquet, a hospital gown instead of a wedding gown, a sick bay instead of a chapel, and a ship captain who had explained that, although everyone is under the impression that captains of ships can marry people, they can't. Fortunately, however, he was also a notary public, so they were in business.

Captain Mitchell stood at the foot of Tammy's bed, and behind him, crammed into the small room, was the entire Moonlight Magnolia entourage.

It had to be the most crowded labor room in history.

But then, Savannah thought, Tammy and Waycross were truly extraordinary human beings, so was it really so surprising that their wedding would be unorthodox?

Tammy was huffing and puffing, her beautiful hair hanging in sweaty strings around her flushed face. Her groom sat on the other side of her bed, opposite Savannah, holding his laboring bride's hand and whispering words of love and comfort into her ear.

Captain Mitchell cleared his throat and said, "Shall we begin?"

"Yes! Begin!" Tammy said between huffs. "Hurry!"

The captain looked down at their hands. "Do we have any rings?"

"No," Waycross said. "Just her engagement ring."

"Wait a minute. Yes, we have rings." As Granny pushed her way through the crowd to the captain, she was removing the wedding ring from her own finger.

Savannah gasped. Not once in her entire life had Savannah seen that simple gold band off her grandmother's hand. She knew that it hadn't left Gran's finger since the day Grandpa Reid had put it there over sixty years ago.

Savannah's eyes filled with tears to see such a loving gesture. Then, as if that weren't enough, Gran reached inside her collar and pulled out a necklace chain. Hanging from the chain was a larger version of her own band. It was Grandpa's. She had placed it on that chain and worn it next to her heart from the day he had passed.

"Here's one for the groom," she said, taking the ring from its chain and offering it to Waycross.

Savannah thought her brother was going to burst into tears, but he managed to contain himself and gratefully accepted the rings from his grandmother. When he did, he lifted her hand and kissed the back of it lovingly. "Thank you, Granny. We'll give those back to you once we've—"

"Shush and get on with it," she barked. "I've seen plenty of babies born in my day, and I'll tell ya that your gal ain't got far to go."

"Okay," Captain Mitchell said. "Let's do this. Normally, I ask the man first. But since the bride has some pressing business to attend to very soon, we should probably let the lady go first."

He paused, then said, "Do you, Tammy Hart, take

this man, Waycross Reid, to be your lawfully wedded husband? Do you promise to—"

"Yes!" Tammy paused to huff, to puff, and to try her best not to push, having been informed by the sick bay nurse and Dora that it wasn't time yet. "I do! I do! I take him. I so-o-o do! Next?"

Captain Mitchell laughed. So did the crowd behind him.

"Okay. We have a definite yes from the bride." He turned to Waycross. "Do you, Waycross Reid, take Tammy Hart to be your lawfully wedded wife? Do you promise to love her and honor her and—"

"Ow-w-w-w-w! Oh, this is a really . . . strong . . . one!" said the bride.

"Come on and breathe, sugar," Waycross said, gazing lovingly at the flushed and sweaty face of his almost wife. He told the captain, "Yes, I do take her. I sure do. Hurry up, sir. We ain't got time to dawdle here."

"Slip this ring on her finger and repeat after me: 'With this ring I thee wed and join my life to yours.'"

Waycross did as he was told, and Tammy did the same in turn.

"Then by the power invested in me as captain of this ship, but more important, as a notary public, I pronounce you husband and wife. Mrs. Tammy Reid, would you like to kiss your groom? If you're too busy, I'm sure he'll understand."

Tammy reached up, grabbed Waycross by his curly hair, and pulled his face down to hers. She planted a quick but passionate kiss on his lips and promptly went back to panting.

"Okay, that's it," the sick bay physician said, shooing the captain and the Moonlight Magnolians out the door.

"Wait!" Tammy said. "I don't want them to go. Let them stay if they want to. How often does a person get to see a baby born? I . . . oh, oh, oh, whee!" More panting, more huffing.

"They aren't all staying in here, Mrs. Reid," the attending nurse said. "You can have two people. Your husband and one other. That's all we have room for."

"My husband and *two* others," Tammy demanded. "Savannah and Granny." She paused, breathed, and moaned.

When the contraction subsided Tammy gave the nurse an evil eye and said, "If I can't have both Savannah and Granny and my husband in here with me, I'm not having this baby. That's all there is to it. Take it or leave it."

"We'll stay out of your way," Granny told the nurse in her softest, sweetest, grandma voice. "I promise. You won't even know we're here."

"They can sit in the corners and watch," the doctor said, ending the argument. "But we need to get ready. I think this little stowaway is just about to be born."

Dora was the last of the gang to leave. "I'll be right outside the door if you need me for anything. Anything at all," she told Savannah on her way out.

"Thank you, Dora. That's so good to know," Savannah told her, and gave her a hug.

As the doctor and the nurse removed all sorts of supplies from cupboards and drawers, Tammy smiled at Gran, looked down at the ring on her finger, and said, "Thank you, Granny. I'll never, ever forget what you did today. Not if I live to be a hund-oh! Oh, woo-hoo! This one's a doozy!"

"You best lay back and conserve your strength, darlin'," Granny told her. "You got some hard work ahead. They don't call bringing another soul into the world 'labor' for nothin'."

Thirty-eight minutes later, Mrs. Tammy Reid delivered a beautiful baby girl with big sapphire blue eyes and bright red curls, just like her father's. The infant screamed with great enthusiasm the moment she entered the world and was instantly placed on her mother's tummy by her adoring dad.

The doctor allowed Waycross to cut the cord.

Waycross kissed his wife and his new daughter, then turned to his older sister and grandmother. "Get out of those corners and come over here. You gotta see this. She's the prettiest baby ever born in the whole world. Just look at her."

Savannah laughed. "You sound like a man in love."

"I am!" he said. "After meeting Tammy, I didn't think I could ever fall in love with another woman again. But I think I just did."

A very tired but happy Tammy laughed. "I can't blame you. I'm smitten, too. Just look at her teeny hands. Oh, Waycross, she looks like a little fairy. Our own tiny, red-haired pixie."

Savannah looked down into the sweetest face she had ever seen and instantly knew she would love this child for the rest of her life. "May I touch her hand?" she asked.

"Of course you can," Tammy said. "Waycross, wrap her up so that she and Granny can hold her."

"Wrap her up?" He looked slightly panic stricken. "How?"

"Like this." Gran took the receiving blanket the nurse offered and within seconds had the wee one lovingly, efficiently swaddled. Then she held her close to her chest and said, "Welcome to my family, sweet girl. I'm your great-grandmother, and I have all sorts of wonders and miracles to share with you."

A few moments later, Gran handed the baby to Savannah, whose heart melted on the spot.

She had held babies before. She had even delivered her sister's twins. But this child . . . this one was special. Savannah looked into the blue eyes, so like her own, and felt she and this baby had known each other forever.

"What's her name going to be?" Savannah asked, gently kissing the tiny forehead that was softer than anything on God's green earth.

Tammy looked at Waycross and they smiled at each other.

"Funny you should ask, Sis," he said.

"Yes," Tammy added. "Because we decided long ago that if she was a girl, we knew exactly what we'd call her."

Waycross looked at Savannah with more love than she could possibly imagine and said, "We're gonna call her Vanna. But her name will be Savannah Rose. If that's okay with you."

Is it okay? Is it okay? Savannah thought as the purest joy she'd ever known, like a golden, life-giving flame, warmed her spirit and every cell of her body. No, it wasn't *okay*. It was the most glorious honor she had ever received in her life.

She wanted to tell Tammy and Waycross how much she loved them, how deeply, wondrously happy they had made her.

But for once, Savannah Reid couldn't speak. All she could do was laugh, cry, and hold her new niece, this magical little copper-haired sprite, close to her heart . . . a heart that was positively overflowing with love.

As one of nine siblings raised in the Deep South, plus-sized P.I. Savannah Reid has experienced her share of family drama. But shotgun weddings and snooty in-laws don't worry her nearly as much as a search for a missing mother and child—especially when it leads to murder . . .

Savannah and her husband have settled back in San Carmelita, California, and life is slowly returning to normal—if "normal" means babysitting newlyweds Tammy and Waycross's incredibly fussy infant daughter. But soothing a squalling baby is kid's stuff compared to the Midnight Magnolia Detective Agency's latest case. Handsome up-and-coming actor Ethan Malloy has enlisted the help of Savannah and Co. in a desperate attempt to track down his missing wife and toddler, not long before the beloved family nanny gets murdered.

With the police involved and paparazzi swarming at every turn, the discreet search becomes a sensationalized homicide investigation, leaving Savannah rushing to apprehend the killer and save the missing child. Famous heartthrobs can attract the wrong kind of attention, and some snooping into the complicated private lives of Ethan and his wife tells Savannah that she's in for a deadly chase. As Savannah dismantles bombshell after bombshell while balancing delicate family matters of her own, she soon finds herself closing in on a terrifying culprit—one who's willing to do *anything* for a moment in the spotlight . . .

Please turn the page for an exciting sneak peek of G.A. McKevett's next Savannah Reid mystery HIDE AND SNEAK Coming soon wherever print and e-books are sold!

Chapter 1

"Oh, for heaven's sake. Of course, I can babysit for a couple of hours. I'm the oldest of nine children. Hightail it over here with that little redheaded punkin'. Auntie Savannah's been aching to get her hands on her."

Words uttered so blithely with such conviction, such confidence, with only the best of intentions.

They were words that came back to haunt a person. Not unlike: "For better or for worse." Or in Savannah Reid's former life as a police officer, "Hey, only five more minutes to the end of my shift; what could happen now?"

As Savannah stood in the bathtub, letting the hot shower water stream over her exhausted body, washing baby urp out of her hair and rinsing even more from between her breasts, she pulled the shower curtain aside a few inches and peered down at her unhappy charge.

The less-than-angelic pixie lay, squalling, in her makeshift cradle on the bathroom floor, snuggly tucked into what had been, only moments before, a towel drawer from the linen closet.

If the drawer had been lined with prickly pear cactus instead of Savannah's softest Egyptian cotton guest towels, Miss Vanna Rose's yowling couldn't have been louder or more piteous.

The sound reverberated around the room, bouncing off the tiles and straight into Savannah's heart. "I'm so sorry, kiddo," she told her tiny niece as she applied a second application of shampoo. "But I'm sure you'd pitch an even bigger hissy fit if I was to bring you in here with me."

The child responded with another plaintive wail that threatened to peel the rose-spangled paper off the walls.

"Lordy mercy, that kid can holler!" Savannah marveled at the sheer volume, not to mention the vibrato that would do a mezzo-soprano proud.

Suddenly, the bathroom door flew open, startling Savannah. She jumped and dropped the shampoo. It hit her big toe. Yelping, she danced around, while grabbing for the closest weapon of opportunity—a bar of her husband's favorite soap on a rope.

Not that she was likely to fight off an intruder with a half-gone bar of soap, but the pain from her mashed toe had shot all the way up her body and into her brain, so she wasn't thinking clearly.

It was simply shocking how heavy a bottle like that could be when nearly full. Whoever had invaded her sanctuary, burglar or babynapper, they were about to become the first person to be slaughtered with a chunk of Old Spice.

Fortunately, it was her husband who rushed inside.

Detective Sergeant Dirk Coulter stood there, taking in the scene. His wife. Her head covered in lather that was streaming down into her eyes. Eyes filled with shampoo, pain, and fury. Her hand upraised, brandishing his soap. The cherub in the drawer on the floor, mouth wide open, screaming, her cheeks red with rage.

Dirk wore his own look of alarm, along with an unsettling amount of blood on his face, his shirt, arms, and hands.

While a typical day in the Reid-Coulter household could hardly be called "mundane" or "ho-hum," Savannah had to admit, this was a bit unusual even for them.

Her anger quickly turned to concern as she watched him peel off his bloodstained shirt.

Tossing it into the hamper, he said, "And here I thought *I'd* had the worst day."

"Oh, sugar," she said, fighting down the fear every police officer's spouse suffers daily. "Are you wounded?"

"Naw. It's all Loco Roco's. We tussled, I clocked him a good one on the nose, and the dude sprung a leak."

"Roco's out of jail?"

"Not anymore. Apparently, in the state of California knocking over a liquor store is a violation of a guy's parole. So's assaulting a police officer. Go figure."

He knelt beside the angel in the drawer and, leaning down with his face close to hers, he said, "I'm sorry, Curly-locks, but I can't even touch you, let alone hold you till I get every drop of ol' Roco's bodily fluid yuck offa me."

He stared at Savannah, the shampoo bottle in one hand, the soap still in the other. "You're taking a shower *now*," he asked semi-indignantly, "with my birthday present soap? Funny time to treat yourself to a luxurious bath routine, when you're supposed to be babysitting my favorite girl here."

Savannah scowled. "I thought *I* was your favorite girl."

"No. Kitty Cleo's my favorite," he said with a grin. "At least, she was, until this little beauty came along. But don't worry. You've always been a solid second. Actually, now you're third, but at least you're still on the podium."

He gave his wife a wink. She stuck out her tongue, responded with a loud, rude raspberry, then ducked back into the shower. "Just for that, I'm not going to jump out of here, like I was fixin' to when I saw you all bloodied up. Figured you'd be anxious to get in. But now I'm gonna take my time and 'luxuriate,' as I've been accused of doing. Might even condition my hair, exfoliate, and shave my legs, too, while I'm at it."

"Fine," he replied. "I'll go downstairs." He looked around and shuddered. "This bathroom always gives me the heebie-jeebies anyway. Flowery walls, lacy towels, perfumey candles. Girl crap everywhere."

Ducking his head closer to the baby's, he spoke to her in the softest tone imaginable—the one he used for cats, dogs, and children. Occasionally for Savannah as well, but only if they hadn't been arguing about such things as overly feminine bathrooms and him leaving the toilet seat up. "Don't you cry, little darlin'," he told the child. "Uncle Dirk will make it up to you as soon as I get out of the shower, and that'll be before Auntie Savannah. While she's still shaving that first leg, you and me'll be all comfy in her big chair downstairs, reading a book."

The baby stopped crying and stared up at him, big blue eyes bright with interest, as though she understood every word and was intrigued by the prospects.

"It won't be no pansy, princess book neither," he added as he stood and walked to the door. "It'll be a good one with some bears or a big, bad, pig-eatin' wolf or two in it."

Savannah watched him, enjoying the blissful silence from the drawer on the floor, while experiencing just a tiny jab of jealousy that he could comfort her niece far better than she.

"Hey, since you have such a quieting effect on her," Savannah said, "why don't you take her downstairs with you and let me finish my shower in peace?"

Dirk looked positively scandalized. "And let her see a grown man shower? *Naked*? No way! That's just . . . just . . . *wrong*. She'd be scarred for life."

Savannah rolled her eyes and sighed. "Oh, for heaven's sake, Dirk. She's two months old. I assure you, she'd never even register it, let alone remember it."

He grinned and waggled a blood-streaked eyebrow at her. "But *you'll* never forget the moment *you* first laid eyes on the Big Monty."

He ducked as a net bath scrubbie sailed past his left ear, then chuckled as he left the room and closed the door behind him.

Savannah could hear him whistling the theme to *The Godfather*, loudly and badly, as he walked down the hallway, heading for the staircase and the more gender-neutral, less female-foo-foo bathroom downstairs.

Actually, she couldn't remember her first sighting of the much ballyhooed "Monty." Undoubtedly, it was years ago when she had still been a cop and they had been partners. It was probably during a stakeout when she had inadvertently caught a glimpse of him "draining the dragon" onto a roadside sage bush. But she knew better than tell him she had no distinct recollection of the momentous event.

Personal experience had taught her that men didn't take such news well.

For the sake of domestic tranquility, she decided to revise their love story, creating a version more in line with his. She decided that her initial glimpse of such manly glory and her subsequent swooning at the sight occurred on their honeymoon night.

What the heck, she thought, mentally dismissing the whole subject. *Where's the harm in a bit of revisionist history, as long as everybody lives happily ever after?*

Anticipating a renewed series of protests from the juvenile on the floor, Savannah quickly rinsed away the last bit of shampoo, turned off the shower, and stepped out of the tub. After a quick "lick and a promise," as Granny Reid would say, with a towel, she slipped into her fluffy terrycloth bathrobe.

In the drawer at her feet, her tiny niece appeared to have been temporarily distracted from her fit-pitching and seemed moderately mollified by the brief, but pleasant, encounter with one of her favorite people, Uncle Dirk.

The baby gave her aunt an enchanting half smile and cooed adorably as she waved her tiny fists.

"Yeah, I know, you like him better than me," Savannah said, scooping her up and cradling her against her chest. "So does Cleo."

Savannah tweaked the tiny rosebud mouth with her fingertip. "That's perfectly okay. I understand."

Savannah pressed a kiss to the child's cheek. Little Vanna squinted as one of her aunt's wet, dark curls fell down onto her forehead.

The baby's tiny fingers tangled in the hair and tugged.

It hurt, but Savannah didn't even notice as she gazed into eyes as sapphire blue as her own. Squalling fits and upchucked milk were forgotten as the bond between the two Reid females tightened yet another notch. Two hearts, forever entwined with Love's soft, but ever-enduring chains.

"I plum adore you, Miss Savannah Rose. You'll never know how much," the former cop, present private detective, all-around tough gal whispered to her tiny namesake as they left the bathroom and headed down the stairs. "I have a lot to teach you. Especially about men. Most of it you won't need to know for a long time, but for right now, let's discuss deep voices. Us gals are suckers for a deep voice, like your Uncle Dirk's. Women are always just hurling themselves at his feet, and all because of that voice of his."

As they reached the bottom of the staircase, Vanna gazed up at her aunt with a slightly doubtful look.

"Okay," Savannah clarified, "not *all* women. To be honest, the vast majority of them don't really like him very much, deep voice or not. Mostly, it's just you, Cleo, me, and sometimes Diamante—if he's feeding her off his plate. It's a pretty small fan club, when you come right down to it."

Vanna cooed, expressing agreement and adding her own opinion on the subject.

"Yes," Savannah replied. "You're absolutely right. He *is* a good guy at heart. The barking and growling are mainly just when he's hungry."

They passed the bay window, where Diamante lay drowsing in the sun, a glossy black panther-ette soaking in some rays.

Normally, Di's sister, Cleo, would have been curled next to her, enjoying the day's last bit of sunshine. Life-giving, bone-warming, soul-uplifting, California sunshine.

But Dirk was in the shower, which meant that faithful, brave Cleo would be standing just inside the bathroom door, staring, terrified, as once again the daily horror unfolded before her eyes. Every muscle in her sleek, feline body would be taut, quivering with anticipation, ready to make the ultimate sacrifice. If necessary, she would leap into that shower and at least attempt to rescue poor "Daddy," should he be overcome by all that vicious water raining down pitilessly on him.

Yes, Cleo adored Dirk and had since they'd met, back when she was a six-week-old kitten. It had been love at first sight for both of them.

She had decided that his lap was the most comfortable and his petting the most satisfying of any human anywhere, including Mom's. She would abandon Savannah and her caresses the moment Dirk walked into a room—much to Mommy's consternation.

Back then, he had even shown his devotion by changing his bank password from "BROKE1" to "MY-CLEO."

Diamante, on the other hand, was far more practical. While she would have fought a rabid Rottweiler, fang and nail, to prevent it from harming her beloved mom, she was perfectly willing to let any human being, even dear Mommy, die a hideous death if they were foolish enough to step into a cubicle where water poured down on them. As far as Di was concerned, anyone who did such a dumb thing was just asking for it and deserved whatever they got.

Diamante scrambled down from her window and followed Savannah as aunt and niece passed into the kitchen. Savannah took a small glass bottle, filled with Tammy's breast milk, from the refrigerator.

"For heaven's sake, do *not* microwave it!" Her friend Tammy had instructed her with what Savannah considered an overly enthusiastic admonition that bordered on Maternal Mania. "There's no telling what nutrients those waves might destroy or alter in some horrible, unnatural way."

"O-o-o-kay," Savannah had replied with an ever-so-slight eye roll.

"No! Not o-o-okay!" was Tammy's passionate response. "I know what that means when you say that and roll your eyes. That means you think I'm being silly, and you're going to do it your own way. But you better not! I'm the mom around here, and when it comes to my baby, what I say goes!"

Savannah had been taken slightly aback, given that Tammy was usually such a gentle, acquiescent soul.

But when Waycross added, "Better do it, Sis. She's got all those postnatal hormones roarin' through her bloodstream, and she's liable to slap ya neckid and hide your clothes if you don't abide by what she says."

Savannah promised, Tammy was convinced, and the topic was discussed no more.

A promise is a promise, Savannah reminded herself when she passed the microwave on the way to the stove. *Especially one made to a woman whose hormones have run amuck.*

She looked down at Vanna Rose and said, "It'd be just my luck that, if I snuck it on the sly, the first words out of your little mouth wouldn't be 'Ma-ma' or 'Da-da.' They'd be, 'Hey, Mom. Guess what? When you weren't looking, Auntie Savannah microwaved my bottle.'"

Vanna watched with a slightly concerned frown crinkling her forehead as Savannah placed the bottle into a shallow pan of water to heat.

"Don't you worry your pretty little noggin," Savannah told her. "I'll get it right. I'm actually a very good cook, as you'll discover in a few years. Your mommy will probably raise you up on celery sticks and carrot puree, but what happens at Aunt Savannah's house *stays* at Aunt Savannah's house. Yessiree. Over here, you'll get introduced to the wonders of homemade ice cream and chocolate chip cookies. If you're lucky and I'm ambitious, maybe on the same day."

Once the milk was heated to precisely the right temperature, Savannah offered it to the child and sauntered back to the living room.

Savannah decided to forgo her own cup of coffee or steaming cocoa with whipped cream, peppermint crumbles, and chocolate shavings. Vanna had quick-action piston leg kicks to rival the Rockettes. There was no point in taking a chance with a hot beverage.

As they settled into the rose chintz-covered, comfy

chair—a cushion at Savannah's back, her feet on the overstuffed ottoman—Savannah adjusted the bottle in the infant's mouth and continued her sage instruction. "As a baby, who'll be a girl and then a woman someday," she said, with a tone of great gravity, "you have to remember a very important thing about the males of our species. Here it is. Don't ever forget it: men . . . if you keep 'em fed and comfortable, for the most part, they're darned near tolerable."

Vanna spit out the bottle nipple and cooed a question.

Savannah listened with utmost attention, then gave a solemn nod. "Women, you ask?" She sighed and drew a deep breath. "Well, that's a different situation all together. As it turns out, us females are a mite more complicated."